THE Escalation CLAUSE

STELLA STEVENSON

This book is for anyone who has ever felt the need to protect themself. Whether you built a wall, stood apart, or put on a mask, it takes courage and strength to put your safety and health first. You should never feel guilty for surviving.

It is never too late for your own happily ever after. When you feel safe and ready, you can choose how your story ends.

CONTENT NOTES
includes possible spoilers

As an author, I take mental health and well-being very seriously. I'm including this warning so readers have the ability to steer clear of topics that may otherwise cause them harm. Reading should be fun and enjoyable. It should be an escape. Protect yourself first, always.

This is an **open door** romance that portrays on-page consensual sexual intimacy, suitable for readers ages **18+.**

This story has a plot line involving criminal and legal troubles. There is talk of **drug use** and sales, and **murder.** While the discussions and ramifications take place on page, the use and crimes do not. The officers in this book are not friendly, which could be triggering for some readers.

This book contains two **emotionally abusive** and controlling relationships. While most of the interactions are off-page, the characters are actively dealing trying to move forward and heal after such connections.

There is a mention of a **parental death (very briefly)** in chapter 7. There is another **death of a side character**. While the incident is not on=page, the cast does experience the fall-out in the pages of TEC. There is also a brief **mention of cheating**

Through my own experiences, research, and the guidance of authenticity and beta readers, I hope I have given these subjects the care and respect that they deserve.

I also need to add that I am not a lawyer. While I have done extensive research on the procedure for this story, please do not take anything from this book as legal advice.

Please see my website **www.authorstellastevenson.com**
for a full list of content warnings.

"All I want is all you got,
Oh what you give is good enough…"

ALL I WANT IS ALL YOU GOT, Steppenwolf

Of all the ways to start a new week, being hauled to the local police station after a traffic stop certainly had to win some kind of award for last place. Eden was a nervous driver at the best of times, so when she saw the flashing lights in her rear view mirror, her hands started to shake and sweat pooled in her lower back.

There were no shoulders on Storrow Drive—possibly one of the most notorious of all Boston roadways—and sheer panic had almost sent Eden driving onto the grassy embankment before common sense prevailed, and she turned on her hazard lights and found a spot where she could pull over

If she'd known then that she was about to be bundled into the back seat of a cop car and escorted to the local precinct, well, she probably would have had actual heart failure.

Eden didn't watch much television, but her stepdad had always liked cop shows. It was the scent that television got wrong. Not that anyone could smell through a screen—no matter how fancy their entertainment center—but she had definitely imagined something different. From the pieces she'd seen, she'd always imagined that the station would smell a bit like the tang of metal, the hint of cigarette smoke, and the earthy sweetness of leather.

It didn't.

Instead, window units hazed the room with a musty dampness that couldn't fully disguise the scent of sweat and weed.

Eden wasn't in a fancy interrogation room like she had imagined, staring down a one-way window disguised as a mirror. She was sitting on an old, lumpy, orange plaid couch in what looked like a mismatched living room full of hand-me-down furniture from the seventies. A sandy-haired man slid an uncovered Styrofoam cup of caffeine onto the coffee table in front of her. It was acrid and burnt, like it had sat too long in a warmer. Eden preferred her coffee loaded down with cream and sugar. The stuff being offered to her was a dark sludge she was fairly certain would eat through the cup itself, given enough time.

"Sorry to take so much time out of your afternoon, Miss Yates," the officer said as he settled back into his chair. "If you wouldn't mind answering a few questions, it would help clarify a few things."

His smile came with a little dimple in his left cheek, and he kept it on full display.

Eden could do questions. She could do answers. It wasn't the officer's fault she was here. He was doing his job. The least she could do was give him whatever information he needed. She wasn't sure exactly why he brought her in—no one was answering any of her questions—but she wasn't in handcuffs so that seemed like a good sign.

"Of course." Eden smoothed her sweaty palms down the length of her skirt. The tiny metal beads on the drawstring tinkled together as she moved.

"Now Miss Yates—"

"Eden," she corrected. "Call me Eden,"

"Right." The officer's smile widened, forming a second dimple. "Eden. Can you tell me how you know Justin Fredecker?"

"He was my boyfriend," Eden said. He'd been a shitty one, but that probably wasn't information the officer needed.

"Was? He's not anymore?"

Eden shook her head. Justin hadn't just been *a* boyfriend. He'd been her *first* boyfriend. Her first real adult relationship. It had been fairly easy to stay single after seeing her mother shrink under the demands and opinions of her stepdad. She'd grown up on romance and love and fairytales and then her mother had met Greg when she was ten and things had changed. It had been easy to spend most of her early twenties keeping her romantic entanglements light and uninvolved, but by twenty-nine Eden had been lonely, dammit. Lonely and hopeful that maybe, just maybe, not every partner was like her stepdad.

And then Justin had been equally bad. Maybe not controlling, and maybe not threatening, but she'd still found herself changing for him. Chipping away pieces of herself until she didn't recognize the Eden who was left.

Wearing her hair just so since he thought it made her more attractive, wearing makeup so she wouldn't look quite so old, putting on certain clothes so no one else would lust after her body. Letting him drive her car wherever he needed to go, making him breakfast, lunch, and dinner, buying his new phone and putting it on her own plan because he just needed to wait until payday to pay her back and that's what you did for someone you loved. Right? Until one day she looked in the mirror and there was her mama, Theresa, staring out from her reflection.

Eden wished that had been enough for her to leave Justin. Wished she'd fought for herself then, but she'd stubbornly hung on. Desperate to have her own happily ever after. Relationships took work, compromise. She could bend for her boyfriend. Except he wasn't bending for her. He was cheating.

That had been enough for Eden to shove him out of her life. She'd taken back her keys—both to her apartment and to her car—stopped his phone line, and told him they were over. And then she'd spent the last two months pretending he didn't exist. That was, until three police cars had pulled her over on Storrow Drive this morning on her way to teach her yoga class. It had been decidedly difficult not to think about him when she had been told to step out of the car with her hands above her head, while two officers pointed weapons at her and asked for the whereabouts of her ex.

"How did the two of you meet?" the officer asked, pushing the coffee cup closer to her clasped hands.

He seemed friendly enough. Keith? Was his name Keith? He'd been the one to apologize for the scare and the misunderstanding. It wasn't his fault they had been looking for Justin and thought he would have been driving Eden's '02 Toyota Camry. It was a reasonable assumption to make. Justin had used the car more than she had.

"We met at an art festival in New Hampshire," Eden said, tucking her hair back to see the officer better, and smiled. "I was there to market my paintings, and Justin was there with a few friends."

"Did you meet the friends?"

Eden frowned. It had been two years ago, so the memory wasn't exactly fresh. She could see Justin, blonde hair falling around his slim shoulders and a scruffy beard covering his pale cheeks. He'd been wearing a collared shirt printed with some abstract swirling design in greens, purples, and muted browns that hung open over his low-slung cargo shorts. His blue eyes had sparkled at her in the bright summer sun as he had offered to buy her a water from one of the vendors.

There had been someone with him, a nebulous figure in Eden's mind, who had waved a quick hello before turning and leaving the two of them alone.

"No," Eden shook her head, "We just walked around the event and spent the whole day talking about our art. The next day, he dropped into my morning yoga class. He was charming."

"Your art," the man leaned forward, arms resting on his splayed thighs. "Sculpture? Sewing?"

"I do a little of everything." Eden returned his smile, running her fingers through the curling end of her ponytail. "My booth at the festival was for my paintings."

"Did Mr. Fredecker have a booth as well?"

"No, he was just a patron. Did something happen to Justin?"

In hindsight, he hadn't bought anything, but that wasn't abnormal for Justin. Funding wasn't something he'd ever been overly concerned with. Why should he? Eden had always been there to take care of things.

"Did the two of you live together?"

Eden shook her head.

"Not officially." She crossed her legs, making the ties on her skirt jangle loudly again, too loud in the small room. "He spent the night a few times a week, but kept his own place."

She had never been to Justin's apartment. He'd had roommates and Justin had wanted them to have privacy. Eden lived by herself. She could afford to because her landlady let Eden teach guitar and piano to her granddaughter in exchange for half her rent.

"And the vehicle is in your name?"

Eden nodded. She thought she had given them license and registration when they had surrounded her, but she couldn't be sure. It had been a whirlwind once they realized she wasn't who they were looking for. Eden was trying not to be offended that she'd looked enough like Justin through the windshield of her old car to warrant their confusion.

"I'm sorry." Eden twisted a lock of hair around her finger. "What is all of this about?"

The officers had mentioned needing her help, but they hadn't been clear on what she was helping them with. The cop studied her from under his pale lashes. He wasn't in full uniform, just a white shirt and a pair of khaki slacks with a gold badge clipped to his waistband like she'd seen on all the cop shows. He wore a pair of leather loafers, and Eden wondered if they were conducive to running or if he needed to change before going out into the field and chasing down suspects. Perhaps that was another thing that only happened on stages and sound lots.

"We need to locate Mr. Fredecker," the officer said. "We know he drove the vehicle we stopped this morning."

"Oh," Eden relaxed into the couch. "Well, He used to. Sometimes. I haven't seen him since April." When she'd dumped him.

"What?" The officer shot his blue eyes to hers, narrowing with the question.

Eden smiled back, calm and serene. See? This had all been a misunderstanding. A terrifying mess that obviously stemmed from her ex. Justin had been a colossal mistake even before she'd seen him with his pants down getting serviced by Gem, the community garden coordinator. Okay, that wasn't entirely fair. She didn't have to forgive his cheating—and she definitely hadn't—but something had drawn her to Justin once upon a time. Probably his passion for his poetry and the guts it took to risk everything to follow his dream. Or the fact that way down deep in the depths of her soul, Eden wanted someone.

"Justin used to drive my car all the time when we were dating. At first, his car had been in the shop, so I let him borrow mine. After his car was fixed, we decided, since I didn't drive much anyway, to sell his car and have him take mine when he needed to go somewhere or do something. That ended when we broke up over two months ago."

The officer leaned back in his chair and steepled his fingers in front of him. He tapped his pointer fingers against his mouth as he stared at her. Eden shivered under his scrutiny but kept up her smile. Of course he seemed frustrated. They'd been looking for Justin and found her instead.

"And he hasn't had access to your car since?"

Eden shook her head. "Not that I'm aware of."

"You gave police permission to look through the vehicle. Do you mind if we do a more thorough search with some of our techs? If Mr. Fredecker was a consistent operator, we may find something he left behind."

"Can someone please tell me what's going on?"

Keith shook his head. "We need to talk to him about something. I'm sorry I can't say more than that, Eden."

She was tempted to agree if it would help them find him. Something awful must have happened for the police to get involved. Eden wondered if it made her a horrible person for not caring what happened to Justin. What if he had been in an accident? Or dead?

She should probably feel something if that was the case. They had slept together on a semi-regular basis. Even if the sex had been mediocre, it should have been weird to think that something could have happened to him. But how long would a search take? She'd long ago missed her class, but she had others. The city made her tense, but having a car was still easier than waiting on the T.

"I promise it will be painless for you. We just need to find him, and your car might hold the key."

"I guess that could be alright." Eden waffled. "As long as it won't take too long. I'm supposed to drive out to Worcester tomorrow for a meeting."

"Don't worry about a thing," Keith waved a hand in front of her face. "Would you like something other than coffee? Water? I'm sure someone in this joint has bagels."

She wasn't really thirsty, but they were nice to offer. "Water would be great. Thank you,"

Keith got to his feet, the chair squeaking against the laminate as he pushed back. The door clicked shut behind him as he left, and Eden was alone with the hum of the AC and her own thoughts.

She pulled her phone from her pocket and thumbed through her contacts. She no longer had Justin's number saved, but she still had a text thread from him. It contained several messages she'd left unanswered. The final one called her a few choice names after she wouldn't return his calls. She'd kept the thread for one reason and one reason only: to remind herself why she was better off without him.

Despite how things had ended, Justin had been a nice guy. He'd listened when she spoke. He'd emotionally supported her chosen work. He'd never once pushed her into going home or seeing her stepdad again. For a few months Eden had allowed herself to believe that she'd found the one. The person who'd love her and support her and let her be herself. She'd been wrong.

Eden opened the thread, refusing to look at the names he'd called her. She clicked the message box and watched the blinking cursor. If the police were asking her questions to find him, then she could try to get them some answers.

There. She'd done her good deed for the day. Now, she could go home and get some work done. When officer Keith came back, she would thank him for his time, give them the name of Justin's agent—he might be able to locate her ex—and let them know they could keep her car overnight. Her yoga things were still in the backseat. She'd ask to grab them before she left and tell them she'd come collect her car in the morning.

The door slammed open, rocking on its hinges. Eden's hand wrapped around her throat as she jumped back, away from the noise and the sound. A second later, the biggest man she'd ever seen strode into the room. He was tall, broad through his shoulders, and thick through his waist. A veritable moving mountain blocking out all light and routes of escape.

His hair was the same color as her bitter coffee and was just long enough to be on the wrong end of a haircut. A thick beard covered his cheeks and chin. His even darker eyes glared out from under a set of thick pinched eyebrows. The man looked out of place in his gray suit as the fabric gripped his limbs like a baby koala clinging to a tree trunk.

Another cop? Eden wondered. He didn't look like a cop, but he could have been higher up the food chain than Keith. Although why they'd need to go further up the chain of command when she had been more than willing to answer the questions they had, she didn't understand. Keith strode in behind the behemoth, taking two steps for every one of the other man's.

"We just have a few more questions for Eden."

The giant glared over his shoulder at the smaller man.

"For Miss Yates," Keith corrected.

"She's done with questions," The mountain said. The mirror on the wall shook with the force of his voice.

"Why don't we let Miss Yates decide," Keith skirted around the stranger.

He held out a plastic water bottle, the blue label crinkling under his fingers. As Eden reached for it, the behemoth stepped in between them, his arm blocking hers. He glanced at her, his gaze raking her from head to foot.

"What are you doing?" He asked.

She smiled her classic it's-all-going-to-be-okay smile. The one she'd practiced all through middle and high school. The one that had calmed her stepdad enough to let her get on the bus, or go out with her friends.

"I'm thirsty," she said. "Keith was kind enough to grab me a drink."

She turned her smile to Keith, ducking around the thick forearm blocking her path, and hoped she hadn't just gotten him into trouble.

The large man closed his eyes and blew out a deep breath. After several seconds, his arm dropped, and she took the bottle, unscrewing the cap and taking a long sip. The man watched as she pressed the plastic to her lips. A strange tickle grew in her abdomen, right below her belly button.

"If you have any more questions for Miss Yates," the man broke his stare to turn his attention to the other officer, "you will contact me. She's not being charged with anything?"

Keith wasn't smiling anymore. In fact, he looked downright pissed. "She can go. For now. But we'll be in touch."

In touch? About what? But tall, broad, and dangerous was looking down at her again. Eden found she didn't care much about Justin or the cops when his eyes were on her like this. She wasn't sure if she felt like squirming under his gaze or freezing, as if he were a predator that could only sense her if she moved.

"We're leaving," he said.

Eden set the water bottle on the table. He picked it up, fingers almost meeting around the middle of the plastic, and handed it back to her. He grabbed her coffee cup too, draining the liquid in a single gulp before crumpling the Styrofoam in his fist.

"These are coming with us," he said. "Let's go."

Eden didn't have a chance to question where they were going before he moved past her toward the door. She followed as Mountain Man led her out of the small sitting room and through a large open space she'd seen in cop dramas. People sat behind their computers, tapping away and answering phones.

This room smelled even worse. It reeked of sour sweat, the burn of ammonia, a sickeningly sweet floral air freshener, and more weed. Her large protector kept walking, past the desks and the reception window, until he pushed open the heavy glass doors to the front of the station. Eden trailed behind him, stuck to him like a shadow.

"I'm sorry," she said as the door slammed behind her, "but who are you?"

"I'm Ted," he held out a hand.

She slipped her palm into his, shaking it. His fingers flexed around hers in a firm grip.

"I'm Eden," she squeezed back. "Your name doesn't tell me much."

"Ted Hughes," he repeated his name as if it was all the explanation she needed. "I'm your lawyer."

TWO

Ted Hughes wasn't a litigator. His firm dealt exclusively with contracts, creation and negotiation, mostly. They left enforcement to other attorneys with occasional consultation when necessary. Ted couldn't speak for his partners, but he knew Will had gone into contract law with some noble idea of helping the underdog, and Logan— while a complete genius with research and due diligence— wasn't great in front of crowds of people, so staying in their comfortable office was much preferred.

For Ted, there were two reasons he had chosen the track he did. The first was that his family had pressured him into law school, but his rebellious nature meant he would absolutely not be joining his stepfather's firm or even his type of law practice. Martin James was the litigator to end all litigators. Other lawyers wept when they saw his name listed as the opposing counsel.

The second reason was that Ted didn't enjoy spending time in court or police departments. And yet here he was at his local precinct on his lunch because Massachusetts had rules about filing reports within forty-eight hours following a motor-vehicle accident, even if both parties walked away unharmed, and the body shop said his bike only needed minor repairs. This was what happened when drivers didn't check twice for motorcycles. They changed lanes directly into them, clipped their fenders, and added a police-department visit to Ted's already busy Monday schedule.

Ted did not have time for any of this. He'd been in meetings all morning, and had another four scheduled for after lunch. When one partner in a three-partner firm left to film a reality television show and found the love of his life, again, then the rest of the lawyers had to double up on work hours. Ted didn't mind, really. He was thrilled for Will and AJ, but they could stand to tone down the happy.

Other people were looking for someone too and didn't need the constant reminders of what they didn't have. Or the constant reminder that Will had found the most perfect woman for him and that his old-money, blue-blood family had accepted her with open arms—the second time. Ted's family would not be doing that. Being married to the wrong person would be worse than staying single. Normally this was the kind of request he'd pretend he hadn't heard, but ultimately it would be wonderful to have someone to share every single day with.

So yeah, he didn't have the time for this. He was working eighty-hour weeks, extreme-dating, and pushing the limit by dropping this report off in person with only twenty-one minutes to spare. But he was still on time and ultimately that's what mattered. He'd expected a quick in and out. He hadn't expected to meet her. He definitely hadn't expected his compulsion to rescue her. It was probably the damsel-in-distress thing. Ted had spent a lot of his formative years putting himself squarely between his stepfather and his mother. It was second nature to jump in when a woman was in danger. Even if it meant even more time at the 1-A precinct.

"I appreciate the help," the woman said, pulling her hand free and leaning back against the brick wall behind her.

Ted closed his fingers around the empty air, a tingle starting in the center of his palm.

"But I don't need a lawyer." She smiled at him as if he was the one about to be strung up by the cops like a sacrificial lamb.

Her mouth–the upper lip a little heavier than the lower–was a deep pink, as though she'd scraped her teeth over the sensitive skin. Her front two teeth overlapped just a fraction. It was the tiniest imperfection, but Ted couldn't look away.

"Yes, you do." Ted tried to keep his tone gentle since she looked like the type who needed calm, sweet.

Everything about her looked soft; her smooth honey bronze skin, her belly curving into rounded hips, her dark hair shining in the afternoon sun as it fell down her back in loose waves. Even the dark lashes framing her big green eyes seemed soft. Ted would have been able to tell she was smiling from only a photo of her eyes.

She shook her head, but her smile never slipped. "Thank you for your help, Ted, but they were just looking for someone."

Her ex.

That's what chatty officer one had been saying to chatty officer two when Ted had turned in his accident report. Ted thought their discussion on the "pretty little thing" that they were about to take down with Fredecker was highly inappropriate, as was laughing over how stupid she was to not realize she was handing herself to them on a silver platter.

From what he'd overheard, both in the hallway and in the interrogation room, they had no reason to arrest or charge her. If they had, they would've already cuffed and booked her. No, instead they'd assumed she was guilty by association, hoping she'd give them the information they wanted to send her down river.

That was what hadn't sat right with him. Instead of doing their jobs, they'd been willing to let some innocent—until proven otherwise—woman take the fall for someone else. Someone male. How many times had his mother taken the heat for Martin? For him? Ted was no longer a hothead teenager who didn't care about the verbal beatdown his mother often took on his behalf. He'd gone out of his way to become the kind of man who not only didn't break rules, but who actively tried to help others.

It wasn't like Ted was actually going to be her attorney. Being a practicing lawyer didn't mean he had the skills to work a criminal case. But he did have connections. He could set her up with one of his firm's recommended defenders and then go home and sleep comfortably knowing he had done his part in helping the naïve woman who had been blindsided.

Maybe he'd also give her some resources to help her with the ex-waste-of-space. He had a few friends who worked with the local women's shelter and he knew therapists who specialized in domestic violence and abuse.

"It doesn't matter what you think they wanted from you," Ted shoved his hands into the front pocket of his dress pants. He tempered his words to sound a smidgeon less harsh. He also fought the impulse to run a finger over the swell of her shoulder to see if she was as soft as she looked. "Any time a police officer wants to ask you some questions, lawyer up."

She frowned and tipped her head to the side.

"Ted," she sighed his name as if he were the confused party.

"Eden." He countered.

Her frown slipped, and she smiled when he said her name. The smile threw him. He'd assumed her placating tone and words were a learned response. Trying to talk down an angry man. But that smile... maybe he'd been wrong, and Eden Yates was just a veritable ray of freaking sunshine arguing with him on the sidewalk.

"Ted, the only time I've ever toed the line was when I turned off my Wi-Fi so my library eBooks stayed on my reader. And even then, I felt guilty after twenty-four hours and wrote the librarian a note." That story shouldn't have been cute, but he felt his lips twitch as if he'd almost smiled. "And that was last month."

"How old are you?" He couldn't help asking, because he'd genuinely thought she'd been sharing a childhood anecdote.

She flushed. Red tinging her cheeks as she glanced away and down the sidewalk. "I'll be thirty next month." She swung her gaze around to pin him to the brick. "How old are you?"

"Thirty-six." He told her automatically. Her smile grew wider.

"That's not too big a difference." She winked.

Was she flirting with him? He couldn't tell. Heat coiled in his belly and he doused it. Ted hadn't asked for romantic reasons—there was a zero percent chance that anything was going to happen between them—but because he wanted to know how many decades she'd made it on this earth with apparently the self-preservation skills of a kumquat.

"I appreciate the concern," she said, laying a soft hand on his arm. Even through his jacket, her skin seared him down to the bone. He resisted the urge to shake off her touch. "But there's nothing to worry about. I'm sure Justin will get in touch with the police soon. I sent him a message to let him know they wanted to talk to him. I'm assuming about his mother, so he should stop by the station or call them."

Lord, help them all. She'd texted the idiot. A message that could very well be construed as a warning. He took it back. Kumquats had more common sense. He wasn't about to be her lawyer, but he'd bet his license that she would probably end up needing one.

She was still touching his arm, so he felt comfortable cupping her elbow and drawing her further away from the door. Not into the shaded alley next to the building, although she'd probably let him, convinced he was a good guy. That he *was* a good guy was completely beside the point. He just wanted to put some distance between them and the front of the station.

"They aren't looking for your ex because they want to relay some important news." Ted said. He rubbed a hand over his eyes. "Other than his Miranda rights."

Eden laughed, a boom of sound he hadn't expected but wanted to hear again.

"They only recite those when you're arrested." She said. As if at least eighty percent of the country didn't know that from watching *Law & Order*. Ted looked down at her, willing her to put the pieces together. "Why would they want to arrest Justin?" A bewildered frown marred her features. She crossed her arms over her chest.

Was it unethical to tell her what he'd overheard in the station? It would be to withhold that information if he were actually representing her. And it wasn't his fault the officers hadn't thought twice before airing private information in the very public hallway of the precinct. She had a right to know what she was up against, and it wasn't like they'd been playing fair in there. They'd known good and well that she did not know what they were angling for. This woman did not deserve to be steamrolled by her ex and a bunch of cops.

"Drugs," he said and watched her mouth drop open in actual shock.

Ted considered himself an excellent judge of character. His instincts had already been screaming that she wasn't involved in whatever her dickhead ex had gotten himself into, but if he'd been on the fence at all, the look on her face would have secured his confidence. Nobody was that good an actress. His faith in her had absolutely nothing to do with the blistering attraction she stirred.

"What?" There was that laugh again, only this time tinged with the high-pitched chuckle of nerves. She shook her head. "No. Justin doesn't do drugs."

The best dealers didn't.

"He's selling heroin," Ted said, and Eden's head was still shaking back and forth. "At least, according to the officers inside that building. They've been staking out his car and his home for months now, but imagine their surprise when he vanished off the face of the earth just last week. And then when they saw his car and pulled it over, ready to make the arrest, they found his girlfriend instead."

"Ex," Eden said, so at least she was hearing him, even if she needed a minute to process. "Ex girlfriend. He hasn't driven my car in months, thank you."

"That doesn't surprise me," Ted said. "They were probably staking him out when you were together, and the car stayed on their radar. No one paid attention to the fact that he hasn't had access to it."

Eden started pacing, skirt swishing between her legs as she stomped up and down the pavement in front of him. Ted watched her move one way, then pivot—the ties of her shirt and skirt flaring out behind her—and march back the way she came. She moved back and forth, back and forth, back and forth, her sandals pounding on the same square of cement several times before she stopped in front of him. Eden jammed her hands on her hips, threw her head back and screamed up into the clear blue sky.

"Mother fucking crap on a cracker!" She yelled, and it was almost too horrible to admit, but Ted couldn't help but grin at her obscenities. "If it's true, then he's not showing up at the precinct," she said after a few shuddering breaths.

Ted shook his head.

"And I sent him a text telling him they were looking for him."

Ted winced, but nodded.

"Well, that settles it then," she shrugged and turned back toward the entrance to the building. "I'll just have to go right back in there and tell them I had no idea what he was up to."

It wasn't his finer moment, but Eden had made it a few steps before Ted locked a hand around her wrist and drew her back to him.

"Negative," he said, looking down at his hand on the softness of her golden skin. He was right. She felt like silk under his touch. "You do not speak to them without a lawyer, and *this* lawyer is telling you to go home and hire a defense attorney."

"A defense attorney?" She reared back from him, pulling her arm out of his grip. "But I didn't do anything wrong! Shouldn't I just go tell them that?

She had a death wish.

And he was going to get a migraine trying to deal with her.

"Listen Sweetness," frustration thickened his Boston accent, broadening the vowel in the pet name. He hadn't meant to use one, it just slipped out. It wasn't Ted's fault that she looked like she was dipped in caramel and chocolate and smelled like vanilla and sugar.

"What did you want me to listen to?"

She was certifiably insane. Hot, yes. The kind of beauty that stopped him in his tracks, but also off her rocker. Good thing they weren't going to be seeing each other again. A girl like this would send him into a tailspin from which he would never recover, and her clothes alone would give his stepfather apoplexy. Actually, that might be reason enough to bring her home. Just once.

"Those guys are not in there to look out for you," Ted said, and Eden opened her mouth to protest, "They were probably hoping you'd give them permission to search the car, although even without your agreement, they can probably seize it if they can argue that your ex had access to it. Considering that they pulled you over in it after staking it out, they can probably make that case. They're looking for a way to tie you to what happened because none of them believe you shared a car, shared an address, and you didn't know what he was doing."

Eden gaped at him. Her lush pink mouth snapped open and shut as she tried to come up with the next thing to say.

"We didn't share an address." She said, her voice small. "He never lived with me. I—he didn't move in." She shrugged. "He used my car. I don't like driving in the city, so it was sitting untouched. It made sense to let him borrow it. I never thought—"

"You don't need to explain anything to me," Ted said.

He had the strange urge to hug her. She just looked so lonely standing there. Ted understood lonely. Sometimes he felt like he was drowning in it. Will was engaged, Logan had siblings and cousins and parents who actually cared about him, and Ted had… no one. He had a weekly call with his mother when they very clearly didn't discuss anything that would upset his stepfather.

That meant most topics were off-limits beyond the weather, Will and his parents—not Will's fiancée, Ted's stepfather did not approve of AJ—and he had a few friends he'd play a round of golf with. A few more who also rode motorcycles when the weather was nice, but ultimately no one he'd go to if he'd made an unimaginable mistake. Isn't that what friends were? The people who'd bail you out of jail if you needed them to? Will might. If Ted decided to call him.

Sitting alone in that precinct, answering questions designed to get her in trouble, Eden had seemed like she was in exactly the same spot as he was. Up shit creek with no one to help paddle her out.

That was ridiculous. Ted didn't know Eden at all. She might have teams of people ready and able to help her. If she'd known she needed a lawyer or a phone call she probably had friends she could call. Seeing her on that orange couch, reaching innocently for a water bottle they were going to grab her fingerprints and possible DNA from, telling him she'd texted the asshole that had let her down, he'd known she was a mess. But she was a mess who needed a friend and some help.

"I'm not supposed to tell you I'm innocent?" Eden took a step toward him, glancing up at him from under her lashes. There was an alarm bell pinging in Ted's brain, but he had to admit that he liked her standing so close to him. Liked her smiling at him. "Aren't you my lawyer?"

"God no," Ted said. Getting her out of the precinct had been his helping hand. Now it was time to shake her hand, send her on her way, and get back to finding his own someone.

"But," she frowned. "You said—are you not a real lawyer? Can you get in trouble for lying?"

"I'm a real lawyer, but you need a defense attorney. Someone who deals with criminal cases. I deal with contracts. You want the big guns if you have to go to trial."

"Trial!"

Shit, he was getting ahead of himself.

"You most likely won't have to, especially if you stop handing them information on a silver platter, but yes. You need to put someone on retainer. I can recommend some names."

Eden worried her lower lip. "I can't exactly afford a lawyer right now. Or legal fees." She looked down the street again and Ted felt like an asshole. An asshole who was seriously considering calling in a favor for a woman he'd known for five minutes and who might not even need legal representation after all.

"It's okay." He said, pulling his wallet out of his back pocket and removing one of his business cards. The HMP logo was visible above his name and other contact information. "If they bring you back in, you can ask for a public defender. If they say you don't need one, you aren't under arrest and you don't have to answer questions. You can get up and leave. They can't detain you without offering legal counsel."

"If they come for me again, lawyer-up. Got it." She grinned up at him before looking down at the stiff card stock in her hand.

"And call me if you need anything."

There she went, worrying her bottom lip again. If she wasn't careful, he was going to rescue her again. Something he absolutely didn't have time to do.

"Anything." Eden repeated; her voice raised the hairs on his arms.

Ted nodded.

"Anything."

"And you'll do it without yelling?"

Ted wasn't really a yeller by nature, but he knew he was intimidating, so he couldn't blame her for worrying.

"I promise not to yell." He agreed.

"Great." Eden looped her arm through his elbow, snugging her body into his side. Ted tensed at the initial contact and then relaxed as she did. The top of her head was even with his mouth. The temptation to press his lips to the crown of her head swamped him. Nothing weird, just something to tell her he was on her side. And he wasn't going to yell. She tipped her head back to meet his eyes, her pupils expanding as they met his, then retracting in the bright light of the sun. "Do you think you can give me a ride home?"

"What?" So she had been flirting before. He'd just have to let her down gently. Eden was attractive. Not entirely off-limits since he wasn't actually her lawyer, and maybe a few years ago he'd have gone for it. A few years ago Will had been single too, they'd been trucking along together. Now the stakes were different. Ted wanted, he needed, the perfect wife.

"I don't have a car," she said, pressing her cheek to the cotton of his dress shirt.

"Didn't they apprehend you at a traffic stop?" He asked, as though he wasn't willing to carry her home if she really needed him to, let alone give her a lift.

"Yes," she nodded, "but unfortunately I didn't yet have legal counsel when I gave them permission to keep and search the car."

A smile twitched the edges of his mouth.

"Come on, Miss Yates. Your carriage awaits."

"**A**nd then he just… dropped you off?" Romy asked, following Eden into her small kitchen.

The space wasn't actually big enough for both of them, and Romy boosted herself up onto the tiled counter so Eden could reach the refrigerator. Eden opened the door, searched the meager offerings, closed the door, and then opened it again on the off-chance that something had changed. It hadn't. She had half a tub of hummus, a shriveled green bell pepper, two soft kiwis, and a jug of fresh-squeezed orange juice. There was a wrapped cheese stick in the back of one drawer. Eden checked the expiration date before peeling back the plastic and taking a bite out of the top.

"Just like that," she said to her best friend.

"And he didn't try anything?"

Ted had been a perfect gentleman. A grumpy one, with a room-clearing scowl, but a gentleman just the same. What she'd first taken for outright rudeness had actually been a gruff version of protection. She'd read his exasperation loud and clear as he'd laid out her situation, but he'd still helped her and given her a ride home. He had also lied for her, probably putting himself on the line to save her naïve butt, and then hadn't blinked an eye when she'd told him that legal retainers were outside her monthly budget.

When Eden had called the precinct that morning about getting her car back, she'd been told that she could provide her receipt—the one they never gave her—to collect her property after the investigation was concluded. So yeah, private defense attorney? Definitely out of her budget, especially now that she was going to need to factor public transportation back into the equation.

And yet...

Ted's dark eyes had traced the lines of her body and heat had poured off his skin. She'd seen his pupils contract as he looked down at her, his gaze dropping to her mouth whenever she spoke. She'd heard the drop in his voice, his already rough words sounding like distant rumbling thunder as he talked her through the next steps. Eden recognized all those signs as easily as if they were glowing neon. He'd liked the way she looked. Even if being attracted to her clearly annoyed him.

And she'd liked that despite the obvious attraction, he hadn't done anything about it. That was a refreshing relief. He'd seen a woman in a vulnerable position and he'd stepped in to help, expecting nothing in return. A prince. Ted Hughes was a goddamn fucking prince. The bar for men was so low it was actually in Hell.

It had been easy, even amid her initial confusion, to appreciate the broad slope of his shoulders under the white cotton and gray wool. Easier to notice the dark wave of shiny hair and the perfectly trimmed beard. Easiest to catalogue his tapered waist as he balled his hands into fists and pushed back the lapels of his suit jacket. Those strong hands, with blunt edged fingers, had handed her a business card and twenty hours later she was still carrying it around, slipped it into the pocket of her flared striped pants. In Eden's experience, noticing someone else's interest was one thing, having an interest in someone else was another, and when the stars aligned…that was the *piece de resistance*.

"He was one of those respectful types. The kind that don't forget their grasp of verbal communication when you say 'no.'"

Romy nodded, green and blue strands of hair slipping over her shoulders. "Did you say no?"

Eden shook her head. "But I didn't give him an opening either." She'd been slightly preoccupied with some of her legal happenings.

"That's—" Romy kicked her legs and looked up at the ceiling light, squinting as if trying to find the right words. "Not like you? Yeah, not like you. Are you sick or something?"

"I feel like I should be offended," Eden said as she crumpled up her wrapper and tossed it into the trash, but she wasn't. Even if Romy wasn't her best friend and the best neighbor, Eden liked to give everyone the benefit of the doubt. That was a conscious choice that stemmed from her early childhood with her mother. One that even her stepdad hadn't been able to stamp out.

Most people lived up to her expectations, as long as she held her boundaries firm. But even if they didn't, seeing the worst in people only left her feeling exhausted and hurt.

"Absolutely not." Romy laughed. "I love how open you are. You see someone you want, you go for it, and you both have a good time. We should all aspire to be like that."

Eden leaned her elbows on the counter and put her head on her best friend's thigh. "I'm sensing a 'but' at the end of that sentence."

Romy speared her fingers through Eden's dark hair. The pressure felt marvelous on her scalp, leeching the tension out of her.

"Do you ever think about getting back into the dating pool?"

Eden frowned. Her "no," automatic.

"I'm just saying," Eden's head moved as Romy snagged her fingers in a tangle, "You said he saved your ass. Maybe he deserves a shot."

"You are completely unhinged. Even if I was looking for a relationship" she wasn't, "I'm pretty sure it's a bad idea to start one on the basis of gratitude."

"It wouldn't all be a thank you," Romy sighed. "You said he was hot, too."

He was.

Eden could see Ted's appeal, feel drawn to the magnetism of his presence, and still recognize that they probably had less than nothing in common. She was assuming he was unattached—better to assume that based on the way he looked at her than to assume he was a pig—but that didn't mean he'd be interested in someone like her beyond the physical.

Call it cliché, or trite, or whatever, but men in bespoke wool weren't usually interested in women who spent ninety-nine percent of their time with paint under their fingernails. Or who made a living as an illustrator, a singer, a piano teacher, a yoga instructor, and a couple other gig jobs that fueled her creative spirit.

"I really really really don't want to be someone's girlfriend" Eden said.

"Okay," Romy shrugged, tugging a little harder. "You know I love you and support you with whatever. But maybe, just maybe, it's about the label and not the relationship."

"No," Eden said. "Relationships destroy you, I watched Greg change everything about my mom because she wasn't the perfect wife he wanted her to be. I let Justin do the same thing to me even after I was sure I wouldn't fall into that trap. Sex? Fun. A weekend fling? A good time. More than that? I don't want to crumble away into nothing, Romy. I can't do that."

"Darling." Romy stopped moving her hand and wrapped her arm around Eden's shoulder. "I know you've been burned. A lot. You just have the biggest fucking heart of anyone I've ever met. Someday you might meet the right person who won't care about your family trauma, or your unorthodox career choices, or the fact that when you get working on a big enough painting you sometimes forget to shower." Eden stuck her tongue out and Romy returned the gesture. "I just don't want you to let that someone pass you by because you are too busy protecting yourself to see the possibilities."

A long time ago Eden may have been the girl reading every romance novel that the library would let her take out, the artist obsessed with paintings that almost exclusively depicted lovers. There had been a brief stint in middle school with a digital camera where Eden thought she might want to be a photographer. Then her stepdad Greg had told her that was a ridiculous job aspiration for *his* daughter—she wasn't his daughter—and his *wife* needed to have a chat with her about smarter choices. Those kinds of comments had squashed a lot of the romance out of her.

"Even if—" Eden narrowed her eyes at her best friend "you're right. Ted is never going to be that person, Romy. He was polite and helpful, but I swear the man starches his underwear. It doesn't matter that he made me the tiniest bit hot when I looked at him. A man like that would melt me down and pour me into his own mold faster than my stepdad could have dreamed."

"Well if he's that uptight he probably still needs a thank you." Romy said, which was annoying because she was probably right.

Ted had given her his card and it had his work address along with three phone numbers, an email address, and a code she could scan with her phone. He worked in one of the big old buildings in the North End. Eden had an early morning yoga class that she taught in Christopher Columbus Waterfront Park a couple of days a week. He was probably a few blocks away at most. She could make a stop. Maybe after her class tomorrow. Or before. She could bring him something as a thank you.

"What time do you think he gets to work in the morning?" She asked. Her class started at 8:30, which meant her regulars were picking out spots and unrolling their mats by 8.

"You mean someone who isn't a starving artist?" Romy asked, and Eden nodded into her best friend's thigh. "Probably around 8 or 9?"

After class it would be.

The building was easy to find, as was the directory with the now familiar HMP logo. Eden had also spent hours studying the different angles of the old stone building and the closest view of the harbor as she mixed watercolors the afternoon before, and that made finding it even easier.

She rode the clunky elevator up to the second floor, stopping in front of a glass door with the names Hughes, Masters, & Paderewski arching across the front in big bold letters.

The waiting room was clean and comfortable without being ostentatious. A leather couch and two modern armchairs faced a wide, square coffee table. A sideboard held a coffee maker and cups. A water dispenser was tucked into the corner next to it. A rounded reception desk faced the front door, and a slender man sat in a plush office chair and laughed into a phone.

He said something to whomever was on the other end of the call, before dropping the phone back into its cradle and giving her a quick once over. Eden suddenly wished she'd done more than pull a pair of overalls on over her yoga shorts set.

"Can I help you?" The man asked, a southern lilt to his smooth voice.

"Hi." She hefted her bag up over her shoulder and smiled at him. "I'm looking for Ted."

"Mr. Hughes?" Another thoughtful look that seemed to touch every feature of her face and trace the sunflowers printed on her loose linen romper. "Do you have an appointment?"

No, she hadn't thought of that. She'd assumed she could just stop by and drop off the gift she'd made. If he was busy, Eden figured she could just leave it on his desk. Except he was a lawyer. He dealt with confidential legal information every day. She couldn't just waltz into his space to leave something for him. Especially not as a virtual stranger. One he'd met at a police precinct, while she was being grilled by the cops. No worries, she could just ask the man in front of her—the placard on his desk said Devin—to deliver it for her.

"I didn't think that far ahead, I just—"

"That's alright, give me your company name so I can look up your file, and we'll make something work."

"Eden Yates, but I don't have a company." She lifted the strap on her bag, accidentally pulling the tie of her romper until it untied and the front sagged. Eden moved her other hand over to re-knot it.

Devin frowned as he tapped something on the computer keyboard. "Do you need an initial consultation? Mr. Masters is available now. All three partners will be out of the office on Thursday and Friday, but Mr. Paderewski and Mr. Hughes will be back on Monday. Is the matter urgent?"

"No, not urgent. I have something for Ted—Mr. Hughes—can I just leave it with you?"

Eden reached into her bag to pull out the carefully wrapped gift. Devin looked at the tissue papered square in her hands and a small smile tipped his thin lips.

"You said your name was Eden?" He reached a hand out to take the package.

"That's what they tell me."

Devin tucked the gift next to his keyboard

"Miss Yates."

Ted stood in the narrow doorway. For someone so big, he certainly took quiet steps. Or maybe it was the expensive shoes and plush carpeting. He was wearing another fancy suit, the navy wool offset by a light blue shirt and a deep gray tie.

She hadn't forgotten how good looking he was, but standing there with his arms crossed over a massive chest and a familiar glower painting his lush mouth, he set her pulse racing. Her lips parted as she sucked in a breath and tried to calm her raging hormones. She'd definitely downplayed his attractiveness.

Eden could have done without the formal address, but it didn't exactly surprise her he'd returned to surnames. They barely knew each other, they weren't friends. Even when he'd been mentally counting to ten to deal with her complete confusion at the station, Ted Hughes had been polite.

"Hi Mr. Hughes." Eden waved a friendly hand.

"Is everything okay?"

Something slick and hot slid through her veins at his gruff words, pooling deep in her belly. They might not be compatible, not in any way, shape, or form, but that didn't mean they couldn't have a good time together. Preferably naked, but she wasn't entirely picky about that.

Another man poked his head out from around Ted's body.

"You're blocking the door," he said to Ted, clapping a hand on one sloping shoulder. He noticed Eden and dipped his chin in a nod.

"This is Eden," Devin said from his seat. He lifted her gift and held it out over the top of the desk.

"Eden?" The second man grinned this time, dark blue eyes sparkling at her. Ted still hadn't moved to let him into the reception area, so Eden waved again. She recognized the dark hair and navy eyes from a reality television show that had aired a few years back. Eden had watched each episode with Romy, waiting for the moment when the man in front of her had finally, epically, admitted his love for the curly-haired woman they'd all known he would do anything for. Eden glanced down at his hand but saw no ring; she wondered how much of the show had been an act.

"She was just dropping something off," Devin said, clearly talking to Will Masters, leading hero of the inaugural season of First Lady and, apparently, one of Will's partners. He leaned into the word "off," putting more meaning on the syllable. Meaning that had Ted's friend smiling wider. Had Ted mentioned her?

"Are you okay?" Ted asked again, stepping into the reception area and moving toward her until the toes of his dress shoes almost touched her sandals. His eyes flicked back and forth between hers.

"I'm fine," Eden said, her heart pounding "I wanted to say thank you. For the other day." And she hadn't expected to find an actual celebrity in his office. A celebrity who was clearly one of his friends.

Ted blinked down at her, the scowl leaving his face.

"Thank me?"

"Hey Devin," Will said, "I'll take Ted's next appointment." He held his hand to Eden, "It's nice to meet you Eden, I'm Will."

She'd already known his name, of course, but maybe it was better to pretend she didn't. Maybe he didn't want all the attention and fawning. Eden could understand and respect that. Right now, she was getting the same feeling she'd experienced in middle school, when she'd walked into a room and known everyone there was talking about her.

There was no malicious undertone here, more like curiosity. As if they'd been imagining who she was for the last twenty-four hours and finally had a chance to see her in person. Like she was an exotic animal on display in a zoo.

Ted held out his hand and Eden slid her palm into his, twining their fingers together on reflex. He pulled her with him down the hall and into an empty office. The door slammed behind them and he took an extra minute, looking down at their hands before he released her and leaned his hip back against the wood surface of his desk. His fingers gripped the small edge as he watched her, a caged predator with a meal just out of reach. It was flattering and exhilarating.

"I owe you for helping me out the other day," she said, stepping closer and watching the knuckles of his hands go white as he gripped the wood harder. "There is a tiny list of people I know who'd be willing to help untangle a friend from that kind of mess. We were complete strangers, but you didn't hesitate to come rescue me."

"Were?" He asked.

"I'd like to think we could consider each other friends now." She said and held out the gift. "I brought you something."

Eden held her breath as Ted unwrapped the blue paper and pulled out the sleek black frame. She couldn't read his facial expression as he looked down at the painting. The one she'd taken hours to get just right. The one she hoped he'd appreciate.

"This is beautiful," Ted said, his voice catching slightly at the end of the adjective. "You painted this?"

Watercolors were her favorite, so of course she'd used them for this one project. Ted ran a slow finger over the picture, then he twisted his body to prop the frame on his desk right next to his computer monitor. Ted spent an extra minute positioning her gift, and Eden stepped into his personal space while he was preoccupied. He'd put her painting in a place of honor, somewhere he'd see it every single day.

Up close, she could feel heat rolling off him. Her core tightened with nerves. With desire.

"Thank you," Ted said as he turned back to her. She was close enough that his hands came up to frame her hips. Tightening on her waist. "Eden?"

"Think of this as a bonus," she said and leaned forward to seal her lips over his.

It took Ted's brain 0.2 seconds to realize what was happening. In less time than it took to blink, he was kissing Eden back, and his hand snaked around her waist to pull her into the cradle of his thighs. With him seated on the desk, she was taller than he was, but barely.

Ted tipped his head back as he sucked at her full top lip and she sucked in a sharp breath through her nose. Eden tilted her chin, just a fraction of a fraction of an inch, and it was like she'd poured lava past his lips to settle in the aching pit of his belly. His hands clenched against her hips, fingers twisting in the soft fabric so that they wouldn't travel anywhere they weren't welcome.

Ted had seen this kiss coming. Her moss green eyes— unable to keep a single secret—had dropped to his mouth once, twice, and then she'd leaned in, dark lashes shuttering that magnificent gaze before she even pressed against him. He could have stopped her. He could have stood up, leaned back, put his hands on her shoulders to hold her off, except some part of him had been thinking about this exact moment since the doors opened at the precinct and he'd seen her perched on the ugliest couch known to humankind.

She'd sat in that room, glowing. He'd imagined this kiss in the interrogation room, standing with her on the sidewalk, and yet again in the privacy of his hell-hot shower, but he'd staunchly avoided even the thought of doing anything about it.

Until she'd kissed him. Handed him his fantasy on a silver platter. It was a reach, but he could justify kissing her back. Pushing her away would have hurt them both. So yes, he leaned into the contact, pressing his tongue against the seam of her lips. Stealing a kiss could still be innocent, especially with him holding their bodies apart, but putting his hands on any other part of this woman would be inappropriate while they were still in his office. Especially when he knew he had no intention of taking anything between them further than this moment.

That was a personal rule, not an office one. Ted sometimes wished he cared a little bit less about what other people thought of him and his behavior. He could blame his family, but Will had been raised in the same tax bracket—probably a few above—and didn't care what anyone thought. Will and AJ had no problem doing things in Will's office. Things involving giggles and muffled thumps and Will walking AJ to the door while they both sported dopey grins. Things that ended with mis-buttoned shirts and a fresh bruise sucked against AJ's neck.

But, not only were Will and AJ three and a half days away from wedded bliss, but they'd fallen back in love on national television. The show had been careful not to show too much, but Will had alluded to some tape of a library that the host had gifted him. Right before the network destroyed the original footage.

Ted suppressed a shudder as he remembered his best friend admitting that they sometimes pulled the footage out during date night. Porn. His best friend had basically made soft-core, public spaces porn. If Will and AJ had been fine with *that*, a little afternoon delight within earshot of the fellow partners definitely wouldn't phase them.

Ted didn't judge. If his best friend wanted to engage in sexual acts in the middle of a duck boat tour, well, Ted would put together a bond check but he wouldn't judge. That didn't mean he himself would be lining up for outdoor sex. He could already imagine the verbal beat down he'd receive from his stepfather, no matter that he was several inches taller than the man and outweighed him by a good fifty pounds.

But there was also difference between defiling your desk with the love of your life, and using it for a random hook up.

It took effort to break the kiss. Ted pulled back by degrees. First his tongue, then his lips, then his face. He locked his elbows to put space between their bodies. Eden blinked down at him, her eyes clouded with lust, pupils swallowing the brown-flecked green. Looping tendrils of dark hair stuck to her cheek and forehead. Ted's hands itched to push them back, but Eden beat him to it. She gathered up her hair and twisted it into a loop before tossing it over her shoulder to fall down her back.

She was wearing a baggy overall thing with huge printed sunflowers. The ties looped over her shoulder. Underneath he could see the shimmery slippery fabric of a sports top, the pearl white emphasizing the golden glow of her skin. A thick green headband held back her long dark hair. The bag tossed over her shoulder looked like the patchwork quilt that Logan's grandma had stitched for him. Each square was a different colored burst of a flower. She'd bitten her fingernails down to the quick, a constellation of freckles spilled across the bridge of her nose, and she was quite possibly the most beautiful woman Ted had ever seen.

"That was—"

"Not a thank you!" Eden said. She pointed at the picture on his desk. "*That* was the thank you, and I was supposed to offer to return the favor anytime. The kiss was just a bonus. I've been thinking about it for a while and really wanted to kiss you. I hoped you wanted to kiss me too, and maybe if you did, we could continue. Kissing. Each other. For fun."

"You're not looking for a boyfriend?" He was a relationship kind of guy, even if he already knew they'd be a bad fit.

"God no," she laughed, the sound a punch to his gut. "I'm all for the benefits, but I'm not interested in the rest of it. You know?"

"Right." Ted ran a hand through his hair and braced himself for the hurt she was bound to feel when he let her down. "It was a delightful bonus."

That was not what he'd meant to say, even if it was true.

"Delightful!" Eden was grinning at him again. She did that a lot. Smiled. At everyone. It was cute.

"Yes," Ted nodded, "but we shouldn't do it again."

He waited, expecting to see her smile dim or her face to fall. Something. It wasn't because he had an inflated ego, but in his experience, no one reacted well to a rejection.

"Fair enough," Eden said, and tipped her head to the side. She shrugged her round shoulders.

Ted hadn't wanted to hurt her—he didn't like hurting anyone—but she could have been a little less fine with what he'd said. She'd kissed him, after all. She'd kissed him and turned his brain to mush and sent all the blood in his body rushing south, and she could care a bit more that he was putting the brakes on that detour. She wasn't even faking it. He was skilled at reading people and she truly was unbothered.

"That's it?" He heard himself ask. Eden nodded.

"Yup. I'm attracted to you, and I took a shot. I think you're attracted to me too, but I'm not entitled to any part of you that you aren't ready or willing to give. So that's it. No more kissing."

Ted frowned. There was enough distance between them he could push off the desk and walk around it to drop into his chair. It was what he told her had to happen, but it didn't sound as nice when she said it. It sounded…fucking awful.

"So no hard feelings," she said, still smiling. Her fingers twisted in the strap of her bag.

"Right," he said again.

"I still owe you a favor," Eden said. "No questions asked. I can teach your niece or nephew or anyone the piano, guitar, or harp. I'm not great on violin but I can give it a shot. Voice lessons, sure, but my best friend Romy is a better singer. I prefer watercolors, but can paint in most mediums and I do charcoal sketches. I'm a RYT—registered yoga teacher—if you want a class or a session. I have good handwriting and can address your holiday cards, or pose as an angry ex-girlfriend to get you out of something. Pretty much you name it and I'll be there."

"It's June," Ted said, and Eden nodded again.

"Yep."

"You said you'd address my holiday cards, but who sends holiday cards in June?"

"Maybe you send Fourth of July cards, or you can call me in November." Eden said. "I'll email you my contact info."

"Because you think you owe me a favor."

"An open-ended IOU," Eden confirmed. "I trust you to use it wisely."

She shouldn't. Trust him, that is. Ted was a decent guy. He'd never hurt her on purpose, but she didn't know that. They'd spent maybe thirty minutes together. Including today, it was an hour at most. He didn't like the idea of her feeling indebted to him, especially when she had no guarantee that he wouldn't take advantage of her offer.

A chime sounded from his computer. A calendar reminder for the meeting Will had taken. It lit up his screen, illuminating the HMP logo he'd set as his backdrop. The one Eden painted was better. He glanced at the picture he'd placed just to the right of his monitor. She'd painted their building, the gray stone composed of muted blues and purples. She'd made it look beautiful. Behind the building, she'd cut out the few blocks between them and the harbor, leaving little red and green sailboats bobbing in a sea of navy and white water.

Across the front of the painting, in big block letters that matched the font of their logo, were the letters HMP. If he was less selfish, Ted would insist that they display the painting in the reception area. The first thing clients saw when they walked in the door. He'd ask their IT guy to replace the logo on their website, too. She'd given him enough. He didn't need some nebulous favor.

What he needed was a date to Will's damn wedding. That sounded bad. He liked Will. He'd been the best roommate freshman Ted could have asked for, and it was an honor to be asked to stand up with him as Will promised to worship, cherish, and encourage AJ's dreams for the rest of time.

Ted possibly loved AJ even more. He'd liked her a lot when they'd first met. Thought Will was dimmer than a single watt lightbulb for not going after her a decade before. Had laughed so hard he'd fallen off a chair when Will told him she was on the reality show he'd starred on. Overnighted the engagement ring Will had never parted with, and blinked back tears when the fucker finally proposed. Now he ached with the need for the same comfort, companionship, and chemistry that his best friend had found with the best girl.

Ted didn't want AJ, he wanted *an* AJ. Someone who would stand next to him and rub soothing circles on his back when his family was intense. Someone who would be a partner. Someone who would fit into the life he'd been working so hard to build from the day his family had dropped him off at college and he realized they were happy to be rid of him.

He'd been looking for that someone for about a year now, with less-than-zero luck. And if, for one moment, he'd thought maybe Eden would be a potential fit for the role? Well, she'd been pretty clear about her thoughts on that.

"How do you feel about weddings?" He heard himself ask. As if he had no control over his own thoughts or vocal chords.

"I love them," Eden said. "I cry every time."

Ted didn't think that was true. She was too smiley for tears. When he told Eden that, she laughed.

"When they first lay eyes on each other, that's the doozy." She shrugged. "I'm a total romantic."

"Just not for yourself." Ted said, and Eden froze.

"Look, it's not that I don't believe in love. I do, or I used to. It's that relationships always leave one person changing for the other. One party loses themselves in the process and that's not great. I'll be the first to admit there are exceptions. I've decided to believe that the weddings I attend happen to fall into that category."

So she wasn't as totally anti-love as she seemed. More like anti-relationship. That gave him the courage to plow ahead instead of backtrack.

"How would you feel about attending a wedding? This weekend."

She didn't immediately say no, which was better than he deserved.

"As a date?" She asked, small lines appearing between her brows as she frowned at him.

"No, I heard you loud and clear. As a…" Ted tried to think of the right word. He'd thrown them both with the suggestion, now it was his job to explain his reasoning. "As a business endeavor." Eden chewed on her lower lip, but still didn't answer. He felt creepy. Like he was pushing too hard against her boundaries and needed to back the hell off. "I was thinking about it to cash in that favor. I'll write up a contract to keep everything black and white. I 'paid' in advance when I stepped in at the precinct. Now you're repaying in kind with an escort."

The smile was back, her demeanor changed. "Oh," she laughed. "You don't need to do that. I'd love to go to a wedding. This weekend. With you."

Now it was Ted's turn to frown. "I feel like I'm coercing you." He admitted. "You seemed a little… quiet."

"I was worried you were angling for something more personal." Eden said. "I know you said you weren't but…Anyway I didn't know how to let you down easy."

"No date." Ted said, and it was the truth. Eden wasn't the one for him, but she was beautiful, and fun, and it would be nice to have someone there for him as he watched his friends begin the kind life he wanted for himself. "See? This is why we have it all written down. Just Party A and Party B attending a weekend event together in exchange for previously rendered services."

"I am formally requesting that I get to be Party B. A seems like too much pressure. Now, who do you want me to be? Your girlfriend? Your date? Your distant cousin? I'm not the best actress, but I can pull out a character for a single evening." She rifled through her purse for a battered notepad and a glitter-covered pink pen.

"Just you?" Ted frowned. "I hadn't thought that far ahead. It would just be nice to have someone there for the festivities."

Eden jotted a few things down on a blank piece of paper, her head nodding as the pen drew across the page. He was telling the hand-to-heart truth here. He'd told Will, when he and AJ sent out invitations, that he'd like to bring a date to the wedding. His best friend had said it wasn't a problem. Will knew he was looking for his future.

The issue hadn't been finding a date; it had been finding the right person to bring with him. Someone easy to get along with. Someone his friends would like. Someone he liked. He'd stupidly assumed that it would be easy to find the perfect woman. Easy to revive his dating career and find the one. He'd been wrong.

Finding women hadn't been the issue. The problem had been finding the *right* women. If his friends liked them his family wouldn't. If Martin would approve, then his friends were only barely polite. Time and time again he'd find women who understood his career and his drive to be the best attorney he could be, but they had less-than-zero desire to hop on the back of his Harley and drive along the waterfront.

Those same women often praised his tattoos and then gave him pointed looks while asking when he planned to shave his beard. He couldn't bring one of those women to the wedding. She'd be in photos, memories, and Will and AJ would forever be stuck looking at a stranger in their photo album that everyone had tiptoed around with chilly politeness.

Eden on the other hand… well, his family—his stepfather—would hate her, but she'd fit right in with his friends. Much better to take her, with her amiable smiles, perceptive gift giving, and her ability to thaw even Devin, than to take any of his recent girlfriends. Besides, going alone would be just as bad as taking someone everyone else couldn't stand. Except instead of rolling their eyes as his friends pointed to his date in photos, they'd be pointing at pictures of Ted standing sullen and alone in each and every shot.

Eden would do great. Ted enjoyed talking to her. He enjoyed being around her. It would cash in the favor she believed she owed him, and okay, he was going to great lengths to justify an impulsive invitation. He just enjoyed being around her. Even if there was no future on the table.

"I'm all in," she said, "just let me know the details and I'll be there with bells on."

Ted should have given her the details before now.

"The wedding is this Saturday on the Cape. Chatham. It's small, just family and friends at Will's family home. I'm going up tomorrow, but you can meet us there before the ceremony."

Eden frowned and Ted thought about what he might have said wrong. Maybe she'd thought it would be an enormous affair, where she could slip away into anonymity.

"You can change your mind at any time. No hard feelings." Ted told her.

Eden shook her head. "No, not that. Um—" she twisted her fingers together and looked down at her feet, glancing up from under thick dark lashes. "The police still have my car? I don't know when I'll get it back, so I might need to find a ride."

Ted didn't know the public transportation options offhand, but he had no problem paying for them. Eden shook her head again when he told her so.

"No, no, no. I'm sure I know someone driving down for the weekend. I'll hitch a ride. It's June. Doesn't everyone go down to the Cape on the weekends?"

"Hitch" was a figure of speech and she didn't mean with her thumb, right? Or strangers? Yes, a lot of Bostonians drove down for the weekend. That's why he and Logan and the happy couple were driving down Thursday. A desperate attempt to avoid hours stuck in traffic.

"When you say friends—"

"Oh, a friend of a friend, I'm sure." She waved her hand as if brushing off his concern. It wasn't working.

"So a stranger." He said, and she shrugged. Very reassuring. "I'll drive you. There's more than enough room at the Big House and I'll give you cab fare in case you want to bail."

"I don't think a cab would drive me from Chatham back to the city. And technically, you're also a stranger," Eden said, her signature grin highlighting those dimples. "But I accept. On one condition."

Anything.

"Did you say never again because you thought the kiss was lousy?"

It had been the best kiss of his entire life.

"No. I said never again because I want to get married."

Eden's green eyes went wide. "Ah yeah. I'm not the right person for that. You need someone—" she looked him up and down, "tamer."

"Tamer?"

Eden nodded, "I'm not the right person for a lawyer. And I'm not interested in being anyone but me."

"That's not a bad thing, Eden." Ted smiled at her.

Eden hoisted her bag higher over her shoulder and backed toward the exit.

"We're hitting the road at noon. I'll swing by your house to get you."

"I'll meet you here," Eden said, pulling open the door and bracing it with her shoulder. "Less messy that way."

Messy. Right. He should take some steps to mitigate any complications.

"I'll draw up that contract for us and send it to you," Ted called after her as his office door slammed closed. Only when she waved over her shoulder, moving down the hall with purpose, did he remember she had his contact information, but he didn't have hers.

Eden met Ted at his office right on time and together they walked the few blocks to the parking garage. She'd actually gotten there fifteen minutes early and walked laps around the block to pass the extra time. Ted struck her as the kind of man who'd care if she was late and for some reason that mattered to her. Not the punctuality—Eden was a free spirit but that didn't mean she played fast and loose with other people's time—she cared about making a good impression on Ted.

So far he'd seen her in a precarious situation at a police station and then he'd seen her throw herself at him. Usually that kind of thing didn't bother Eden. She'd spent years making sure other people's opinions didn't bother her.

The fact that she already cared about what Ted thought… well, that was just another reason that he was right to push her away. She should keep her distance.

"Don't worry," Eden said as he opened the passenger door for her and took a hold of her overnight bag. "I left all of your contact information and the house address with my best friend. If I don't check in and offer proof-of-life updates, then she knows to contact Uncle Earl." She slid into the leather seat and grinned at Ted. "I have full faith in you, but Romy worries. She says I'm too trusting."

"Romy may be right." Ted said, low enough that Eden had to strain to hear him, and shut the door with a click.

Ted slid her bag into the trunk and then jogged around the back of the SUV. It was the same car he'd driven her home in at the beginning of the week, and Eden had to admit that it was impressively clean.

There were no food wrappers, no watery half-full Dunkin' cups, no random articles of clothing stashed along the crumb-strewn floor mats. Every single time Justin had borrowed her car, it had come back with enough stuff piled into every nook and cranny that she'd wondered if he'd been living out of it. Given her recent run-in with the authorities, it was quite possible he had been. She was certain, now, that he'd been conducting business out of it.

Ted's car was the shiny pristine epitome of someone who regularly picked up after themselves. He probably wasn't someone who panic-cleaned right before someone slid into the passenger seat. He was someone who took care of others, who took care of himself and his own things. He'd be the type to take care of her, and in Eden's experience that meant she'd end up changing what she wore and said and did just to make his job easier.

The cleanliness of his car almost made her feel guilty for toeing off her sandals and sliding her feet along his dashboard. Almost. His gaze moved to her feet, and she wiggled her toes. Out of the corner of her eye, she saw Ted's mouth tip up into an almost smile as he positioned himself behind the steering wheel.

Ted had either embraced Casual Thursday or changed his clothes before she showed up, which was a good thing. The one and a half hour drive—longer if they encountered any form of traffic—would be rough in a suit and tie. Maybe he hadn't fully changed. A long-sleeved button-down hung open over a white t-shirt and he'd swapped his dress pants for a pair of cargo shorts, but Eden was still sure his shirt cost more than her rent.

"I like the color." He glanced at her feet again and Eden smiled, grateful that she'd let Romy swipe the bright yellow over her toes. She could feel Ted's eyes moving up the length of her leg and she tugged at the hem of her denim shorts, twisting her fingers in the frayed edges. "Sorry," Ted started the car, pulling out onto the road.

"Don't apologize," Eden said as they merged onto 93. "If I minded people looking, I wouldn't have worn these shorts."

Something hot and needy coiled low in her belly when he switched lanes with ease, one hand draped over the leather steering wheel. It only grew when he raked his gaze along her legs and up to the faded denim.

"I like them." His voice was deeper than normal, his dark eyes hot on her skin. It sent a shiver up through her core and out through her limbs. Good old-fashioned lust. Eden didn't know if it was better or worse that it was affecting both of them. Ted's pupils expanded as he flicked his gaze between her bare legs and the road.

"Listen, Ted," Eden licked her dry lips, "I am more than interested in what you're offering, if it's just for the weekend, but I thought we agreed—"

"You're right." Ted shook his head, as if he were clearing his thoughts. "You do—"

"Casual."

"And I—"

"Don't."

"So it's best we keep the naked stuff off the table."

It *was* for the best. "Technically, you don't have to be naked for the fun stuff." Eden couldn't help but add, and Ted took in a ragged breath. "Sorry." She grinned at the slight flush that was climbing his neck. He didn't strike her as the type to blush. "I'm stopping. I'm done. Want me to cover up or something?"

Eden was wearing one of her favorite white babydoll shirts. It was comfortable and breezy but didn't pair well with a bra. It had also come out of the dryer two inches shorter than the last time she'd washed it. Eden frowned. She wasn't used to dressing for someone else. Growing up, her mama had encouraged free expression, especially with clothing. Theresa Yates had been heavily influenced by the 60s free-love movement, and Eden had been heavily influenced by her mama.

That hadn't lasted past the "I do's". Theresa had gone from peasant skirts and bright colors to sedate sweaters and khakis because that was what Greg liked best. The few times her mama had tried to branch out, she'd been met with the silent treatment or the harsh reminder that she was a wife and her job wasn't to embarrass her husband but to support him. Eden's wardrobe had changed too. Greg had approved every article of clothing that came into *his* house.

It wasn't just wardrobe. Greg wanted final say in anything *his* money paid for. Theresa had left her job with the local theater company and had transitioned into the role of a stay-at-home wife and mother. Eden was forbidden from getting a part-time job because it was more important that she study and get straight A's.

It had chafed, following each and every one of her stepdad's rules, but arguing only made things worse for both her and her mother. Eden stayed carefully between the lines until her eighteenth birthday. Then she'd packed a small suitcase full of her personal things—the clothes she left in her dresser and closet—and told Greg she was done. From that point on, Eden had made every decision firmly for herself. She wasn't interested in changing her personal style for someone else, ever again. Greg had been mad, of course, but that had no longer felt important. Being herself made her happier than her stepdad's disappointment scared her.

That being said, she could put a blanket over her legs for the span of a car ride. That wasn't the same thing as changing her style. It wasn't. It was a courtesy. Eden was a firm believer that clothing was *not* an invitation, but she also knew there was simmering chemistry between her and Ted. She didn't need to stoke the flames just to pass the time.

"No," Ted said, "You don't have to do that for me."

Something tugged in the center of Eden's chest at the horror in his voice. It was just once, a minor hiccup in the regular beats of her heart, but it was disconcerting and unwelcome.

"Not willing to give up the view?" She asked.

Ted turned his eyes back to the road instead of answering.

Eden had the strange urge to apologize. If there was one thing Ted had made very clear, it was that he was respectful of other people. Her own offer, and his rejection, had thrown her off guard. Years of her own insecurities had swamped her like a tidal wave and she'd reacted with jokes, humor. She hadn't meant to offend him, just to tease. Something to get under the edges of his skin the way he had under hers.

"I'm sorry." Eden said. She felt like they spent a lot of time apologizing to each other. "I don't really like being told what to do, and sometimes I'm a little sensitive about it. I feel like people are trying to change me and I automatically get tense." Or crack jokes to diffuse the situation.

"I wasn't asking you to change."

"I know," Eden said, "Like I said, sensitive. You've been nothing but respectful of my choices. You even offered to write up a contract to make me feel comfortable. I have nothing to worry about with you, Ted."

"Right," Ted said and lifted his hips, slipping a hand into the back pocket of his shorts. He pulled out a piece of paper, folded into quarters. He passed it over the gearshift and Eden took it in her fingers, eyes searching him for any hints about what it might contain. "Normally I wouldn't fold a document like that, but I figured this was a unique situation. "

She pulled back the corners, smoothing the folds until she could see the HMP logo at the top of the paper and a lot of small words printed underneath. She saw her own name and…

"Theodore?" She grinned at his side profile. "Theodore Norman Hughes. Do you ever go by Teddy?"

"No." He shook his head. "Only binding if we do it right."

Binding.

Eden took another look at the document. A little wordy, but Eden understood most of what it said as she read each line.

"A partnership agreement? You actually wrote a contract." she laughed, "You didn't have to do that."

"I told you I was going to. I thought it would help us keep this—"

"Platonic?" Eden offered.

"I just thought we'd both feel better if everything was in writing. You know, about me not expecting anything out of this trip."

Eden scanned the third line down under the heading titled **Contributions**. *Sexual activity, sexual contact, and sexual advances are neither expected nor acceptable contributions to this partnership unless mutually agreed upon.* Eden read further down the page. Her finger skated over *either party can dissolve the partnership for any reason and at any time. If such dissolution occurs while the partners are in the same location and over five miles from the HMP building, address above, then Partner A (Hughes) will immediately find agreeable transportation for Partner B (Yates) or provide adequate compensation.*

"I don't want you to feel trapped, uncomfortable, or pressured," Ted said, merging back into the right-hand lane. "You can leave anytime and I'll make sure you have a ride, no matter what."

So he'd written it out in a contract. Even if it wasn't legally binding—she didn't know if it was or not—his expectations or lack thereof were in writing. Her escape plan was in writing. Eden hadn't assumed she'd need one. Ted had given her no reason to doubt him so far, and she'd jumped into this weekend with both feet. With this contract, Ted had made sure that she'd jumped into a full swimming pool, not a shallow puddle. Eden didn't know if it was insanely attractive, or if she were waiting for the other shoe to drop.

The need to define and list and categorize. The need for everything to have a place and line up in an orderly fashion. His subtle high-end fashion choices. The clean car he drove.

The careful way he'd put space between them after she'd kissed him in his office, even though he could have had her. Ted was fastidious and organized and everything she wasn't. There was no way his friends and family were going to approve of her. She knew his type. Even for this short getaway, at some point he'd either decide the disapproval was too much and cut his losses from her, or ask her to change. At least if that happened she knew she'd be able to walk away.

"Are you afraid I'm going to forget why I'm here?" A favor for a favor.

"No, it's because I want you to know you're safe," Ted said, even though the pounding of her heart proved he was wrong, "with me."

"Thank you," Eden said, the words not feeling weighty enough for how deeply he'd touched her soul. "I'll sign it when we get there."

She swallowed past the lump in her throat and looked out the window. Route 3 wasn't the prettiest drive, just long stretches of road buffeted by thick trees, but she couldn't complain. The warm summer sun burned through the car windows and heated her skin.

There were other drivers out, but not as many as she'd expected. In another twenty-four hours, families and beach vacationers would pack the road, turning their ninety-minute drive into hours of standstill traffic. Today it was just the two of them. Eden and Ted, his shiny black Volkswagen, and the weekend's potential.

They lapsed into silence, neither heavy nor uncomfortable, just the still lack of conversation normal between two relative strangers. The Animals played through the car speakers, the low hum comforting if barely audible.

She was humming along, tapping the triplets out on her thigh, before she realized Ted was humming too. She refused to take that as a sign.

"I didn't peg you for a classic rock guy," Eden said.

"Yeah," Ted said and the corner of his mouth twitched up. "The Yardbirds, Steppenwolf, The Rolling Stones, if it's a garage band from the 60's I'll probably know the words."

"Me too," Eden said. It was the music her mama had played when she was little. Greg had hated it, but those early memories were powerful. She'd gone right back to her favorite artists

"My stepfather wasn't a fan of top 40 music, but he didn't mind the classic stuff."

"You didn't want to piss him off?" Eden could understand that. Everyone did what they had to in order to survive.

"Oh I never minded pissing him off." That lip twitch again, almost like Ted was smiling. "But I got used to this stuff. I'd rather die than admit it, but it's actually good stuff."

Eden looked out her window. One tiny thing in common didn't outdo all the differences between them. Even if he'd gone back to humming her favorite song.

It was the *pop-pop-pop* alerted her first, and Eden twisted in her seat to glance out the rear driver-side window. A big red bike passed the driver's side of the car, its engine growling as it outpaced the Volkswagen.

"Motorcycle," Eden said and pointed. It was a game her mother had taught her as a child. Some kids played punch-buggy. Eden and her mama had racked up points finding motorcycles. Learning to spot them on the road, learning to look for them, could save lives. That had been her mama's reasoning. Eden hadn't thought about that as a kid.

"A Harley," Ted said, turning to watch as the rider passed them. "You like bikes?"

His forehead furrowed with his words, as though he hadn't expected Eden to be a motorcycle girl. Maybe someday she would be. She didn't shy away from anything else. Eden had asked Santa for a motorcycle five years straight. Even when she'd started to doubt the beard and the belly and the magic. The closest she'd ever come was the old teal Vespa that Romy used to have stashed in their landlord's garage.

"I love them. Never ridden one, though. Maybe someday." There was no way buttoned-up Ted was a biker. He was probably the guy who rolled his eyes when they roared past his little suburban home on a Saturday morning. Actually, the eye rolling didn't seem like Ted at all, but she couldn't picture him on a bike.

"I have a Softail Standard." Ted said, darting a glance at her.

"You have a motorcycle?" Had her jaw dropped open? It felt like it had. Her laugh was high-pitched, manic. "You ride bikes?"

"Remember when I said I liked pissing off my stepfather? Well, old habits die hard." He shrugged one big shoulder. "We could amend the contract." He said it so casually, as if he wouldn't mind spending extra time with her. That thought was… attractive. Even more so than the width of his chest, or his height, or the shiny wave of his warm brown hair.

"Partner A will contribute one motorcycle ride during the course of the partnership?" Eden curled her toes into the warm dashboard. "Do I have to file a motion or get a notary?"

Ted's brows tipped together as he glanced over at her, but he was smiling. "My bike's in the shop right now, but I should get it back next week. I'll take you any time."

"After our contract is up." Eden sighed. "There goes that idea."

"We can just amend the agreement, add an additional clause to the document."

"Is there a term for that? When we have to change things in our agreement? I didn't know we were writing up a full contract. Should I have my lawyer look it over?" She tried to widen her eyes and give him her most innocent look. In return, Ted raised a single dark brow and pinned her to the seat.

Eden wanted a ride on his bike, but a tiny voice in the back of her brain was pinging like a smoke detector, warning her that it was a bad idea. Both extending their time together beyond this trip, and plastering herself to his back for a ride on his bike. That was boyfriend stuff. Date stuff.

"*I'm* a lawyer." Ted said.

"Should I have gotten my own representation?" It was a joke. Especially considering the first day they met. Eden couldn't afford a lawyer for the very real possibility of a criminal defense. She definitely wasn't about to throw away an exorbitant hourly rate so someone could read over a fake contract.

"An escalation clause would allow for changes to agreed upon pricing or compensation. It would need to specify when those changes would go into effect and why. They're common in construction or real estate contracts because the market determines the cost of materials and home values fluctuate."

"Not exactly applicable to us," Eden said. The thick trees surrounding the highway had given way to rolling green golf courses.

Ted's fingers were drumming against the top of the steering wheel. Eden watched his throat work as he swallowed. He lowered the radio volume until she could barely make out The Kinks over the soft sounds of the car's engine.

"I know we don't know each other well," Ted started, darting glances between where she sat and the road. "But I hope you know I wouldn't take advantage of you like that. Not of anyone. Will, Logan and I—we started our own firm to be sure that the big guy couldn't bulldoze the little one. You know?"

The funny thing was, she *did* know. She might pride herself on seeing the best in people. She might work hard to see strengths instead of flaws, but she also knew what Ted was saying was the absolute truth. He was not the man who twisted situations to benefit himself. He wasn't the big guy bull-dozing, the little guy. He was the one who took down the bully. He protected. He played fair. He listened.

"Yes," Eden said, and for the first time she got a glimpse of an actual smile as it broke over Ted's handsome face. Eden wrapped her arms around her waist, layering her limbs like a coat of armor against the brilliance of that smile. "I'll make you a deal. Our own little escalation clause thingy. If this partnership ever goes beyond this one weekend, then you owe me a ride on a motorcycle. Deal?"

Ted held his hand out for her to shake and although the grip was awkward with them sitting side by side, she shook it once. His skin was rough against her palms. She wondered how she felt to him. If he'd noticed that she also had rough calluses on her fingers. Eden's were from all her guitar work. She wondered what Ted's were from.

"You're nothing like I thought you'd be," Eden said as his hand slid from hers. "I doubt you got those callouses signing on the dotted line."

"They're from my bike," he admitted, "What about yours?"

"Guitar," she said. "And harp, although I don't play that one as often."

"How did you get started playing so many instruments?" Ted asked.

"Orchestra was an acceptable extracurricular, but no one can control how you connect with the music you hear or play. The more instruments I played, the more time I was encouraged to practice. My stepdad didn't feel quite the same about my artwork. He thought it was a waste of time." Eden leaned across the gear shift. "Want to hear something ironic?"

Ted leaned in too, only inches separated them.

"Greg thought painting was a waste of time, but illustrating pays most of my bills. Most of my music is just for fun. I wonder what he'd think of that."

"He doesn't know what you do?" Ted frowned but didn't shift away from her.

Eden shrugged. "I haven't spoken to him since I graduated high school," and she had no plans to change that.

Half an hour later, Eden was shivering under the heavy air conditioning when he twisted in his seat. Ted shrugged off the outer layer that he'd been wearing and handed her the shirt. Despite the movement of his upper body, the car never swerved on the road, and Eden clutched the shirt close to her chest, trying not to be obvious as she inhaled the clean scent of him.

His warm sunshine and salt water scent seeped out of the stiff collar and she barely resisted the urge to bury her face in the warm cotton. Eden was a sucker for the clean scent of a man, but even she had some self-preservation. Not a lot, but some. Sniffing his shirt right after they'd agreed to a platonic weekend was not a good look.

She pushed her arms through the sleeves, letting the fabric settle over her chest and stomach, obscuring the happy points of her nipples. It took her a few moments, positioning herself under the starched cotton, before she let her eye alight on Ted as he maneuvered the car down the highway. The muscles in his arms bulged and flexed as he swapped lanes, but it was the tattoos she couldn't look away from. Vibrant, colorful ink painted the lengths of both of his arms. Intricate drawings she'd need time to study. Time she could not give herself.

First the classic rock, the stepfather, the motorcycle. The respectful way he cared about what would make her comfortable. And now tattoos? Was this some sort of test?

"So you want to get married?" Eden asked, her eyes tracing the outline of a photo realistic grizzly bear.

Ted nodded.

Eden had seen tons of bear tattoos where the animal's mouth was wide open in a ferocious roar. Ted's bear stared back at her calm and assessing, as if sizing her up with stoic calm. Her fingers itched to grab her charcoal and sketch the image. It could be a little piece of Ted that she could keep beyond this weekend. A reminder of this journey with a man who was already surprising her. In a good way.

"Tell me about the kind of woman you want to shackle yourself to."

Ted shot her an inscrutable look at the word shackle, but Eden ignored him. She couldn't explain why her heart was pounding as she waited for his answer. She'd assumed she knew what kind of wife he wanted. She'd assumed she knew what kind of man he was. So maybe she'd jumped to conclusions. Did that matter?

"I want—" Ted started and then sighed. "I want a partner. I want an equal. Someone who gets me and can be the other half of my unit. Us against the world. My family isn't… easy… to get along with. They're big on image and deportment so someone that would fit in with them, get along with them, would be ideal."

Eden's pulse pounded in her ears. For just a moment there it almost sounded like he wanted the same thing that—deep in the dark recesses of her bruised heart—she wanted too. A partner. An equal. But no, he also wanted the perfect fit for his family. It didn't matter if the real inner Ted was tattoos and motorcycles and hard rock and artistic expression. It didn't matter if he could be her picture perfect soulmate. He wanted someone who wouldn't make waves. So she'd just keep her hands and thoughts to herself.

Easy enough.

No matter how many times Ted visited the Masters's summer estate, rounding the bend in the gravel driveway and seeing the house always took his breath away. Light gray siding, large colonial gridded windows hugged by tall black shutters, the octagonal widow's walk looking out over the dark Atlantic Ocean. It was the pure embodiment of old family money.

Even Ted's stepfather, a man who preferred sleek modern design and minimal décor, often expressed his envy at the sun-soaked rooms and the perfectly manicured grounds. Ted wasn't the only one admiring the home as he pulled the car up in front of the garage and guest house off to the right. There was a sharp inhale from his passenger seat that made him almost smile, although he ducked his head to hide it.

"Holy fucking shit." Eden spun around in her seat so she wouldn't lose sight of the main house. "You didn't tell me this wedding was at the fucking White House."

Maybe she hadn't made the connection between his partner Will and the Massachusetts senator. That was fine. Maybe even better. Will was close to his parents, but he wasn't the politician so many people expected him to be. He was just Will. Even his season on a dating show hadn't changed much about Ted's friend.

Ted had grown up around similar expectations—his stepfather was an old college friend of Will's father—but the lifestyle that fit Will like a well-tailored suit always fit Ted like a rental tux on the way to junior prom. Maybe that was because Ted's mom hadn't been a part of this lifestyle before Martin came along. They'd gone from a modest suburb to a mansion in a gated community almost overnight. His sweatpants and t-shirts had been traded for tailored chinos and polo shirts that cost more than he'd made in a whole year on his paper route.

"Don't worry," Ted pulled the keys from the ignition, "The Masterses are—" are what? Not like his stepfather? Not obsessed with money and image and prestige? That reminder never seemed to help him relax when he visited. Not to mention there had been a point in the not-too-distant past when Eleanor and George had cared. A lot. Ted had just never been on the receiving end of their judgement.

"Oh, I'm not worried." Eden's dark hair shifted over her shoulders as she turned to look at him. "I'm me. If they don't like me, then it's only one weekend and we can dissolve our agreement. I mean I won't go out of my way to cause problems, but I don't care much about what other people think."

Ted coughed to cover up the acidic burn in the back of his throat. "I'm not going to dissolve our agreement."

Eden's eyes traced the lines of his face, a soft smile dimpling her cheek. "I'm not either," she said. "Should we go in?"

"Proof of life," he prompted. She'd mentioned her friend's request for a check-in when she first climbed into his car. He'd want the same if any of the women in his life went off with a strange man. "Call your friend, family, whoever you need to."

Eden patted her pockets down before twisting to reach her bag sitting on the floorboards. It occurred to Ted that he hadn't seen her phone once on the drive. That was...abnormal for most people their age. Even Ted, not the world's most connected citizen, still had his smart phone connected to his car for music and GPS. Eden finally pulled a small, slim device out of her purse and tapped the screen. It stayed dark. She pressed a button on the side. Nothing happened.

"It's dead." She shoved the phone back to where it came from. "I'll charge it and text her later."

Did he once think she had the preservation skills of a piece of fruit? She had fewer.

What if he'd been a creep? He wanted to ask. What if something had gone wrong and she'd needed a rescue?

"Here," he unplugged his phone and held it out, "Call her with mine."

Eden took the device. She held it up to Ted's face, and he glowered to unlock the screen. She tapped away at the buttons, putting in her friend's number or whatever. A brief chuckle, some more frantic tapping, and then she was handing the phone back.

"I texted her," Eden assured him and reached for the door handle again.

He didn't recognize the number, but the message was still up.

> Hey Rome. It's me, Eden. Im using my kidnapper's phone to tell you he's not a kidnapper at all. No need for a search party just yet. He's been great. But honestly, even if he offs me, this will be an adventure of the highest order.

> Plus he's fun to look at.

Three little dots appeared at the bottom of the screen as "Rome" typed back a response.

> Are you fucking kidding me Eden?

> This had better be Eden.

> I require either a FaceTime call, a phone call, or proof Eden. Real proof. Not the kind of proof an axe murderer would coerce out of you.

> And if you aren't Eden, then I'm collecting your personal info from under her mattress and calling Uncle Ernie. They'll never fucking find you buck-o.

> ...

"I said call," Ted watched in horror as those dots kept blinking at him.

"I sent a message. It was fine."

"A message that read like I had a gun pressed to the back of your head as you typed it." He scrubbed a hand down his face as he took a deep breath. "She's worried about you."

He showed Eden the novel that kept coming through his phone, the device buzzing over and over again. Eden laughed but took it and keyed in an actual call to her best friend. Ted tried not to eavesdrop, no mean feat, when he was sitting so close to her.

"I'm fine. I'm good. We're here." A female voice said something through the line, and Eden laughed into the phone. "Ted said the same thing... no, I don't need our code word. I can't FaceTime you, he's an android guy. Yes.... I know." She tipped her head to the side as her gaze drifted over Ted's face, then shoulders, then dipped to his chest. "Yeah, no change there, Rome. I gave it a shot...what?" Her eyes went even lower and Ted resisted the urge to cant his hips under her gaze. She turned away and dropped her voice, but not before he'd seen her blown pupils. "Still fucking gorgeous, Rome, so fuck me...I'll charge it...and text you." Another bright laugh. "I love you too. Bye, babe."

Eden ended the call and handed the phone back to Ted. Their fingers brushed over the smooth silver shell of the device

"How was that?" She winked, then got out of the car before he could answer.

Ted grabbed their bags from the trunk and they walked to the front door, each step crunching on the fine gray stones. Eden tipped her head back, and the sun painted her skin in a golden glow. That view was almost enough to lighten the pressure squeezing his internal organs in a vice. It was the same heavy sensation that tripped through his bloodstream on the rare occasions he ventured to his childhood home.

Being around any of these people put Ted on edge. George and Eleanor, Will's parents, had never been anything but polite and approving of Ted, but he knew that what they approved of was the version of him that his stepfather had created. The Harvard alum, the well-regarded attorney, the man who hid his tattoos behind long-sleeve button downs and traded his bike in for a shiny new car whenever he was around them.

All of that was the person he'd become in order to keep the peace. In order to ease the smallest amount of guilt he still felt over the lucky break he'd received after his stepfather had made a series of phone calls after a spectacularly bad night. Most teenagers who got picked up by the cops ended up with some sort of record or disciplinary reaction. Unless they had wealthy and connected relatives to bail them out and expunge their records.

So yes, George and Eleanor knew about the tattoos and the bike—impossible not to after almost two decades of friendship—but it didn't matter. No matter how kind the Masterses were, no matter that Will's parents had spent no time with Ted's mother and stepfather—not since he and Will roomed together their freshman year—Ted never felt like he could relax around them.

The need to maintain his public persona followed him into the house, tension seeping deep into his bones even as he crunched up the walkway with a gorgeous woman next to him. Because not that long ago, Ted had learned that Eleanor's judgment had almost cost Will the love of his life.

They started up the brick walk to the arched front door. Eden stood close enough that their fingers brushed against each other with each step. What was he doing? He'd felt the same surge of discomfort at the thought of a weekend in this mansion on the cliffs, and he'd invited a relative stranger on a whim. A stranger he'd met when she was faced with legal troubles. There wasn't a single facet of Ted that thought Eden had done anything wrong, but he knew better than most people how insidious the whispers could be.

Guilt washed over him. He shouldn't have invited her here. Not with him. Not with the chemistry burning between them. There was no way they were coming out of this weekend without emotional damage. Both of them. The kind caused by having to fake happiness in front of his closest friends and people she'd never met.

"If you want to leave, we can leave." Ted said, "This weekend might not be all that fun."

Ted's hand tingled as Eden's pinky skimmed along the edge of his. Her fingers traced the line down the center of his palm as she slid her hand into his. She wove their fingers together, squeezing until he felt the grip clear up to his elbow. Her hand was warm and dry against his, the skin rough with a smattering of callouses. He froze on the top step, his fingers flexing against her slender ones, needing one last moment before they walked into the crowd.

She tugged gently on his arm until he stopped moving, looking down into her big green eyes.

"Why did you ask me to come?"

Because he wanted someone on his side. Everyone in that house knew he was chasing his own happily ever after and if he'd shown up alone there would be pitying looks and sad smiles and he hated that. Because walking into Will's family home reminded him too much of his stepfather's house and he hated facing the snide criticisms and the chill alone. Because she'd genuinely wanted to return his favor to her—despite not needing to—and he hadn't wanted her to worry about when or how he was going to cash in. Because despite the fact that they knew they could never be anything beyond this one weekend, he'd wanted more time with her.

"You don't have to tell me," Eden said, her fingers stroking the back of his hand. "I'm here to help you out, remember? Let me?"

And just like that, the vise grip in his chest loosened, and he looked down at her. He wanted to say something about how glad he was that she was here, but the words stuck to the roof of his mouth like a glob of peanut butter. It was a blessing, really. A chance to rethink, evaluate, choose his words carefully. He'd just spent an entire car ride putting her at ease and then the walk to the door second-guessing. Anything he said right now was going to be a shit show. Before he could figure it out, the front door opened and distracted them both.

"Mister Ted," the older woman said, stepping back to usher them into the white foyer.

"Mindy," Ted nodded his head to the Masters' housekeeper. Mindy had been a long-term employee when Ted first met Will almost twenty years ago. She ran a tight-ship. Every corner dusted, proper seasonal decorations displayed, and an endless supply of fresh white linens. Ted had never seen her in anything but her starched navy uniform dress, hair pulled back into a severe twist, and absolutely no hint of a smile on her thin mouth, but she was a big softie underneath it all. She kept his favorite Godiva Dark Chocolate Cocoa mix on hand and an endless supply of mini-marshmallows. He'd also caught her humming as she swept and dusted.

It had been Mindy who was tasked with taking over the care of Will's father while Will and his mother had been in L.A. filming their season of First Lady. George Masters had suffered a second heart attack in the months leading up to the show and had been vehemently opposed to the new life-style measures that were being foisted on him. The consensus had been that Mindy was the only one who wouldn't take no for an answer. She fussed incessantly, but with the same amount of cuddliness as a porcupine.

"This is Eden," Ted said, and Eden waved her hand and said, "Hello. Nice to meet you."

"Miss Eden," Mindy inclined her head and for a moment Ted thought Mindy might have twitched the corner of her lip. It was more likely Mindy was suffering some sort of stroke than smiling, but she gestured down the wainscoted wall. "Mrs. Masters is in the kitchen with the other guests. I'll have your bags brought up to the blue room."

Ted wasn't sure if he should correct Mindy about the room situation. He'd never intended for them to share a room, although he probably should have. Not in a creepy way, in a "this house only has a finite number of bedrooms and it made sense his date would share with him" way. Honestly, he had completely forgotten all about it, which was so unlike him he went a little dizzy at the thought. Eden hadn't said anything, and Mindy was already clacking down the wide-plank flooring.

"The room has a couch and a queen-sized bed." Ted said into Eden's ear as they followed the housekeeper. "I can take the couch."

She bumped her shoulder into his and grinned. "I'm not concerned. We have our iron-clad no-sex contract, Ted. We can share the bed like two adults. This isn't some sort of romance novel."

"You're sure?" Ted asked. He could hear the murmur of people from the gourmet kitchen.

"Of course." Eden furrowed her brow and tipped her head to the side. "I wouldn't say I was fine if I wasn't. If you turn out to be a bed hog, then I'll flip you for the couch."

Ted opened his mouth to ask her one more time, just to be sure, but she squeezed his hand and followed Mindy into the next room. She tugged on his hand to bring him with her, and Ted followed, still trying to process what she'd said.

Most of the other guests and family members were milling around the kitchen and family room. Will's grandparents sat on the tufted loveseat sipping dainty cups of tea while chatting with AJ's parents. Will's father had a newspaper unfolded in his lap as he ignored the conversation flowing around him. Eleanor Masters stood behind the large marble island, cutting up a fresh cantaloupe with a sharp knife.

Three women Ted recognized from the reality show were sitting around the counter and chatting. Logan stood by the far set of windows chatting with a tall Black man Ted had never seen before. He slowed his steps and tried to slow Eden's down too so that he could introduce her around slowly, but she towed him right into the crowd, aiming unerringly toward Will's mother.

"Hi," Eden said, holding her hand out to Eleanor. "I'm Eden Yates. Thank you so much for inviting me into your home."

Ted slipped an arm around her waist and braced himself for Eleanor's reaction. Will's mother always had impeccable manners, but the reaction was second nature. His stepfather would have said something cutting in response to Eden's friendly greeting. So far, Eden had been a bright spot on this trip. He didn't want anyone or anything to dim her light.

"Yes, Eden!" Eleanor wiped her palms on a fluffy white dish towel and then took the younger woman's hand in both of hers. "You must be Teddy's girlfriend. My son mentioned you'd be joining us this weekend. We are so happy to have you, dear. Can I get you anything? Water? Wine? Soda?"

Girlfriend? No. He should say something about that. And Will had already told his mother? About Eden? He'd met her for about ten seconds the day before and okay, yes. Ted had mentioned her after that first meeting at the station, but the goal had been to source help for her should she need it. Not to talk about the way her hair shone in the sun, or the way her eyes reminded him of uranium glass—glowing and dangerous.

"Soda?" Eden asked and Eleanor nodded.

"We have just about any kind you can think of."

Eden doubted that, her all-time favorite was a drink that no one ever stocked. She'd had one once, with her mom. The sweet, cherry-red liquid had been exactly what she'd needed after their multi-hour hike. It was a good memory, one from the summer before Greg walked into their private world; but more than the nostalgia, it was her mom telling her that the drink had also been her dad's favorite—not her stepdad, her real dad—that really clinched the lifelong choice. Even when no one had it, Eden still had to ask.

"You don't happen to have Cheerwine, do you?" She was fairly certain she already knew the answer.

"My apologies," Eleanor said, "I'll add it to the list for Mindy tomorrow. Can I offer you something else?"

Eden assured her host it was fine and asked for water instead. Eleanor handed her an individual plastic bottle as the other women continued with introductions.

"Alex," the tall Black woman held out her hand and Eden shook it. "My fiancé, Michael, is the big guy by the windows." The man talking to Logan raised his hand to wave, and Eden waved back.

Tandy introduced herself next, looking like she was ready for the Miss Universe pageant more than an afternoon on the Cape. Eden commented on the other woman's colorful beaded earrings and immediately earned a megawatt smile. The woman next to Tandy grinned as she leaned forward to take Eden's hand too.

AJ's closest friend, Chloe, was next. Chloe was AJ's maid of honor and she and Ted had been thrown together for planning often enough. Her hair was a lot shorter than the last time he'd seen her and either the nose stud was new or he hadn't noticed it before. Chloe took Eden's hand in hers and leaned forward to press a kiss to her knuckles, even as his wedding date snuggled closer into the bulk of his body.

"Eden," she said, letting her gaze trip from the top of Eden's dark hair all the way down her body, down her long expanse of leg, and then back up. "How have you been?"

"Can't complain," Eden said, and Ted opened his mouth to ask if they knew each other, which was absurd—how would they have known each other? Chloe lived in Colorado.

She was only in town for the wedding—when Eden tipped her head back to look up at him. Her soft hair caught in the rough stubble from his beard, and he didn't move to free the strands. Instead, he tightened his fingers around her hip, his fingers catching on one of her belt loops. "I lucked out in the date department," Eden said, and a collective "awe" went round the counter.

"You picked a good one," Chloe said with a wink, and Ted went dizzy for a moment. He wasn't one hundred percent sure which one of them Chloe was talking to, but either way, he didn't know how to respond.

"Will and AJ had to make a stop along the way," Eleanor said, resuming her slicing. "They mentioned not waiting for them to eat. Since this entire weekend is about them, I say we let them fend for themselves tonight."

"A little alone time is probably well-earned, considering they need to put up with all of us this weekend too," Tandy said, snagging a piece of melon.

"Right, alone time." Alex arched a perfect brow. "I'm sure they're enjoying it."

"The people getting laid absolutely can fend for themselves." Chloe added. "Worry about the rest of us lonely assholes."

"Not all of us are lonely," Alex said. "Some of us have wonderful fiancés."

"That's a delight for some of us," Chloe countered, but the two were smiling at each other, which ratcheted down the tension considerably.

"Chloe," Tandy widened her baby blue eyes and tipped her head toward Will's father and grandparents. "This might not be the right audience for these conversations."

"Nonsense," Eleanor moved the knife and cutting board to the wide apron sink and turned the water on. "She's just saying what everyone is thinking, dear."

"Why Eleanor," Tandy's gasp of shock was pure actress. "Whatever has gotten into you?"

"I honestly do not know." Eleanor dried her hands on another towel and turned back to face the room. "It just slipped out."

"Weddings do that," Eden said from where she was still tucked against Ted's side. "It's part of what makes them so magical. Anything can happen at a wedding and it's still considered normal. I once saw my stepfather lead a conga line with a tie wrapped around his forehead. All because of an open bar." Ted wondered if anyone else noticed the way her smile dimmed just the tiniest bit. "My stepdad is all about image. No one even knew he was drunk before he got started dancing. He was the talk of the family for months, but that night no one blinked an eye. Everyone just joined in."

Ted wondered how much trouble Eden had been in when the night ended and her stepdad's hangover kicked in. Ted would've been in trouble. Of course, teenage Ted would have been the one swapping the old man's drinks out with real liquor. Adult Ted would have done the opposite.

"My vote," Chloe said, sending another wink his date's way, "is that Eden leads the conga line."

"I concur," Tandy said. "I see you as an essential piece of the party."

"I'll need to borrow a tie," Eden said. "Unfortunately, I didn't think to pack my backup, and my dancing tie is at the dry cleaners."

"That's what he's for." Chloe pointed at Ted. "Just steal his and count it as foreplay."

"Foreplay, huh?" Eden was looking up at him with a lot more heat in her eyes than someone who'd recently reminded him of their no-sex contract should have.

"Don't tell me you haven't ridden that man like a log floating down the amazon river," Chloe said, shock clear in her voice. "Did you just start dating?" Chloe turned to look at Ted with confusion scrunching her nose. "Don't tell me you brought the girl to a wedding,"

"An out-of-town wedding," Eden helpfully supplied.

"—an out-of-town wedding. For your first date?"

Of course he hadn't. Because this didn't count as a date. They'd been clear on that one. He had the contract to prove it. Or, rather, Eden had the contract.

Ted was trying through sheer force of will not to let his tension be obvious. His muscles had locked down over the sex talk in front of his best friend's parents. The last thing he needed was for Eleanor to think he brought a woman to their home just to fuck her. He hadn't done that. Ted slowly counted out his breaths, hoping to ease his heart rate back into the range of normal, when Eden's hand moved from his stomach to his back. She slowly started rubbed soothing circles into the stone-hard muscles along his spine. Each pass loosened the tension and spread heat down the length of his legs.

"Hey Bear?" Eden asked, this time when she tipped back to make eye contact. Her head fit perfectly into the hollow of his armpit. She kept rubbing where no one could see. "Think we can pop up to our room? I'd love a shower and a change of clothes."

Bear. Had she seen his tattoo? Did he say something about the nickname? Did he like it?

Ted nodded, unable to find words in the moment.

"We'll see everyone in a bit," Eden said, and waved. "It was wonderful to meet you all. Thank you again for having me, Ms. Masters."

"Oh please," Will's mother said, "Call me Eleanor. All the ladies do."

Eden nodded, the movement shifting Ted's arm just a fraction of an inch.

"Thank you, Eleanor," Eden repeated, before using her body weight to shift them both toward the hallway and out of the kitchen.

No one's eyes were on them any longer, but Ted could still hear the conversation like a muted hum. He'd have to regain enough control over his body to lead them to their room, since Eden would be lost otherwise. From behind them he heard Chloe's voice call out, "They're totally going to go do it," she said. "Lucky bastards."

Ted thought about calling out something back. Anything. But previous experience told him it would only make the teasing worse, and they were teasing. All the sex comments were made with love.

He heard Alex's voice come through loud and clear too, "Michael," she called to a fiancé who evidently gave her his focus even if he said nothing. "Remind me to google elopement. Thank you."

"I'll still make sex jokes," Chloe's voice told the other woman, and Ted led Eden to the flight of stairs. The roar of laughter behind them succeeding at loosening the last of his tension.

Ted had left the building. Not literally, they were outside after all, and to be fair they only kind of knew each other, but something was off. Eden had noticed the minute they started up the walk to the front door, but she'd written off his initial withdrawal as fatigue from the drive. Almost twenty-four hours later things should have gotten better, right?

He wasn't quieter than usual because Ted was always pretty quiet. He wasn't grumpier than usual because he always had the stoic thing down pat, but something was off. He'd left Eden to pretty much introduce herself and carry on conversations without him. It hadn't been too hard; Eden had liked his friends. It seemed like a tight-knit group, one who shared inside jokes and bone-deep affection.

That probably had something to do with the fact that all the women had been on a reality show together. Eden wondered if it was weird for AJ to have other contestants in the wedding party as she married the man they'd all fought for. Probably not. Will's fiancé was just as beautiful in person as she'd been on TV, and she seemed genuinely delighted to meet Eden and to see the other women.

When they finally retired to their shared room, he'd taken an extra pillow and a thin blanket, and set himself up on the too-small couch for the night.

So no, Eden wasn't sure exactly what was wrong, but she was keeping an extra eye on him just in case. Or maybe there was nothing wrong at all. Maybe she'd misjudged him and Ted was actually the buttoned-up suit he tried so hard to portray. That seemed so wrong that Eden shivered as she shook off the thought. He'd barely looked at her since they'd walked into the house and he'd said even less, but maybe this was the reason he'd invited her. Hadn't Ted said he wanted a partner? Someone on his side?

"I have been looking forward to this game for months." The bride, AJ, pushed a pair of dark sunglasses over her eyes and tucked her corkscrew curls back behind her ears. "Does that make me a pervert?"

With whiskey brown eyes, and hair the color of volcanic glass, AJ was stunning to look at. She reminded Eden of an Ancient Greek statue, round and soft and utterly comfortable in her own skin. When she and Will had stumbled into the main house after dinner, her cheeks pink from the cold and her hair a thundercloud, Eden had wanted to paint her. She'd wanted to immortalize the wide smile, the kiss-swollen curve of AJ's lips, the glow pouring off her skin as she leaned into the solid bulk of Will's chest.

"You fuck that man like it's your job," Chloe said, flopping back on her beach towel. "I refuse to believe ogling him as he plays beach volleyball will get your rocks off more than that."

Will's parents had taken AJ's out on their fancy boat, Will's grandparents were taking a nap in the main house, some of the older guests were exploring the town, and Eden and the other women had laid towels and beach chairs out on the private strip of sand while the men set up a volleyball net. Will was supervising the post placement. Logan was securing one side of the net while Ted tied up the other. Alex's fiancé, Michael, was using a hand pump to blow up the ball. All four men were conveniently shirtless, their skin gleaming under the hot sun and a thin sheen of sweat.

The colorful shapes and swirls of Ted's tattoo were visible even from Eden's vantage point in the sand and Eden wanted to trace each line with her fingers. Or her tongue. Ted had been careful to change his clothes in their attached bathroom the night before, something Eden was sure was meant to keep things platonic and appropriate between them.

This was her first view of his naked chest, rounded with thick muscles, and covered with dark hair and bright pops of colorful artwork. For all her daydreams of inked men, Eden had never considered what tattoos would look like covered in chest hair. They looked like Eden would need to get up close and personal to see all the fine line work and intricate details. Close enough to touch.

"Will and AJ spent a month reconnecting and eye-fucking each other from across the room while the entire country watched. This is probably pretty reminiscent for them." Alex adjusted the sarong around her slender hips.

"Who cares?" Tandy asked. "Some of us are in the middle of a dry spell and just want to enjoy the view because they brought their gay boss as their wedding date and as wonderful as he is, there's no action headed their way."

"We invited Cooper on his own. You both could have brought anyone you wanted." AJ said, and Tandy shrugged.

"You know we've both been too busy to find our own dates," Tandy said. "Cooper has that big show coming up, and I've had a lot on my plate since my dad died."

Eden put her hand on Tandy's shoulder in a show of solidarity, an apology ready on her tongue, but AJ rolled her eyes.

"Hey, no fair using your dead dad to make me feel guilty for teasing you."

"He was *my* dad." Tandy shrugged. "I'll get to use him how I want."

"Not the *best* father-daughter relationship," Alex said to Eden as Tandy laughed. The sound rang across the sand like a shiny bell.

"That's an understatement," Tandy said. "He had so many expectations about who I should be and how I should act that he couldn't see me standing right in front of him."

"I can relate to that," Eden said, and Tandy gave her a soft smile.

"I left," Tandy said. "Hard for him to make my decisions from another state."

"I stopped caring," Eden replied. "Nothing was going to be good enough, so I might as well make myself happy."

"I wish I'd done that," Tandy said.

It had taken Eden years to get to that point. To get to the place where she stopped chasing scraps of approval from a man that wasn't even her real father. Where she stopped changing her outfits, signing up for new classes, and biting back the words she was thinking.

One day she'd been counting down the minutes until she never had to look at his alcohol-red face while he spit through gritted teeth that she needed to change into something less inappropriate, dammit, counting down the hours until she didn't need to see the tear tracks on her mama's cheeks after another one of her fiesta ware dishes was packed into a cardboard box to be donated.

The next day she was trading her cardigans for loose peasant shirts and burning her bra in the gas fireplace to make her point. Staring her stepfather directly in the eye and telling him to fuck right off the next time he'd called her an embarrassment had been good too.

"Yes, yes, we all have daddy issues," Chloe said from behind the battered paperback she held to block out the sun. "Except for Will with his mommy issues. Can we move on?"

"To ogling?" Alex asked, fixated on Michael as he pulled his arm back and smoothly served the white ball over the net. "Yes, please." Ted got his arms under the ball and popped it up into the air before Will slammed it back over the net. Logan dove for it and sent it spiraling back into the air.

"Oh, I'm ogling," Chloe said, peering over her sunglasses to grin at Eden.

Seeing Chloe Calder-Marshall had been a surprise. A familiar face in an unfamiliar place. It had been roughly three years since she'd spent a weekend in the Colorado Rockies with the other woman. They'd met at an art expo where Eden had been painting the stunning bouquets that Chloe put out on her table. The flowers kept selling before Eden finished any of the pictures. A few too many drinks, hours of constant conversation, and they'd ended up sharing a single person tent and a can of refried beans heated over the fire and spooned up with Tostitos scoops. Not that Eden was complaining.

Chloe was beautiful, her hair longer than Eden remembered, but with the same bright feathers peeking out of the layers. She'd been devastatingly sexy, handing Eden a long stem with a rounded pink flower. A ranunculus, Chloe had called it. Something to symbolize the receiver's dazzling beauty and charm. As if the move itself wasn't dripping in charm.

The day after her trip into the mountains had seen Eden bumming a ride in the backseat of her friend's car as they drove all the way out East. She hadn't seen Chloe again unless you counted the television show. They sent occasional text messages, were friends on social media, and seeing Chloe on First Lady had been a sort of nostalgic fun.

Maybe Eden should find it weird that one of her ex-flings—she refused to call Chloe an actual relationship when they hadn't progressed past the thirty-six hour mark—was here, but it wasn't. Seeing Chloe again was nice, even if she wasn't sure how to explain their past hook up to Ted. Did she even have to explain it?

"She's here with Ted, Chlo," AJ said, nudging the other woman over with the tips of her indigo painted toes. "No seducing other people's dates."

Eden hadn't seen a point in correcting Will's mother the night before, but she should probably say something now. Maybe that was what had set him on edge. Giving his friends the wrong idea about what they meant to each other was probably a bad idea. Eden hadn't considered it dishonest, letting everyone believe what they wanted to believe; it wasn't like she was making up meet cutes and talking about the future. She just hadn't seen the point in correcting any assumptions. She'd assumed Ted would have done that if it bothered him. It was actually *being* a girlfriend that sucked the breath from her lungs, not pretending.

"Ted and I—" she started, but Tandy cut her off.

"Are adorable together." She shifted the triangles of her hot pink bikini and leaned forward in her beach chair. "How long have you been together? How did you meet? Tell us everything."

"We're just—"

"It's recent," Chloe said. "As of our last Best People video call, Ted wasn't bringing a date to the wedding. That was last week."

"Love at first sight." Tandy nodded. "So romantic."

Eden shook her head. "It wasn't really like that." Lust? Sure. Attraction? Definitely. Love? That wasn't a real thing. Not in an instant.

"Can confirm," AJ said. "Will met Eden Wednesday when she stopped by the office. He swore he could see the hearts pulsing in Ted's eyes."

Eden laughed along with the other women. "No hearts," she said. There were no hearts. Some impulse control issues, but that was purely physical. "Shouldn't we be focusing on the bride this weekend?"

"Sweetie," Alex looked over the top of her sunglasses. "As much as we love AJ and Will, and we do, most of us had a front-row seat to them falling in love. We watched every sappy, heartfelt moment. They are disgustingly, euphorically in love and we're bored with them."

"Hey!" AJ said, but she was grinning. "Rude."

"Don't whine. We love you." Alex said. "But we know everything there is to know. We're moving on to a new story."

"It's my wedding," AJ protested.

"Right. You get to appear in an interconnected standalone. This isn't your sequel. It's time for a new couple. Ted and Eden."

No, it wasn't. This was not a cutesy love story. She and Ted were acquaintances turned into potential friends. This wasn't a love story. At least not one about her. She was a supporting character in AJ's story, or maybe even Alex's or Ted's. Maybe she'd be the one to jumpstart his actual story about his journey to a wife, a brief mention in the prologue.

She'd be a better fit for a mystery novel. A cozy one. Where the plucky artist solves a mystery to clear her name. She'd had a recent run-in with the law. It was plausible. Maybe he'd be an extra in her book. Maybe he and his wife would stop by her art stand and she'd paint them. Or teach their kids to play piano, and then they'd go their separate ways.

Why did that thought make her abdomen cramp up and the edges of her eyes burn? A romance novel would never work with her as a heroine. Romance novels needed love and relationships and happily ever afters. Eden wouldn't mind love, actually she'd *love* love, but the other two were things she'd learned she couldn't have.

Happily Ever Afters in romance came alongside relationships. She'd never find someone who didn't expect her to compromise her own sense of self in order to be together, so no relationship would work for her. Actually, maybe Eden had that backwards. She'd *only* find love if she were the heroine of a romance novel. A novel would guarantee that she'd find someone who loved her for exactly who she was. Someone who understood the relationships from her past that had shaped her current need to build twenty-foot stone wall that no one could possibly scale.

"Nope," AJ said, her eyes wide as they watched Eden. "We aren't doing this to Eden. I like her and we aren't about to scare her off Ted. He's a great guy and his last million girlfriends were just—" she let out a strangled sound of frustration.

"That was extremely descriptive," Chloe said, and AJ stuck out her tongue at her friend.

"Poor baby," Tandy clucked her tongue. "He's had his heart broken?"

AJ shook her head. "I wouldn't say he was that invested with any of them, more like they were just an awful fit. He kept picking these gorgeous women. They wore fitted suits and held high-powered jobs and had three-hundred-dollar haircuts. It was like he picked them all out of a catalogue, different versions of the same model. And at first, things would seem fine except that no one ever smiled." She looked at Eden. "And Ted needs someone who smiles because he already doesn't do enough of it."

A celebratory shout drifted up from the volleyball net and all five women turned together to look at the game. Logan was dancing. Gyrating his hips with his hands raised above his head. Michael was doing an off-tempo version of the robot, complete with swinging arms. Will had fallen to his knees in the sand, his hands braced on strong thighs, and there was Ted. His hands were on his hips, his chin dropped to his chest, and even from a hundred feet away she could see the barest hint of a smile quirking his lips.

"He's smiling right now," Eden said as Ted looked up from his feet and his eyes found hers. It was definitely a smile—a tiny twist to his lips, but still a smile—and she couldn't resist sending one back along with a wave of her fingers. She turned her focus back to the women and found all the sets of eyes now glued to her.

"See?" AJ said, "Smiling. He needs that."

"Are you sure this isn't just misplaced rage?" Alex asked, "The women Ted dated sound a lot like the type of girl Eleanor wanted for Will."

"It's been two years, AJ. Time to move on." Chloe said.

"This isn't about me and Will. This is about Ted."

"Go on darling," Tandy patted AJ's leg, "All these women were prim, proper, and perfect, and it never worked out because they were too similar? To Ted or to each other?"

Even in their short time together, Eden knew Ted needed a woman who could match him. Someone to go to firm functions with him. Someone to wear conservative clothes in muted colors. Someone to drive the minivan full of children in starched matching uniforms. Someone to impress his business associates and someone who was clearly nothing like her. Not that she was volunteering. Why did she need to keep reminding herself of that?

"No," AJ said, real heat in her voice. "They weren't similar enough. They didn't get Ted at all. On the surface he's all put together and ambitious, all about work, but when he finally got comfortable enough to loosen up and be himself with them—"

"They bailed." Eden said.

AJ nodded. "I know we just met, but I feel like you could get him. You could be the one who understands his family, and the pressure he's under, and still helps him be himself."

"No pressure," Chloe said. "Seriously AJ, that's a big request for a new girlfriend."

It was a big request. Good thing she wasn't his girlfriend. Also, AJ had to have that wrong. Ted wanted the Stepford family thing. He'd told her so himself.

"See?" Alex gestured to the men. "It's definitely his turn for a love story."

"He'd certainly make a nice-looking cover model," Tandy added.

Down on the beach, Ted turned to look out over the water. He ran a hand through his hair and Eden watched his muscles contract and release with the movement. He had the powerful bulk of a man who took care of what he ate and was conscious of his activity levels.

God, she was no better than Ted's previous girlfriends, assuming she knew who he was from the barest of impressions. Every single word he said to her, every time he put her comfort first, every glimpse at his taste in music and art, and yes, even his tattoos, made her forget they wanted different things.

The game seemed to be over and the guys were making their way up the beach.

"You got lucky that the accident wasn't worse. Just a headache to deal with." Will was saying as they neared the bank of towels and Eden shamelessly eavesdropped.

Ted glanced up and met Eden's eyes and instead of busying herself with something else, she raised an eyebrow and grinned.

"I don't know," Ted said. "So far it's made things interesting."

Will started to reply, but AJ jumped out of her seat, meeting her almost-husband halfway. Her arms went around his neck and his hands dropped to cup the swell of her ass. His mouth took hers in a kiss that had Eden pressing her own thighs together. Michael scooped up his fiancée, dipping her back over his arm for a kiss, too. And then Ted was there, standing in front of her with one big hand outstretched and her heart was a runaway truck barreling down a windy mountain road. It thundered in her chest as he stared down at her.

This was the danger, too. Because if he looked at her too long, she was going to remember those moments in his office. She couldn't even be honest with herself. She already remembered those moments in his office. She'd never quite pushed them all the way to the side. He wasn't for her. Neither of them were interested in what the other had to offer. She needed to screw her head back on the right way because she was slowly losing her mind and she'd drive him absolutely insane if they even considered this.

Except there were those tattoos. And his Harley. And Chloe liked him—Chloe wouldn't be friends with him if he were exactly what he seemed. And AJ truly believed he didn't need the kind of woman he seemed to think he did. So maybe he wasn't just a career-obsessed suit after all. Maybe she'd been hasty in her impressions. She slid her hand into his as he pulled her to her feet. She was standing too close to him now, but he didn't move away. The heat from his chest saturating the floral bathing suit she'd slipped on.

Dangerous.

Dangerous, dangerous, dangerous.

Ted knew the weekend was going well. Or at least it was going better than he'd expected. Bringing Eden with him might have been the smartest thing he'd ever done. He knew that because Will had clapped him on the shoulder and told him so.

It also might have been the stupidest because every single time he saw her, he felt drawn to her like a magnet. She was wearing some floaty green skirt that caught between her legs as she walked and a short white shirt that slipped off her left shoulder. She'd twisted her long dark hair up into a giant plastic claw thing, but a few strands at the base of her neck had escaped to curl down over her shoulder blades.

"I didn't realize I'd be at the rehearsal dinner," Eden had whispered up in their room, her lips pressed to the shell of his ear. He'd felt the zing straight down to his toes. An electric throb that pulsed even after she'd stepped away from him to swipe mascara over her lashes.

"It's okay," he'd answered, biting back every compliment that threatened to pour out of him. They'd agreed to be just friends. Just a casual…date wasn't even the right word, even if every person here thought they were a couple. Even if he wanted… no. The *last* thing he wanted was to be half of a couple with someone who didn't want to commit. But he did want Eden. Being honest about that wasn't violating their contract. It wasn't like he was going to do anything about his lust.

"You look beautiful." The words had sat between them, resonating, and Eden's cheeks had flushed pink. "That wasn't a pass." He'd added, and she'd nodded her head.

"I know." She'd straightened his navy blue tie before adding, "I'm not your type, but thank you just the same." She'd patted the lapels of his jacket, a touch he felt clear through to his bones, then she'd stepped back with a smile.

Now she stood with him as he carried on a conversation with Will's father, and her hand rubbing tight circles into the small of his back was the only thing anchoring him to the here and now. George was a good guy. Ted liked his politics and his mannerisms. At one time he'd pushed his only son to follow in his footsteps, but he'd also been the first to support Will's decisions when they differed from what George and Eleanor had planned for him.

It was George who'd helped provide the start-up capital for HMP. He'd been generous with the loan details and the repayment plan. Much more generous than a bank or any other investor would have been. And yet, standing in front of the man in his custom-tailored suit, Ted felt like he was holding his breath, waiting for George to do something to indicate his displeasure and disapproval.

Ted's stepfather would have taken notes. Martin would have mentioned how Ted should have shaved for his friend's big night. That Ted should have gone with the full Windsor knot since it was a formal occasion. That a tiny bit of his full sleeve tattoo was visible when he brought his drink to his lips. That he should've, would've, could've.

Nothing Ted did was ever good enough, no matter how hard he tried. Ted hadn't spent time alone with his stepfather in close to a decade, but that didn't mean the words didn't linger. Didn't ache. It didn't mean they still didn't influence the way he dressed, the way he spoke, and the way he carried himself.

Martin would have hated Eden. He'd have said something rudely calculated. Just sly enough to feign innocence if she got offended. Just nasty enough that he could seem vindicated if she turned angry or teary. Just thinking about it had Ted clenching his jaw. As the tension turned his muscles to stone, Eden's fingers slipped under the hem of his jacket to press hot against the cotton of his shirt.

His shoulder relaxed by degrees as she found the knots on either side of his spine and applied the barest amount of pressure. Her face tipped up as she watched him. Up close, her eyes had a dark green ring at the center, and brown flecks speckling the irises. It would be so easy to drown in those eyes. To melt under the heat of her touch. To forget everything and everyone else.

"I'm going to sit down," she said, her voice sliding over him like a mountain stream. Smooth and refreshing. Cleansing all the negative thoughts that circled his head. She paused as if waiting for him to answer and then her dimple came out to play as she smiled. "I think you guys are going to get started. I'll just be over there."

Ted glanced toward the far end of the yard where Will was standing under a giant white pergola with Cooper Wells, the wedding officiant and designer to the stars. Will inclined his head and Ted saw Logan sliding into place behind the groom. He'd missed George excusing himself, too caught up in his own head, but the Masterses had taken seats in the white chairs on the lawn. Eleanor was already dabbing at her eyes with a lacy white handkerchief. Will shot his mother a stern look.

Eden's hand dropped from his back and he shivered despite the warm evening and his full suit. Losing her touch was like a blast from an over-powered air conditioner ghosting over damp skin. It was the dive into the normally warm pool after spending wonderful moments in the jetted hot tub. It was unpleasant, jarring, and if he just waited it out, things would return to normal. They *had* to return to normal.

Ted stepped into his spot behind Will and clapped his best friend on the back. He didn't look at Eden as she slid into a chair in the back row and propped her feet on the seat in front of her. He didn't watch as she pulled a small white notebook out of her knit purse along with a small orange pen. She propped the book on her knees and pulled her lower lip in between her teeth.

"I like her," Will said as AJ and her dad stopped at the end of the row of chairs. A terrifyingly competent wedding planner was standing on a pair of ice pick heels in front of the bride. Based on her wildly gesturing hands, Ted assumed she was telling AJ and her father where to go. Over the top of the small woman's head, AJ stuck her tongue out at Will.

"I'd hope so." Ted crossed his arms over his chest. "You're marrying her."

"He didn't mean AJ," Logan said from Ted's other side. "He meant Eden. I like her too."

Ted grunted in response. He was trying not to think about Eden. His friends could do him the decency of being a little more accommodating.

"We know you aren't together," Will said. "The women think you are."

"Not that Eden's been telling them that," Logan added.

"But we also know that you want to be." Will nudged his shoulder. "Even when you continue to insist that you met through a case."

"We did," Ted said. Maybe not one of the firm's cases, but it was still a case. "Focus on your wedding."

"It's just a rehearsal," Will said. "AJ and I almost bailed."

"Do not tell me that," Logan said. "I put on a suit for you."

Ted looked down the row of chairs at Eden. She was sketching, drawing, something, her hand flowing over the page with slow passes and then quick jagged movements. Will seemed far too cavalier about this entire wedding process. If it was Ted? If he was watching the woman he loved walk down that aisle toward him? Toward the promise of forever? Well, he wouldn't be gossiping with his groomsmen and he wouldn't have missed the rehearsal unless he and his fiancée were… never mind.

Ted had walked in on Will and AJ enough times to have a good idea about how they were planning to spend their own wedding rehearsal. If it were him? He'd probably meet Eden halfway down the aisle and walk her up himself.

No.

Not Eden.

Her.

He'd meet *her* halfway down the aisle. Why did he think it would be Eden?

"Make your move," Will said, and Ted jolted back into his body as if someone had electrocuted him.

"There's no move to make."

He wanted the wedding, the promise, the forever. He was thinking about Eden because she was here. She was pretty—beautiful—and kind and grounding. She always knew exactly when to press her hand to his back. His friends liked her. He liked her. And none of that mattered because his family would hate her and she'd hate them right back. Martin would take one look at the paint drying on her skin, or the flowing skirts she liked to wear, and he'd be unbearable. He already was unbearable. Eden wasn't a shrinking wallflower. If his stepfather was rude and callous she'd call him out, and then every family function—the ones he already barely tolerated—would be so much worse.

And yet, Ted still liked her. He still caught himself staring at her mouth, or wanting to twist their fingers together. He had to continually remind himself that Eden wasn't interested in a relationship with him either. She'd give him a casual fling. He knew that. She was respecting his boundaries, but if he showed an interest he could probably have her naked and spread across the baby blue guest room comforter in less than half an hour. Did he want that? Yes. No. Ted was just getting himself twisted. Like a contact high. Wedding romance was catching. He must have been absorbing pheromones or something from Will during all the prep.

The truth was that if Ted let himself go for the physical with Eden, a craving that got stronger each time he smelled the sunshine and vanilla scent of her skin, he was going to want the rest. He'd been watching her interact with his friends. He'd felt the way his pulse kicked up when she directed her smile at him, and the way it calmed when she rubbed her palm against his spine. He'd been broken before by women who affected him less. Eden, with her soft voice, her ability to put everyone around her at ease, and their sizzling chemistry, would be the one to annihilate him. He'd be a smoking wreckage once she'd gone.

"Bullshit," Will's voice was a little too loud, and AJ stopped her step-together-step-together march up the aisle to give him *the look.* "She's as into you as you are into her."

"Trust me." Ted shook his head. "We've already had this discussion. She's not interested in a relationship. I am. That's all there is to say."

"Not everyone flattens someone in the park like Will and knows immediately that he wants to spend his life with her," Logan said. "Just give it time."

"I don't have the time to give." Ted glared at his two best friends and business partners. "I'm too busy working at our practice. Thank you very much."

"You work too much," Will said. AJ and her father were close to the first row of chairs, so at least this conversation was almost over.

"It's not like I have a choice. You're too busy fucking your fiancée on your desk, so the rest of us have to put in the overtime."

"Rude," Will said, and the tone was so much like AJ that Ted had to smile.

That. That was what he was looking for. A partner. A friend. A lover. Someone who understood him. Someone who fit him so perfectly that he could barely tell where he ended, and she began. He wasn't asking for too much, just a soulmate. He'd dated too many women to settle for the wrong one. It couldn't be that hard to find someone who fit those parameters and would also get along with his family. But that was why he didn't have time to play with Eden. He needed to focus on finding that unicorn of a woman. He imagined it was going to take some time.

"Take it from someone who's been there," Will said. He'd dropped his voice low as AJ and her father stopped to chat with the planner again. "When you know, you know. Trying to force yourself to pick someone else doesn't work. Not when your heart has picked for you. We've watched you date too many women and refuse to let them get close. You don't show them who you really are and then when you do, you're surprised when they leave." Will cleared his throat and spoke even faster. "That's not cool. You deserve someone who sticks. You deserve someone who sees you and gets you. Not someone you have to pretend with. But that doesn't mean she'll just fall into your lap. You'll have to put in some work too. So put in the work."

It wasn't that simple. Will seemed to have already forgotten the eight years of abject misery he'd spent after his mother had sent AJ packing. The years where his grumpy stoicism had given Ted a run for his money. It apparently slipped Will's mind that he almost sold his third of the practice to make a run for political office, all because he didn't give a damn about his life without AJ.

Two years since the woman of his dreams had walked back into his life, a few weeks of throwing himself at her feet, and he'd forgotten what a shit he'd been to deal with when she wasn't there. Honestly, it was a wonder Will spoke to his mother at all after everything that had happened. Not that Ted could judge. He also knew plenty of people who'd walked away from family for less than what he still put up with.

"I'll take your thoughts under advisement," Ted said as AJ drew even with the pergola.

Logan leaned around the back of Ted, grinning at Will as he took his fiancée's hand. "One hundred bucks says she doesn't go running from the real him."

"No bet," Will said. "We already know she won't. One hundred bucks says he pulls his head out of his ass and makes his move before the end of tomorrow."

"Are you seriously making bets at our wedding?" AJ asked Will, smiling up at him as he dropped his hand to her waist and pulled her in flush against him.

"I'm so deliriously happy with you, that I want Teddy to be happy too," Will said, dropping a kiss to the tip of AJ's upturned nose.

"He is happy," AJ frowned. "With Eden."

"That's what we're working on," Logan said. "Keep up, would ya? They aren't in love yet, but Will and I know they could be by the end of the weekend. Ted just needs to get out of his own way."

Will nuzzled into the curve of his fiancée's neck and Ted turned away to give them a modicum of privacy.

"You boys are idiots." AJ shook her head. "They don't need until the end of the weekend."

"You think you know better? You want in on the bet?" Will asked. AJ looked at Ted through narrowed eyes. It felt a lot like the dreams he'd had as a kid. The ones where he showed up naked to the school science fair. Or any of the times Martin had dressed him down for his behavior.

"Yes." AJ nodded her head once. "I want in. You boys are already finished. One hundred bucks says they're already in love and just don't know it."

"You can't fall in love without realizing it," Logan said. "They only met a few days ago."

"You know I bow to your superior wisdom," Will said to AJ as Cooper cleared his throat to get everyone's attention. "But that would be really fast. Most people don't fall in love like people do in romance novels."

AJ shook her head. "You had me the first day, but I don't mean undying devotion and professions of forever love. I mean that subtle tug toward another person. When they stay on your mind and star in your thoughts and no matter how you try to think of something—someone—else, you can't. It's instant attraction and chemistry and curiosity. It's a magnetism that pulls you back over and over and over again until you know for sure that you can't—and don't want to—be without them. It's all of that before the I-love-yous and it can absolutely happen in the first day. First hour. First minute. It did for us."

"You had me too," Will kissed his fiancé as the officiant sighed and checked his watch, and Ted let AJ's words sink into his gut and bury themselves in the back of his brain, a buzz he was sure he'd have zero chance of ignoring.

Ted couldn't find Eden.

The plates had been cleared. The guests were milling around with glasses of champagne. AJ and Will had made speeches and handed out gifts, and a low-level hum of conversation sizzled along his nerve endings. He knew she'd stepped outside for a moment, but he'd assumed she'd be back.

The problem had been that when she leaned in close to tell him where she was going, she put her hand on the front of his chest and her lips brushed his ear lobe. He hadn't heard a word she'd said over the sound of his pulse thundering in his chest. That had been twenty-eight minutes and forty-four seconds ago. Not that he was counting. Or watching the door. Or ignoring the man talking to him while he waited for her to come back.

Cooper Wells was a great guy. Not only was he Will's godfather and one of L.A.'s hottest fashion designers, but he ran an after-school program for underprivileged kids. A program that Ted and Will had both written some checks and done some pro-bono work for. Ted liked the guy. He respected him. Hell, he'd known Cooper as long as he'd known Will—the wedding officiant was more of a pseudo uncle than a family friend—but despite the energetic retelling of a Christmas tree debacle, complete with minor electrocutions for Cooper's longtime boyfriend Silas, Ted couldn't focus on a single word the other man was saying.

Wait for a lull. That was what his stepfather would expect. Wait for a lull in the conversation, then politely excuse himself. It was bad enough that his mind was wandering when he should be listening. He didn't need to be obvious about his need to escape. He was paying attention. Just not to the man in front of him.

"I have to go," Ted said, cutting Cooper off mid-word. Screw waiting for the lull. What if Eden had walked down the dock and tumbled into the churning Atlantic? Okay, so the barrier islands protected the Cape from most of the temperamental weather, but climate change was real and North Beach Island was changing every day.

Also… sharks. Chatham was a hotspot for Great White sightings during the summer months, and yes, most of them were around Monomoy Island—a little further south—and yes, sharks had earned a bad rap from Hollywood, but that wasn't a guarantee that Jaws wasn't sitting under the Masters dock with its mouth open, just waiting for a midnight snack.

"I was wondering how long you were going to last." Cooper sipped the dark amber liquid in his glass. "You've been eyeing every exit and your watch in a rotating cycle. You're about to gaze longingly across the back patio, I assume, looking for your woman." Ted didn't answer. "She went down the steps towards the beach," Cooper said. "If anyone else tries to head your way, I'll direct them to the far side."

Ted didn't need Cooper Wells to run interference for him. This wasn't some lover's tryst. Eden wasn't "his girl," and he certainly wasn't planning to do anything that needed privacy. He just wanted to make sure she was okay. Both emotionally and physically.

"You can say 'Thank you Cooper,'" Cooper said before holding up his now empty tumbler. "Would you look at that? I appear to need a refill." He shot Ted an exaggerated wink.

Ted didn't wait for the older man to move toward the bar. He was out on the back patio, head down to avoid any other distractions, before the other man had even turned away.

The night air was cooler than Ted expected and he was glad he'd grabbed his jacket. He didn't need it, but Eden might be cold. Especially if she was down by the water. Ted jogged across the perfect lawn and took the narrow stone steps two at a time down to the sand. There were no lights down here, but there was still a faint glow from the big house and the nearly full moon took care of the rest. The waves rolled in, soft whitecaps breaking and spreading across the dark, wet sand. Ted saw a set of footprints leading towards the surf and then…nothing.

Don't panic, he ordered himself. She didn't walk straight out into the void and become shark bait. The waves simply washed away the prints. He wasn't actually *worried* about her. He had just been itchy inside. Uncomfortable. As if someone starched his boxer briefs after shrinking them in the dryer.

The dock and boathouse were to the left, a wooden platform on spindly stilts. There were a set of steps leading down to the sand, but the footprints hadn't started there. To the right, the beach spread out from the rocky embankment and then rounded a bend, disappearing from the house's line of sight. Ted glanced out over the water but didn't see any dark shapes bobbing on the waves.

He set off to the right, not running, but striding with purpose. It grew darker the further he got from the house, but he kept going. In the back of his mind Ted thought maybe he should take out his cellphone, use the flashlight to see better, but the contrast from light sand to dark water was visible even as the party lights dwindled, and he didn't want to slow down to fiddle with the settings.

Ted rounded the bend in the rocks, the house still visible, but barely. He could just see the jut of the dock when he looked back over his shoulder, just hear the jazz from the party slipping through the night air. He scrubbed a hand down his face and sucked in a breath. And there she was. The white of Eden's shirt glowed as she sat among the breaking waves, knees pulled up to her chest, arms looped around them, and stared out into the water. Her skirt floated around her, absolutely soaked, and she didn't even care, just stared out into the darkness. Ted stepped closer, and she tipped her head to look his way, her cheek now pillowed on her knees. She smiled.

And the tightness in Ted's chest eased as his pulse picked up speed.

Eden hadn't intended to be gone long, but once she'd stepped out into the crisp night air, and heard the shush of the waves even over the soothing slide of the saxophone, it had been almost instinct to find her way to the smooth stone steps and head down to the sand.

She left her shoes on the grass, taking the extra minute to line them up just in case someone came across them, and was grateful she could feel the sand move beneath her feet without having to lug them around. She'd walked right up to the breaking waves, digging her toes deep into the sand and feeling the ground pull out beneath her as the water slipped back out toward the dark of the horizon.

She'd needed a break. Ten minutes away from the crowd. Not that the wedding party was a crowd. There were maybe fifteen people, tops, but they were all connected. They all had a history that Eden couldn't touch. She wasn't jealous, and she wasn't uncomfortable—everyone had been nice—but there was a significant awareness that she once again didn't fit. Given enough time, she probably could, but one weekend wasn't that kind of time. She and Ted were down to their last thirty-six hours together.

A few minutes in the waves had turned into a few more, the salt water splashing over the bottom of her skirt. Eden held it up at first, determined to keep it dry for her inevitable return to the house, but after the first crash of water caught the hem, she'd given up the fight.

Eden sat in the wet sand and let the hem billow around her as the surf rolled in and over her legs. She could look out into the darkness and see the line of jagged foam as each wave broke, or she could tip her head back and look at the smattering of stars glittering in the blue-black sky. Feeling lonely in a crowd was a lot worse than feeling lonely all by herself.

Something shifted. A scent, although Eden only smelled salt water and the earthy scent of seaweed, a sound, although she could hear very little over the crash of the surf, a pull, like a giant magnet drawing her inexorably closer to the man who was standing on the beach. A man who clasped enormous hands together over the top of his head and stared at her as she sat in the surf.

"Hi," she said when he continued to stand there. Staring but not moving.

He should have been hard to see in his dark suit, but nothing could completely block the breadth of his shoulders or his staggering height. The man was his own lighthouse, drawing her in even as he warned her away. The danger was practically stitched into the lining of his fancy jacket.

"Hi," Ted said, and Eden shivered as his voice washed over her, warmer than the waves but still raising goosebumps along her exposed skin.

"Coming to rescue me again?" She asked. She'd be willing to admit that she needed a rescue that first day, even if she didn't need one now.

Ted moved closer, the pointed toes of his loafers sitting just beyond the reach of the waves. That made sense. Not everyone felt like soaking their clothes just to sit and admire a nonexistent view.

"You don't need a rescue." Ted said, shoving his hands deep into his pants' pockets.

"Ah, just looking for a quick breather?"

"Maybe *I* needed the rescue." he leaned back on his heels as a small swell of water floated a little too close to him.

"A rescue from your own friends?"

Ted bent his knees and scooped a handful of wet sand. He let it sift through his fingers, piling onto the dark beach in a twisted spiral. Eden gave herself a moment to admire the thick blunt ends of his fingers, the shadowed hint of the sleeve tattoos hidden under his suit. Those hands were big enough to span the width of her hips when she'd pressed her mouth to his. That said more about the size of his hands than anything else. She wasn't a skinny woman.

"It's not them," Ted said. "Have you ever felt alone, even in a crowd of people?"

Ted's eyes met hers, and her throat worked on a swallow. Eden felt stripped bare under his gaze. Her cheeks heated, skin prickling as he stared across the dark expanse of sand and water. She sucked a breath in through her nose. Right before a large wave caught her off guard and smacked into her chest.

The cold water took her down to the sand, flooding her mouth and nose with the sting of salt. She was fine. The water didn't even cover her chest and stomach, so she stayed flat on her back for a moment, feeling the tug as the sand slipped out from underneath her. The pull on her shoulders and hips felt like the perfect stretch after a long workout. Eden reached her fingers towards the retreating waves. She smiled up at the spray of stars scattered across the inky blackness. Stars like that weren't visible from her apartment in the city.

A pair of warm hands gripped her shoulders before one slid under her back. Strong arms pulled her up as another wave broke over her body. It was instinct to lean back into the heavy weight of the arm banding around her. Instinct to turn her head and rest her cheek on the rounded shoulder. Instinct to blink the salt water out of her eyes and bring him into focus. He was frowning at her. The same look she recognized from the Boston police station. The same deep furrow between his brows as he glared down into her eyes, his own darker than the water.

"Are you okay?"

Eden barely heard him over the rushing in her ears. She hadn't realized she was cold until the heat of his body seeped into her skin.

"I'm fine," she said, but she didn't move away from his hold and he didn't loosen his grip.

"My stepfather and Will's dad go way back," Ted said. He settled her against his chest, not caring that she was dripping seawater over his fancy coat. Plastering the shirt to his solid chest.

"How far back?"

"Harvard Class of 1980."

Eden thought back to the battered red baseball hat she'd seen on AJ's head for most of the day. Will had taken great pleasure in tapping his knuckles against the curved brim, before tipping her chin up to seal his mouth to hers.

"Harvard," she said. A bead of water worked its way down Ted's jaw and she had the strange urge to touch her tongue to the drop.

"Will and I are class of '08. Logan too. We shared a suite freshman year."

"That must have been nice," Eden said. "School with a close friend."

She'd gone to community college. Any money that had been set aside for her tuition had vanished into the ether when she'd stood up to her stepdad. In the long run, it was probably a good thing. She hadn't finished the program. Halfway through the second year, she'd had an opportunity to illustrate a picture book for a local author.

It hadn't been an overnight success, but the book had brought in enough attention that Eden had had steady commissions ever since. So she'd quit school, packed a bag full of art supplies, and traveled across the country. She'd made the personal commitment to never look back. To never regret her choices.

"We weren't friends growing up," Ted said. The frown was still there. "Will and I met at school. My stepfather and his dad set up the roommate situation. They hadn't spoken in years before that, but Martin worked hard to get me an acceptance and thought Will could keep me in line. I got a stern lecture about not dragging him down with me."

It was Eden's turn to frown. A successful law firm wasn't somewhere to be dragged down to. It also wasn't just any firm. She'd been listening this weekend. Ted, Will, and Logan took on clients that needed help. Not just the ones who could afford topnotch legal representation. Even if she hadn't been keeping her ears open, absorbing every facet of information dropped at her feet, she'd have known. Their first meeting was proof. She told him so.

"Will was expected to run for President. Senate, at the very least. Not start his own practice, especially not in a no-guts-no-glory sector of the legal profession."

That made sense. The cape house did have a sort of Kennedy compound feel to it. There was only the main house and the guest house, but the décor, the staff, the atmosphere all screamed old world money and status.

No one had been overtly snobby, but there was no missing the designer life. It hadn't bothered Eden. She'd spent years practicing her lack of fucks. Also, whatever expectations Will had carried back in his college days, his family certainly seemed loving and supportive of him now. Either that or they'd learned to keep their mouths shut. She'd have paid good money to watch that interaction.

"Did your parents help them come around?"

Ted's laughter poured into her like a roll of thunder. Had she ever heard him laugh before? Goosebumps broke along her arms. She wanted to blame it on the chill of the water, but it was him. It was Ted. His body was a furnace behind her, pumping heat into her organs, her being. This is what she imagined it would be like to ride a motorcycle. The heat of the motor. The cool of the wind. The rumbling vibration pouring through her. It was a rush.

"My parents—" Ted shook his head, his beard scraping over the top of her head. "My stepfather expected me to join his firm. It's the only reason he was willing to pay for my fresh start, the Ivy League education, and the law degree."

Her nose brushed the underside of his jaw as she looked up at him. He smelled like sandalwood and musk and a hint of leather. "Fresh start?"

Ted's arm tightened around her for a heartbeat. A squeeze she felt to the very core of her soul. A comforting weight. Like all of her parts were being held together by that one bit of pressure, compressing her body and her organs until they smashed together into the right form, as if she were made of hunks of clay.

"There was a lot of pressure in my home growing up. I didn't get along with my stepfather, and I didn't just toe the line. I took a battering ram to it."

Eden tried to imagine straight-laced Ted missing curfew because he was studying at the library. Overstaying his parking meter so he could play another round of go-fish with his Granny at the retirement home. Threatening single-minded assholes who made inappropriate comments about the quiet kid who played the tuba. Eden swallowed down a laugh. Then she imagined a strange man that looked a lot like her own stepdad berating him for any of those choices, and it took a concerted effort for the red to bleed away from her vision.

"Whatever you're thinking, is not it." He raised his thumb to trace a lazy line down the underside of her arm. He didn't even seem to notice that he was doing it, but Eden's whole being seemed to focus in on that one point of contact.

"How would you know what I'm thinking?" She countered, her voice hitching as she sucked in a breath. Her chest felt tight as his fingertips brushed her skin.

"When I got into fights at school, it was because I decided someone looked at me wrong. When I stole things, it was the neighbor's car that I took for a joyride. When I skipped curfew, it was because I was getting arrested for vandalism, not because I was doing some sort of good deed."

Ted was right. She hadn't been expecting that.

"A lawyer, an Ivy-educated lawyer, with a criminal record? I'd say that's hard to believe, but I bet it's actually more common than you think."

"Ah, see? That's the perk of Martin." Ted's voice was flat. "Call a few buddies, write a few checks, and nobody ever knows. No criminal record to be found. Write a big enough check and no one presses charges and people look the other way."

Ted's arm dropped from her back and he propped himself up in the sand. She missed the touch immediately. Missed the heat and the pressure and him. Eden stopped herself from leaning into his chest. This conversation was more intimate than she'd expected. If he needed some space, then she could give it to him.

"I'm not proud of it, Eden. I'm not proud of my past and I'm not proud that I got off without paying for it. I've worked hard to be different. I'm not wasting the opportunity."

He had paid, Eden thought, studying the harsh angles of his face. He'd spent years feeling guilt and shame and falling into line. It was almost like he'd done a full 180 and never been allowed to find the happy medium. The pieces of him that could be expressed without the risk of handcuffs and jail. She'd done the same thing. The minute she'd ducked out from under her stepdad's control, she'd been wild. Throwing caution to the wind as she did what she wanted when she wanted. Until Justin things had always worked out.

"So the tattoos, the motorcycle, the prison record. That's the real you?" She nudged his shoulder, hoping she was going for playful. "Because I happen to think bad boys are extremely hot."

That last part was a stretch, but not entirely a lie. Just look at her last relationship. He'd apparently been Breaking Bad all over the city when she wasn't watching. Actually, Justin was her only past relationship. Eden had always done better with short and sweet flings. She'd stayed friends with all of those.

Chloe was a perfect example. They'd spent a handful of days surrounded by pine trees and mountain lakes and wildflowers and then parted ways with a smile. Justin and Eden had parted ways and then the police had seized her car and hauled her down to the police station for questioning. Not the point. Chloe had tattoos and brightly colored hair. See? Bad girl.

With a heart of gold.

Just like Theodore Norman Hughes.

"It's easier," he licked his lips, "to put on the suit. There are expectations in my family, and I can hate that he used his name and his connections to get rid of all the consequences I should have faced, hate that I walked away from something that would have ruined other kids, and still be overwhelmingly grateful that he did it. Would it be noble? Or a slap in the face to ignore what he did for me? I can ignore his practice and his plans, and still try to smooth things over just the tiniest bit. So yes. The suit is easier. Maybe not better, but easier."

It probably was. It had certainly fooled her. Eden had packed him and his suit up into a neat little box and tied a ribbon on top. She'd assumed he was the roughhewn exterior and almost missed the sparkling crystal facets that made up his insides. She'd almost ignored the tiny hints, the shimmer trying to break free. Except Chloe liked him. A honey bear, she'd called him. Growly on the outside and sweet gooey sugar on the inside.

"It's okay if it's easier." Eden rubbed her hand along the sodden material covering his back. "It's okay if it's a part of you. As long as you don't destroy the other parts. Easy isn't worth losing yourself."

Ted studied her, his face so close to hers that their noses almost bumped. His throat bobbed as he turned to look back over the water.

"Will and his family, the Masterses, they've never made me feel like I have to be a certain way, or play a certain part. They made Will feel that way, but never me." He shrugged his big shoulders. "Sometimes being here, surrounded by what my stepfather wishes he had, I feel like I'm stuck right back in that place. I hide too much."

Except he was sitting in the surf in a custom wool suit. Water was pouring over his expensive shoes, soaking his dress socks and pants, plastering the white of his shirt to a solid torso. When he'd first found her, Ted had purposely kept himself just beyond the reach of the water. Then he'd run into the waves to help her, even when she hadn't needed help. He hadn't stopped to remove layers or to protect his fancy clothes. That was a very not-suit-like thing to do. That was a honey bear move. That was a bad boy with a heart of gold.

"Lonely in a crowd," Eden said, and Ted gave a short, quick nod.

"No one has ever seen behind the suit unless I wanted them to,"

"You're sitting in the surf with your shoes on, Bear. You're not hiding it all that well."

"Bear?" He hadn't wrapped his arm around her again, but the edges of his fingers were brushing her hip. "You called me that before, too."

"Bear," she grinned at him, feeling loose and warm and… happy. "As in Teddy." Or honey, although she doubted he'd appreciate that metaphor. "And you have that tattoo."

"I feel less lonely when I'm with you, Eden." Ted looked down at her, but he wasn't smiling. His mouth pulled into a solid line, his brows tipped together, his lips parted, and Eden swayed toward him. She was sure that whatever came next was going to be another something that would carbonate her blood. She placed her hand high on his thigh as she overbalanced. Ted's muscle turned to stone beneath her hand.

"I'm about to do something stupid," he said, and Eden leaned even closer. "Something dumb and impulsive and necessary."

His gaze dipped to her mouth, and she knew where this was going. The tingle rushed through her body, settling into the base of her stomach. Her fingers flexed against him. She could have this. He was offering himself up with the look in his eyes. It didn't have to mean anything. Just a teeny tiny escalation, a change to their previous contract. This moment was the catalyst, and the stakes were different now.

"Necessary," she repeated, and he nodded, his chin dropping as he angled his head closer.

"Yes," he said. "Inevitable too."

"So do it," she said, smiling as she angled her chin the opposite way. Her skin sizzled as the water rushed over it. He was right. This was stupid and necessary and inevitable. It had been building since the moment they met. "Kiss me."

Ted closed the gap and sealed his mouth over hers.

Ted had wasted far too much time trying to keep his mouth off Eden's. Her lips were soft under his, slightly parted, and wet from a brush of her tongue. She'd seen him coming a mile off and it was a relief when she pushed her chin up and kissed him back. There was no tentative brush of lips. No back-and-forth dance. He pressed into her and she pressed back.

He sucked at the softness of her lower lip, pressing his teeth into the flesh and dragging her ragged exhale into his own lungs. She smelled like sunshine, even covered in salt water and sitting in the moon's glow. Sunshine and vanilla, bright and sweet, as she blanketed his senses. He'd been inhaling that scent since she brushed past him at the police station. Breathing her in so he could hold on to the tiniest piece of her after all of this was over.

Should he slow down? Pull back? They'd agreed on one weekend. They'd agreed on friendship. They'd agreed to keep their body parts to themselves. They had it all written down.

Ted had wanted to be sure that she knew nothing was expected of her. That he hadn't invited her with the sole purpose of having a warm body in bed with him each night. There was a balance of power he knew he was pushing. Ted had rescued her and then invited her to a wedding to return the favor. He'd momentarily lost his mind and figured if the move was good enough for romantic comedies, it was good enough for them.

This wasn't a romantic comedy. There was no guaranteed happy ending. They weren't going to fall into a storybook love as he watched his best friend marry. Eden had been clear on her boundaries and he got it. Her last relationship had singed pretty badly. Burns were always worse on the inside. Worse where you couldn't see them, where they festered and stung and bubbled until you sought treatment. The tricky part about burns was that the healing was often worse than the initial scorch.

The best way he'd thought of to respect her boundary had been to avoid this scenario. To avoid touching, kissing, sex, because he'd known. The awareness had barreled into him at their first meeting, and it had roared to life like a fanned flame when she'd kissed him in his office. He could love this woman. He could love her humor and her smile. He could love her kindness and her optimism. He could love her face and her body.

Ted had been looking for someone who could blend into both his work life and his personal life, and here was Eden. Making friends with every wedding guest without even trying, rubbing her hand along his spine when he struggled with flashes of his past, seeing the real him underneath all of it. She liked the real him. Even Eden, who wore and said what she wanted, when she wanted, had understood why he didn't do the same. Why he couldn't. She understood and she didn't judge him for it.

So yes, he could absolutely see them taking this past the weekend. He could absolutely see himself falling in love with her. It was possible he already had. A ridiculous thought. People didn't fall in love in the blink of an eye, but AJ's words from the rehearsal were clanging through his head on a loop he couldn't break. Words she'd seemed to pluck directly from his heart and soul.

Eden's tongue touched his lower lip. A soft swipe from the very tip and that was all the permission he needed to deepen their kiss. Ted pushed his tongue into her mouth, skating it along the length of hers. She moaned as he increased the pressure of his mouth. The sound sent a shudder down his back, and he brought his left arm up to grip her jaw as he angled her head just so. He pulled back his tongue, sucking lightly at her mouth, nipping, then soothing, and after she took a shaky gasp of air, he pressed his tongue against hers again.

They were sitting shoulder to shoulder in the surf, trading open-mouthed kisses, but that wasn't conducive to plastering their bodies together from top to bottom. With his hand on her cheek, Ted had one arm currently propping up his body, but the need to touch her was overwhelming, especially when she smoothed her hands over his chest and popped the button on his shirt.

"Undershirt," he breathed into her mouth when her seeking fingers encountered more cotton.

Eden pulled back to look into his face. The corners of her lips tipped up into a smile, even as she panted sweet hot air over his chin. She trailed her hands down to his waistband and tugged his shirt free from his pants. Then her fingers were sliding up and over his abdomen and he could barely think through the heat that melted his brain out of his ears.

"Your suits are hard to get out of," Eden said, nipping his throat along his collar. "I prefer easy on-easy off."

Ted's right hand was still braced in the sand, barely touching the very edge of her skirted hip. He flexed his abs to keep them upright and lifted that hand to brush against the skin bared between her waistband and the flowing edge of her shirt. If they both leaned forward, they could stay upright, but that would impede Eden's ability to explore his chest and stomach. Her fingers gently twisted in the hair that circled his navel and he'd rather set himself on fire than stop her. Her mouth brushed his again, and Ted lost himself for breathless minutes, trading hot wet kisses back and forth.

More, he thought. He needed infinitely more of this woman and this moment. He used the arm around her hip to push her up and over his body until she straddled the tops of his thighs. Ted pulled out of the kiss and moved her hips forward until her center dragged along the ridge of his erection. He saw the shudder wrack her body, felt the tremor against his, and heard the sharp inhale of breath as she rocked her hips into his. He relaxed his body back into the sand and held her still as he ground up against her. He barely heard her curse over the sound that ripped from his chest.

He rolled his hips again and moved his hands up the sides of her ribcage. He stopped just under the heavy weight of her breasts and waited for something, a sign, permission. Eden circled her hips over his, the friction euphoric, and he took it as a green light, sliding his hands higher to cup her in his palms. She wore a soft lace bra, the kind that made it easy to swipe a thumb over her nipples without pushing the cups out of the way. She ground down on him, pushing her chest into his hands, and Ted lay back on the wet sand before his muscles gave out.

Eden surged against him and he knew the head of his cock had bumped her clit just from the breathy whine she made with each move.

"That's right Sweetness," he said. "Take what you need."

"I can't," the words pulsed out of her on a ragged breath. "My skirt—" the material was soaked and twisted around her thigh. The fabric was loose, but it had no stretch. She rocked her hips again, and he paid attention this time. Not just to the way she felt against him, but the way she couldn't follow through on the motion. She was stuck. He hadn't noticed because he was caught up in the friction and the heat, but she couldn't slide her hips the way she wanted to. He could fix that.

"I've got you," he said and surged upright to tuck a hand around the back of her neck. The other he anchored on her hip. "Hold on to me. I'll fix it." And then he rolled her under him, cushioning her against the soaked sand.

They were even more twisted now, her skirt wrapped under her legs. Ted pushed one hand flat against the sand and used the other to ruck up the fabric, pulling it out from under her curves, until it pooled at her waist. Her panties were the same flimsy lace he'd felt under her shirt. Soaked from the water and from her arousal, they hugged every dip and fold of her pussy. Ted dropped his head to her neck and pressed a fevered kiss to her damp skin. His teeth scraped her throat, and she moaned, tipping her hips as she wrapped her legs around his waist.

"Better?" He let his erection nudge the hot place between her thighs.

"Yes," she moaned into his ear. She twisted a hand into the wet hair at the nape of his neck and pulled. He bit down on the slope of her breast through her shirt. The white fabric was completely see-through, but there was something exciting about leaving it to cover her. He ground against her pussy again and her breath hitched on another groan. "There. Don't stop."

Ted was pretty sure the entire wedding party could do a conga-line down the beach and stop to take pictures of them in the surf and he wouldn't stop. The clip had fallen out of her hair, and she threw her head back, digging the dark strands into the sandy shore. He kept up the rocking motion of his hips. Driving his cock against her body over and over as she moved under him. The waves were still pouring over them, but Ted didn't care and he wasn't sure Eden even noticed.

She was a siren under him, her gasps and moans the song that would lead him down into the depths, never to be heard from again. And he was happy to go down with her. Eden stiffened under him. Her chest heaved, and she sucked in a breath. He pressed kisses to her exposed throat, quickening his pace to get her there. She was close. He could practically feel her pulse slide over his dick. Even through her panties and his pants. Her eyes were closed tightly and no, Ted didn't like that. It was the only thing he didn't like.

"Open your eyes," he said, barely recognizing his own voice. "Look at me, Sweetness. Look at the man who makes you come."

Eden's lips quirked into a smile as her lashes fluttered open. Even in the dark, he could see the green of her irises. If the ocean didn't swallow him, her eyes surely would. She detonated like a bomb. One hand clutched his suit coat, the other fisted strands of his hair. Her body jerked like she'd been plugged into an electric socket and Ted buffeted the movements with his chest and hips. He tried not to lose his mind as her body arched into his. Ted breathed out through his nose, sounding like a rampaging bull, his teeth clenched to ride out her orgasm as Eden screamed out into the night, the sound of his name on her lips almost taking Ted over the peak with her. She relaxed under him, her body supple and loose and glowing. She'd kept her eyes on his the entire time.

"That was amazing. Thank you." Eden tightened her thighs around his hips, brushing her panties against the stone length of his dick, and Ted's eyes crossed. He grunted, trying to control his racing heart and the throbbing ache in his balls. He needed her to move. To stay still. To disentangle. To press closer. She slid her hand in between them, her fingers grazing his erection as she reached for his belt. He jerked against her with a low curse, and she let out a breathy laugh. "Your turn Bear,"

Ted dropped his hips to still her hand on his waistband. The little minx had gotten the belt undone one-handed.

"No?" She stilled her searching fingers. "I can't remember the last time a man actually made me come, and I want to return the favor, but if you're not interested—"

Not interested? His brain was barely functioning past the fantasy of her wrapping her hand around his dick or sinking into her wet heat. He was so close to the point of no return that it would probably take only a few strokes, and he'd go off like the illegal fireworks he'd set off during his teenage rebellion. And yes, Ted wanted to finish what they had started, but if this was a one-night stand and nothing more, then he didn't want to come in her hands as if they were fumbling behind the bleachers.

He didn't have a condom with him, didn't assume that sex itself was an option. But if it was? Well, if it was, then he would not lose himself in her fist on the beach. He was going to take his time. Something that wasn't possible in their current situation. The water still swirled around them. The tide was heading out, but they were still getting soaked with each wave. Eden was shivering, not the good kind either.

Not the full-body shudders she'd had when he'd gotten her off, but the tiny quaking shivers that usually came before chattering teeth. She was freezing. A good reason to move them somewhere other than water that averaged fifty to sixty degrees during the day. Water that felt a lot colder now as he held himself still against her.

"I'm interested," Ted said because it was true and Eden was frowning. She wasn't supposed to frown. She even smiled when she came, for fuck's sake. "I'm extremely interested."

And there it was. Her grin rounded her cheeks. Eden wiggled her fingers against his stomach and slipped them past the waistband of his pants. She wrapped her hand firmly around the width of his cock and gave him a firm stroke. Ted's stomach hollowed out, and he bucked his hips into her grip.

"Not here," he said as his body rolled on its own. He should take her inside. To the baby blue room with the wide bed. Where it was warm and he could strip her naked and didn't have to worry about her catching hypothermia while he got off in her hands. She gripped him tighter, swirling her palm over the sensitive tip, and he dropped his mouth to her neck, cursing against her pulse.

"Okay Bear," she slid her hand up to cradle the back of his head. "Let's move fast."

Fast. Right. He could do fast. That's probably the only speed he was going to manage for this first round. He'd have to make the next one last. He didn't want her to have a single regret about this escalation in their relationship. They were blowing his carefully written contract out of the water, but they were doing it together.

Ted levered himself off her body, trying not to sob when her hand left his dick. He could feel his pulse thundering away in his erection, the tip leaking milky white fluid. He pulled her out of the surf and along the sandy beach. The water had plastered her skirt to her thighs and he could see the lace of her bra through her white shirt. It also clung to her body, showing each rounded curve and soft divot. His own clothes were dripping salt water down into his sodden shoes. It was a good thing he had a spare pair in his car. And an extra suit. He wasn't sure this one was salvageable. He *was* sure that he didn't care.

Eden shivered again and Ted slipped his jacket off. He snagged her hand, the one she'd wrapped around him with the perfect grip, and tugged her back. Spinning her like a dancer until she was pressed against his chest. He looped the jacket over her shoulders, swallowing hard as she slipped her hand up the front of his wet shirt. Her hand blazed heat clear to his heart. Her eyes caught his, darting back and forth as she focused on his face. Then, so slowly he almost missed her moving, she pushed up on her toes and kissed his mouth. Her fingers laced through his, squeezing his hand tight. He hadn't touched her yet, not without her clothes between them. He hadn't tasted her, not where he wanted to. Suddenly teleportation felt like it would take too long to get her to a bed.

At the far side of the beach, tucked in against the stone retaining wall, was an outdoor shower. It wasn't much, but it had a door, and the water was heated. Ted maneuvered her towards the small building. He shouldered the door open and reached in, cranking the water as hot as the dial would go. He toed his shoes off and left the sandy mess just outside before backing Eden into the relative privacy of the shower.

"I thought we were headed to a bedroom," she laughed as he moved her under the steaming spray of water.

"Too far." Ted took his jacket and looped it over the top of the door. He pressed a kiss to the curve of her shoulder. He slid his hands to her hips, gathering her skirt in his fingers and dragging it up her thighs. "Do you mind?"

"Not at all." Eden pulled her shirt over her head and dropped it on the wood slat floor. Ted's gaze dropped to her breasts, hugged in pale lace. Through the sheer fabric he could make out the dark circles of her nipples. His mouth watered. "It reminds me of you," she slipped her hands into his hair as he bent and sucked the under curve of her breast into his mouth. Underneath the salt, she was warm and soft. "Outside and not outside. Risky and safe." She dropped her head back as he gently bit her nipple. "Is it my turn to play?" She reached for his waistband again.

Ted grunted into her skin and dropped to his knees.

"It's my turn again," he said as he shouldered his way between her thighs and slid her panties to the side. "Yes?"

Ted looked up at her from his knees. The shower steaming around her, her cheeks flushed from heat and arousal, eyes bright and wanting as they stared down at him.

She grinned and spread her legs wider, gripping the back of his head for support.

"Yes." she'd barely finished the word when he'd swiped his tongue along her center and circled her clit. She tasted of salt and sun and woman. Tangy and musky. He could stay here for hours. Days. Years. Her fingers tightened in his hair and he used his free hand to hold her open and spear his tongue deep into her center. His thumb rubbed her clit as he fucked her with his mouth. Above Ted's head, Eden praised a god, cursed, and then moaned.

"If you make me come again in under ten minutes, I'll return the favor with *my* mouth," she said, and Ted grinned against her core. He always did like a challenge. Especially one he knew he could beat.

"How about five?" Ted asked and then slid two fingers deep inside her while his mouth found her clit.

Ted snored like a MAC truck. Eden wasn't surprised to learn that fact, so much as she was surprised that she hadn't noticed. They'd been sharing a room for over twenty-four hours and even if she'd been alone in the bed the night before, the room wasn't so big that she hadn't been able to find him on the couch.

Probably because that night he'd curled up on his side, face pressed to the back of the upholstery, muting the sound or opening his sinus cavity or something. Tonight he'd pressed against the back of her neck, breath fanning over her skin in waves of heat. When she'd slipped out from under his arm, he'd sprawled back across the mattress and the snoring had gotten louder.

It had been cute. *He'd* been cute.

Not a phrase she ever thought would describe Ted, but it was accurate. When he'd looked up at her from his knees, a blush tinging his cheeks. When he'd slammed his hands palm down on the shower wall and shook with the need not to thrust himself into her mouth. When he'd gathered her up into his arms and carried her back into the house, both of them dripping estuaries of sea and shower water all over the Masters' wide plank flooring. He'd marched them both past the dwindling party and up to their second-floor bedroom, not sparing a second thought for anyone. She'd had to call over his shoulder that they were both fine when Chloe asked if they'd fallen in.

Fine. They were both *more* than fine. They'd stripped down to their naked skin back in the room and he'd all but shoved her into another shower. This one alone.

"No condom," he'd told her as he handed her a bottle of shampoo, his erection bobbing as he moved around the bathroom, completely unconcerned with his lack of clothing. Before she'd been able to tell him she was on birth control, and she trusted him enough to consider an exception, he'd closed the bathroom door and headed out into the main room. By the time she'd followed him, scrunching her wet hair in one of the softest towels she'd ever used, Ted had donned a pair of thin gray pajama bottoms. A pair he wore into the bathroom for his own shower. When he returned to the bedroom, they were already back in place. Clearly a defense mechanism.

Ted had pulled back the covers on the bed and waited for her to climb in before tucking the comforter around her like a mummy. Eden had barely struggled free enough to sit up as he backed his way to the couch.

"Ted," she'd said in her most serious voice. "We've seen each other's O face. I think we're safe to share a bed."

He'd grumbled out a laugh, and there it was again. That cuteness she'd never expected.

"I'm not used to being vulnerable, Eden, and I'm trying for some self-control," he said, which was even cuter, but she pulled back the covers and patted the mattress, sending him her sweetest smile. If he was serious about not trying anything, then she could respect that, but she wasn't going to watch him spend another night on the damn loveseat. It was too small for her, let alone six-foot-plus of muscled man.

He'd hesitated, staring deep into her eyes, and Eden refused to think about why her heart had squeezed in her chest. She'd simply patted the mattress again. "Come to bed, Bear."

She didn't regret offering to share. Not when he stalked to the far side of the bed, his eyes pinning her in place like a wild animal. Not when he pulled back the covers and slid in next to her, the soft fabric of his pants brushing against her—freshly—shaved legs. Not even when he'd turned to her, practically glowing in the pale moonlight from the big window, and asked if she was okay. She was. Eden was an adult. They could share a bed after a handful of delicious orgasms. She'd done that before with other partners. Chloe, for example.

And yet when midnight tipped them from late night to early morning, she was wide awake, still trying to slow her heart rate. Trying and failing because some time while they'd slept, they'd both shifted toward each other. Now their legs were hopelessly tangled, a heavy arm was thrown over her waist, and light snores were ruffling the damp hair at the top of her head. So yes. Now she recognized the snoring.

That was a good enough reason to extricate herself from the bed. It had to be the snoring that was keeping her awake, not her pounding heart or the itchy tendrils snaking their way through her limbs, urging her to move. Eden half expected

Ted to wake up when she pushed away from him, but he just rolled to his back, his head turning away from her. One of them had kicked the covers down and she could see his flat stomach, dark hair crisp against his skin, and rounded pectorals. The muscles in his arms bulged as he scratched an absent line across his belly and sighed into the darkness of the room. It took Eden a moment to recognize that his other arm was underneath her.

Once she was out of the bed, leaving the room was easy, as was finding the kitchen. Will had told her a million and one times to make herself feel at home, so she could help herself to a bottle of water from the subzero fridge and enjoy it on the sun porch. Alex had whipped up some homemade cookies and Eden was fairly certain she knew where those were, too. A late-night snack was just what she needed. She wasn't avoiding Ted, or the baby blue bedroom, or the snuggling… she was just hungry.

The hanging lights over the kitchen island bathed the room in a soft yellow glow, and it took Eden longer than she'd care to admit to notice the woman sitting on the loveseat. Eleanor had a book in her lap and was slowly turning the pages while sipping from a large ceramic mug.

"Hello Eden," Eleanor called out, just as Eden was contemplating backing out of the room. "Come join me."

She closed her book and set it on the end table, then stood up and moved toward the counter, mug held in her elegant fingers. Even in her pajamas, Eleanor was elegant and sophisticated. She reminded Eden of Jackie O with her dark hair and her matching silk separates. The woman even had a pair of cream-colored slippers. Eden was in a pair of men's boxers—not Ted's, but Eleanor probably would assume they were his—and a thin camisole. She crossed her arms over her chest to disguise her lack of a bra.

"Can I make you something? Tea? Coffee?"

Was it polite to help herself when her hostess was offering? Usually, these kinds of interactions didn't bother Eden. She reacted with her gut, and assumed that others would recognize that her actions came from the right place, or they wouldn't. Now she cared. She just didn't know why.

"Thank you, Mrs. Masters. I was just going to grab some water." Eden opened the fridge herself and pulled out a bottle of Evian. It was cool in her hand. The plastic was smooth as she clutched it to her chest like a lifeline.

"Trouble sleeping?" Eleanor asked. She slid onto a stool and pulled another seat out for Eden.

She *was* having trouble, but she doubted the reason was an appropriate conversation topic for her and Ted's best friend's mother.

"A bit," she admitted, opening the bottle to take a sip.

"Do you have everything you need?" Eleanor asked, and Eden shook her head.

"Everything is great. We really don't need anything."

"It's a lot," Eleanor said, and took a sip of her own. "I was having trouble sleeping, too. I haven't been a night owl in years, but I have a lot on my mind this weekend."

"That's probably normal, given the wedding tomorrow."

"Yes," Eleanor agreed, "but I've been focusing most of my introspection on the past."

Eden studied the other woman. She was flawless, perfection achieved with money and time, but there was something else there too. Her eyes seemed heavy, weighted. Like she hadn't slept well in over a year. Maybe more. It wasn't a chill. Eleanor might not be cuddly, but she was kind. This looked almost like sadness.

"Weddings are complex," Eden said. "There's beauty and magic and love. They're a beginning, a start, but they are also an end. They close a chapter on a portion of someone's life. No matter what happens next, nothing is quite the same."

Her mother certainly hadn't been the same after marrying her stepdad. One minute it had been Eden and Theresa bouncing from small town to small town, riding old scooters to the farmers' market, picking up basket weaving or *papier-mâché* for a fun weekend activity. Then it had been family Christmas cards in matching sweaters, perfectly applied make-up, and extra-curricular activities that would look good on a college application.

"You're right. Of course," Eleanor said, "but I have a lot of guilt surrounding my son, his bride, and this wedding. I've done things I'm not proud of and it has taken the last two years to recognize that the reason behind my behavior does not absolve me of the consequences."

"Well, whatever it is, neither AJ nor Will seem to be the type to hold a grudge." Eden said. She almost put a hand on the older woman's arm, but that seemed a tad forward. "It's also pretty clear they are absolutely perfect for each other."

Eleanor nodded. Even now, in her pajamas, the dark bob of her hair didn't move.

"You and Teddy make a fetching pair," Eleanor said. "We've all been hoping he'd find the right partner, and we were thrilled when he mentioned a date."

This was probably the perfect time to tell Eleanor that they were just a pair of acquaintances turned into friends who'd recently given into a few moments of temptation. Ted had mentioned that his stepfather and Will's dad were close.

Would it be worse to blow their arrangement wide open? Or to let them continue to think he was dating someone. Someone who definitely wouldn't fit into the suit his parents clearly wanted.

"Will says the relationship is new?"

Depending on how Eleanor wanted to define relationship, it was at most a few days old. At least a few hours.

"Very," she said instead, and Eleanor smiled into her tea. "He's a good guy," she added, confident that it was one hundred percent true.

When Eleanor looked at her like that, it felt as though she were peeling back each of Eden's layers and peering into the spaces in between. Like she was looking for the glue or stitches that held Eden together. Looking for whatever Eden was made of and how long she'd last. Eden was positive that Eleanor saw more than most people. It wasn't just her quiet watchfulness. She had a presence that seemed to demand answers.

"May I be frank, Eden?" Eleanor asked. She waited for Eden's cautious nod before continuing, "I never liked any of Ted's former partners. They were all too concerned with appearances. Too self-important to put in any sort of work, but you—" she let her gaze roam Eden's face before she smiled. A genuine one, even if her teeth stayed hidden behind the curve of her lips. "I like you, Miss Yates. I like you a lot."

"Thank you?" Eden said, because what else was she supposed to say to that kind of pronouncement? If her words tipped up at the end, turning her statement into a question, well, it wasn't quite the confidence she wanted to portray, but ultimately that didn't matter.

"Do you agree? That you and Ted are a good fit?"

"I'm not sure that's any of your business." Eden said. "I appreciate your honesty, and I like you too, Mrs. Masters, but ultimately, the only person who would need to like me to make a relationship work would be Ted."

Ted did like her. She liked him, too.

She also braced herself for Eleanor to turn frosty. In Eden's experience, most people didn't like their opinions being written off. Especially not people who held a particular place in society. People who were used to being heard.

"You're right," Eleanor said. She set her mug down on the counter and pushed it away with a sigh. "Although I'd argue that *you* need to like you too, in order to have a successful relationship."

That was definitely the truth. Eden hadn't particularly liked Justin by the end of their time together. Now she wasn't sure she'd really liked him at the start of their time together, either. And if she was being completely honest, she definitely didn't like herself by the end of their relationship.

She'd been disgusted with herself. Angry that she'd let someone take such advantage of her. Enraged that she'd spent far too long not realizing she bent and bent and bent until she was in danger of snapping just so he could stand upright. Furious that she'd allowed someone to box her into his own idea of who and what she should be. The worst part had been that she'd entered the relationship believing that he was different.

She'd thought Justin understood her. Thought he recognized her need to create and express herself through her art. And maybe he had, just that he'd cared more about his own needs and desires than about what she needed to survive, let alone thrive. The clues had all been there. Perhaps the most important of all was Romy's immediate dislike for the man, and yet Eden had felt defensive.

She could acknowledge that even if the only opinions needed were hers and her partner's, that didn't mean that other people couldn't potentially see warning signs she had missed. It was drastically different to wave off a friend who liked your partner as opposed to one who disliked them.

Eden had no one to blame but herself. After almost a decade out from underneath the shadow of her stepdad's relationship with her mother, she had been lonely. Eager to find someone to prove her fears about love and relationships wrong. Maybe it didn't matter who she'd have picked. Maybe romance and love were dangerous and deadly and would never work for her. Or maybe she shouldn't have rushed into things with the first guy who seemed to share some of her interests.

"I overstepped and I apologize," Eleanor said.

"I was overly sensitive," Eden admitted.

Eleanor clasped her hands in front of her, carefully interlocking her fingers as she started blankly into the kitchen toward the stainless steel restaurant-grade appliances.

"I overstepped with my son and AJ, too. This whole wedding almost didn't happen," Eleanor's voice more subdued than it had been moments before.

"I wouldn't be too worried," Eden said. "They seem to have a really strong foundation and they're crazy about each other. I doubt anything could shake them or stop them from launching down the aisle tomorrow." The clock on the stove glowed in the dim light. "Today."

"It wasn't today." Eleanor said, "It wasn't this weekend or this year, or at any point during their engagement."

Eden frowned.

"I first met my son's fiancée just about ten years ago. They'd been together for a few months, we'd never been formally introduced, but I met with her so I could tell her everything that I thought made her wrong for my son. Then I offered her a large sum of money to avoid Will for the rest of her life."

It said something about Eleanor, that she was willing to be so upfront about her behavior. It also said something about AJ that the woman could forgive her soon-to-be mother-in-law enough to have her wedding at the woman's family home.

"You know AJ well enough to guess how that went over, but it still took her out of my son's life. Some of the things I said, things that I thought mattered beyond any sort of affection they might have shared, stuck enough to make an impact. And I watched my son wither away for the next eight years. He retreated into a shell of himself. He went to work and went home. He didn't date or smile or laugh. He let me control his life because he didn't care what happened to him after she was gone." Eleanor's voice wobbled, tears making the words a husky rasp of sound.

Eden had seen most of Will and AJ's season of First Lady. She'd been entranced by the way Will watched the dark-haired woman. Energized every time AJ—although they'd called her Jane on the show—lit up when he walked into a room. Their chemistry had burned white hot. She'd asked Justin to take dance lessons with her after she watched them waltz around a dusty old study surrounded by leather-bound books. He'd said no, of course, and Eden should have taken that as the red flag it was and run for the hills. Or danced for them.

She hadn't known that Eleanor had been so opposed to their relationship. She'd seen two people gloriously in love. Their differences notching together like pieces of a puzzle forming one beautiful picture. Two people worried that their past troubles might stop their future. But never would she have guessed that there was an issue with AJ and Eleanor. She had so many questions. Questions that would be wholly inappropriate as the couple said their I-do's.

"Have you met Teddy's parents yet?" Eleanor broke through Eden's thoughts. "I've never been a fan of Martin, which I think is fair to say since I'm not the one who has to be married to him and neither are you." Given what Ted had told her about his stepfather, Eden was tempted to agree with Eleanor. "I think what I dislike most is how much he reminds me of my own horrid behavior. He's never pushed away one of his son's romantic liaisons, but his opinions have had a drastic effect on Ted. These women that he dates fall for the version of Ted that Martin has inspired him to create. They don't get to know the real Ted at all."

Eleanor reached over and took Eden's hand in hers. "I will forever regret the pain that I caused both Will, my child, and his AJ. Despite our rocky start, I really do love her. I don't think Martin cares if his child hurts, so long as he maintains his perfect image. But I do. So yes, I am glad Ted met you and brought you here this weekend. And yes, I like you, Miss Yates, but I also like you for Ted."

She squeezed Eden's hand in hers. Eleanor's skin was cool and dry against Eden's overheated palm, her fingers long and tapered. There was no relationship. It didn't matter if Ted liked her or she liked him. It didn't matter if they were great together. It didn't matter if Eleanor liked her. Or liked her for him.

They wanted such different things that even letting her brain sit with the thought of them together was dangerous. Dangerous because wanting more would hurt both of them, no matter what Eleanor thought. No matter what Eden thought. The same danger that sent her skittering out of bed in the middle of the night, when an attractive, kind, honorable man wrapped his arms around her waist and held on tight.

Ted hadn't seen Eden in almost fifteen hours, which was a problem given the night they'd shared. They'd fallen asleep facing opposite sides of the bed, and he'd briefly woken up when she slipped back beneath the covers around one in the morning. He'd waited, eyes closed in the dark, as she settled onto her side.

He wasn't sure if he should reach for her, touch her. One second passed. Two. Then she scooted her body back, her hips nestling into the curve of his, her back pressing into his chest, and he wrapped an arm around her waist. She sighed into the dark room—a happy, soft sound—and then her body relaxed into sleep and he went back under too.

She'd been gone in the morning. He'd heard her voice in the kitchen as he'd made his way to breakfast. Should he kiss her? Hug her? He hadn't been this unsure around a woman since his first middle school dance, and even then he'd bluffed his way through asking Rachel Schreiber to be his date.

He'd almost made it into the sun-drenched room when Will clapped a hand on his shoulder and dragged him out the front door. He'd been shoved bodily into the front seat of Logan's Subaru and within ten minutes, Ted, his partners, and Michael had been ensconced in a corner booth at the Chatham Filling Station, ordering coffee and waffles. Apparently, it was their job to stay out of everyone's way so that Will didn't accidentally glimpse his bride.

By the time they'd made it back to the house, Eden was gone with the other women for a morning of pampering. He'd hauled flowers and chairs, helped the catering company set up tables in the formal dining room, and kept one eye on the driveway for her return. The longer she was out of his sight, the more Ted worried she wasn't coming back at all, not emotionally. Now he stood in his navy blue suit with the summer sun bathing the garden and grounds in golden light, and he still couldn't find her in the small crowd slowly filling up the white chairs.

"You seem more nervous than Will." Logan stepped up behind him in matching blue.

He probably was. Will had shown zero nerves so far, just the confident surety of a man who had been waiting for this moment for a decade. Probably because he had been waiting a decade.

So yeah, Will wasn't nervous in the slightest about today. He knew AJ was going to come down that aisle and say "I do," and kiss him on the mouth in front of their friends and family. Probably with tongue. AJ was spunky like that.

Ted had no guarantees. He didn't have a years-long history to fall back on with the woman he liked. He had a single—okay, slightly more than single—sexual encounter that singed that blood in his veins, and an easy camaraderie with a woman who'd told him that she wanted nothing more than casual. Nothing more than a friend.

And as Ted stood under the flower-covered arch, and watched the groom buss his mother's cheek and shake hands with one of their guests, Ted realized that not only could he blur the lines and see himself in the role of groom, but he could see himself there with Eden playing the opposing role.

The seats were filling up faster than he'd thought and still no Eden. Which was fine. Perfectly fine. It wasn't like she'd left—he'd driven her to the Cape—and even if she had left it wasn't like she was breaking up with him. There was nothing to break. They weren't a thing. They weren't together. He could see whomever he wanted—not that he wanted to—and so could she. Although he had to admit that it helped to know that Eden had no intention of dating anyone. Not just him.

"I'm not jealous." Ted hadn't meant to say it out loud, but he had anyway, something he realized when Logan nudged his shoulder.

"I'm not sure there was anything to be jealous of. It was just that one weekend." Logan said, and the way Ted saw red proved that he was the world's biggest liar. He rounded on his friend, fists clenched at his side. The only thing stopping him from hitting first and asking questions second was the sea of witnesses. Logan threw his hands up to protect his face. "Not me," he said quickly, peering out from around his fingers. "It wasn't me."

It didn't affect him. Even if it was Logan, it didn't matter. Ted had no right to the information, especially if it came from anyone but Eden herself. No right to be upset. No right to anything. That hurt almost more than the news that she'd been with someone else.

"Who?" Ted asked and Logan dropped his hands, grinning.

"Never thought of you as a liar," Logan said, before nodding towards the back door of the estate where AJ's maid of honor had poked her head out to survey the crowd. "It was Chloe. They had a weekend fling a few years ago. And you didn't hear it from me."

Ted swallowed down his surprise. He never would have guessed. He knew Chloe was bi. Even when she'd starred on the show with Will and AJ, she'd been open about that. Ted hadn't known that Eden was into women, but her sexuality didn't faze him. He genuinely didn't care beyond the grip of jealousy, but never in a million years would he have thought that Boston-based Eden would have had a history with Colorado-based Chloe. That was the kind of coincidence that appeared in movies and novels. Not in real life.

"How'd you find out?" He couldn't resist asking, and his friend shrugged.

"Hard not to notice, plus I guess AJ, Tandy, and Alex already knew about the fling, just didn't have a name to pair with the story. They're still on good terms. That bodes well for your future."

"My future?"

"Yeah, when your fling with Eden peters out, she'll still leave you an opening to fall in love just like we all said you would."

"Fling?" Ted parroted. The last time they'd discussed him and Eden, his friends had been positive that there was nothing going on between Ted and the woman, but that they were a perfect match.

"Will hasn't noticed, so don't worry about the gossip train. He gets a pass given that it's his wedding, but dude." Logan smirked, his head shaking. "First she disappeared from the rehearsal dinner, then you disappeared, and then you stormed the castle with her in your arms, dripping *everywhere,* and when you reappeared this morning you were humming." That got Ted. He frowned at his friend. "Yeah, Mr. Grump. You. Humming. Around a stack of waffles. So either you had a lobotomy, were kidnapped by the pod people, or you got laid and you know what they say about hoofbeats."

"Think of horses." Ted said as the first strums of classical guitar floated through the air.

He hadn't remembered Will or AJ mentioning a guitar. He thought there was supposed to be a string quartet. That's what Eleanor had suggested and Will and AJ had agreed, because who didn't love a string quartet? The woman singing sounded fantastic. Her voice was clear and strong, holding the right notes until the perfect resolution.

The guests clearly felt the same way. Conversation hushed and seats were taken. Chloe's head appeared at the back door again, and Will gave her a slow nod before making his way to stand with Ted and Logan. The bridesmaids stepped down the aisle in perfect step-together-step-together rhythm. Tandy went first in baby blue, followed by Alex in a deeper royal. Chloe brought up the rear in navy. He still couldn't find Eden, but he valiantly searched the familiar and unfamiliar faces, hoping for a sight of her.

There was a brief silence, and then everyone stood and turned to face the top of the aisle as the guitar picked up again. He knew the song. It was some peppy number, usually sung by a woman with neon orange hair. Something about holding hands, butterflies, and wondering. And the woman singing it poured her soul into the words, slowing them down into a soft croon. A caress to the senses. All eyes were on AJ standing with her dad in white silk, curls pinned back with a pearl band. Except for Ted. Ted's eyes were elsewhere because he'd finally found Eden.

He didn't know how he'd missed her, especially once the music started. Eden stood off to the side. She had an acoustic guitar strapped to her front and her fingers deftly picked the strings. Ted did not know where she'd gotten the guitar—it definitely hadn't come to the Masters' in his car—but that was the least of his concerns. She was almost unrecognizable.

Her long dark hair was smoothed back into a fancy twist, the kind he'd seen on flight attendants. Her dress was simple and sedate and looked like it had come out of Eleanor's own closet. Eden's shoulders were bare, round in the warm sun, her long arms flexing as she strummed the strings and plucked out chords. Her eyes were closed as she swayed along to the music, lashes dark smudges against her full cheeks.

She looked beautiful. She sounded otherworldly. She sang a line about meeting someone's mother, and smiled around the words. Ted's heart constricted in his chest, the dull ache intensifying as she opened her gorgeous green eyes and locked them on the bride walking down the aisle. Despite the space between them, Ted watched a tear track over the swell of Eden's cheek. It glistened, sparkling like a diamond against her tanned skin. She never faltered, her words clear even as she cried. She believed in love. The proof was staring Ted right in the face.

Something scratched at the surface of his brain. Even as Cooper Wells welcomed everyone to the wedding and Chloe started a reading from *Pride & Prejudice*. Like the cat he'd loved as a kid, the one who would beg to be let out of a room only to demand reentry less than a minute later.

Those demands often came with scratched door frames and Ted could remember like it was yesterday, the day he came home from school, calling for Gizmo, only to face down his stepfather as the man explained with cool indifference how he'd re-homed the animal. The house couldn't take the damage. Ted had snuck out his bedroom window that night with a can of spray paint tucked into his back pocket.

The itch persisted as Will and AJ shared vows, promising forever and ever. Eleanor was blotting her eyes with a white handkerchief, careful not to smudge her eye makeup, and Chloe was sniffing loudly from her spot holding AJ's bouquet. Ted knew it was inappropriate to tune out this part of the weekend, but he kept feeling like he was missing something. Something big, something like his cue to hand over the platinum wedding bands. He fumbled them out of his pocket and handed them to Cooper. Neither AJ nor Will seemed to have noticed the hesitation.

Among the guests, Eden ducked her head and a wry smile twisted her lips. She was sitting in the last row, hands folded sedately in her lap and Ted felt the corners of his lips tip up as he smiled back at her. Her shoulders shook as she—no doubt—laughed at his wandering attention. It hit him like a two-by-four to the chest, like the rogue wave that had crashed her into the surf the night before.

As he looked down the rows of chairs at the stranger he'd brought to the wedding, he couldn't help but imagine her standing up at the altar with him, imagine losing himself in her and missing the cue to get his own rings or recite his own vows. Because the longer he stood up at the front, watching her there at the back, the more he realized he wanted a wedding—yes—but he wanted a marriage more. He wanted the partnership, the loyalty, the camaraderie. He wanted it with Eden most of all. He wanted her bright sunshine soul lighting up every single minute of his days and heating up every second of his nights.

"It's the dress," he said to himself as Cooper asked if Will would take AJ to be his lawfully wedded wife. Logan bumped him with his shoulder, eyes narrowed as he motioned back toward the happy couple with his chin. It was okay, though, because Ted had figured out the problem, and once he explained, Logan would understand. The itching had abated to a dull tickle.

"She's wearing the wrong dress," He said, at least remembering to keep his voice low.

"No, she's not," Cooper leaned in to add, not nearly as quiet as Ted had been. "I designed it."

"And I love it. It's absolutely perfect," AJ added with a wink, "But I don't think Ted's talking about me."

AJ tipped her head towards the guests and every member of the bridal party turned to look at Eden. She was shaking her head, still smiling and quaking with suppressed laughter. Now she raised her hand and waved too. She shone, brighter than the June sun glinting on the caps of the waves. She glowed up at him, one hundred percent herself. One hundred percent confident. One hundred percent everything.

And he completely missed Cooper Wells introducing Will and AJ as husband and wife.

The dress itched like it was made of stinging nettles, and Eden rubbed the insides of her arms along the side seams to find some kind of relief. It wasn't helping. Maybe she shouldn't have brought the black sheath dress. Romy had handed it to her before she left, reminding her that she was there as a favor to Ted and he might want her in something more "classic." Romy rolled her eyes when she said it, the dress was one she held onto for funerals, but she'd been right. Eden had set out on this weekend almost like she was going to play a role, and if she was going to do that she'd need the right costume.

Now Eden was thinking she shouldn't have put the damn dress on, or matched it with the plain pair of black heels. She'd been feeling more than a little raw after her chat with Eleanor, and she wanted to do right by Ted. Make a good impression, or a good something. Give him the partner he said he'd been looking for. It was probably her own feelings making her itch, more so than the dress itself. Or maybe it was the way Ted was staring at her from the front of the aisle.

Half the discomfort was that the dress was clearly made for nuns in the winter, but the other half was the niggling reminder that no matter how many times she told herself that she was wearing this dress as a costume, acting the part of Ted's date, she was once again bending for someone else. Between smiles and nods she had to constantly remind herself that this wasn't the same thing as losing herself. She couldn't burn Romy's dress, not without permission, but she could stuff it back into her suitcase and never wear it again.

Eden had felt it the minute Ted's eyes found her, the tingles moving down her arms as she strummed the guitar. The song had been a gift, one she'd offered on a whim when the violinist had to cancel. His youngest had come down with a rogue case of chickenpox, which left the quartet without a leader.

Eleanor handled the setback with the remarkable calm that came with knowing the world would bend to her demands. Eden had played her share of weddings, and it had been easy to offer her skills. Both the bride and mother-of-the-groom had been happy to accept even without hearing her play. That kind of trust was staggering. Intense enough that her breath had caught as the two very different women had given her twin smiles and thank yous.

Playing a wedding had never moved Eden to tears before. Usually she reserved the waterworks for the vows and the groom's first glimpse of his bride. She blamed the bubbling joy arcing between Will and AJ for her sudden sentimentality. It was absolutely not related to Ted's eyes skating over her body. Definitely not connected to the way she felt when he was near her.

And if she had a sudden bout of sentimentality? A resurgence of the desire to find someone all for herself? That had to be wedding magic dripping all over everyone. It was the ambiance. Nothing more. No one would ever love Eden the way she'd learned to love herself. She'd just have to keep telling herself that, especially when Ted stared her down like he was a starving man and she was a freshly baked loaf of bread.

Eden was holding firm to that line of thought through the readings, personal vows, a strange pause and hushed murmurs during the ring exchange, and the first kiss. She held onto it with both fists until the moment when she could bypass the receiving line and step into the room set up for cocktails. She just needed to drop the façade for a moment and take a deep breath. One breath before she could go back out there. Eden steeled her will as Ted dodged his way through the fancy suits and garden dresses. Clung to her resolve like it was the last thing she would ever do as he stopped in front of her, his broad chest blocking out all the light and noise.

The dress felt like it was cutting off her air supply. It had zipped with no problem, but that didn't mean it couldn't be too small, right? She and Romy were built nothing alike, and it would actually be more surprising if the dress fit. It had nothing to do with her desire to sketch Ted staring down the aisle at her, as though he were the groom and she was about to walk toward him and their future.

"You're supposed to be taking pictures," Eden forced a smile. She twisted her hands together in front of her rioting belly. Anything to stop from reaching out and touching him.

"Yeah," Ted said, grunting the word like it was ripped from his gut.

"But you aren't taking pictures." There was no reason for him to be in front of her, looking down at her with a frown, pinching his brows together.

"No," he said.

Some people might not think that one-word answers let out a lot of information. Eden disagreed. The way his jaw locked and unlocked between his single syllables. How he cut the word "yes" down to "Yeah." The way each word seemed to vibrate out of his chest. The pitch low and slipping over her senses until she almost shivered. The sunroom was a comfortable temperature, with the AC running despite the open doors, but it wasn't chilly enough to cause the goosebumps that broke along her skin.

"You need to change," Ted said, his eyes dipping to trace the line of her collarbone, the swell of her chest, the width of her waist, the roundness of her hips. She felt each move like a caress, enough to get her damp between the thighs.

"Excuse me?"

"Your dress," he stepped a fraction of an inch closer, the toes of his leather shoes—not the same ones from the ocean—touching the shiny tips of her pumps. "Go take it off." He punctuated each word with a sharp inhale of breath. As if each one was its own little world holding living breathing organisms, capable of thought and art and exploration. Capable of greatness.

"Why?" The word was a challenge—a quiet one—but it wasn't weak. Eden placed it between them, a dare to explain his reasoning. One option could make both of them extremely happy. The other… well, the other and she'd be snagging a ride back to Boston tonight. She'd wanted to think the best, but the tone of his voice, the furrow in his brow…she wasn't holding out hope that she was about to get lucky.

Ted's fingers touched the fabric over the center of her chest. He steered clear of her breasts, pinky grazing the skin along the front of her shoulder. It was like a brand, a moment of stunned heat that spread and spread and spread until it threatened to incinerate her. Judging by the way his pupils expanded, he was feeling the same burst of something.

"Because..." his hand traveled down the front of her chest, dipping between the valley of her breasts. She watched the tanned skin against the itchy black fabric as it moved over her belly and rested against the curve of her abdomen. Eden held her breath as his fingers flexed against her body. "It's not you. I want—we all want—you to be you."

Whatever she'd been expecting, it hadn't been that. Eden's heart hiccupped. A little squeeze that she refused to acknowledge was anything beyond indigestion. Too much champagne and the lobster bisque shooters they'd served for lunch before standing in the sun. That's all it was. She swayed toward him, just a tiny infinitesimal shift, but it was enough for him to drop his hand.

"Okay," she said, wishing she could have his hand back on her body. "I'll go change."

Twenty minutes later, her blue dress swishing around her thighs, Eden stepped back into the cocktail room.

"This is a much better choice," Cooper Wells said, fingering the floaty sleeves. "That black thing looked like something Nell would have worn." At Eden's confused frown, he said, "Don't tell Eleanor I called her that. She buried the nickname around the time she got engaged to George."

Eden mimed locking her lips and throwing away the key.

"It was my friends. I was worried this one might be too much." she admitted. "I wasn't sure about the blue. Isn't it considered impolite to wear the same color as the bridesmaids?"

"As the man who designed the bridesmaids' dresses, my official opinion is that *that* opinion is crap. You aren't in the same family of blue, your dress is nothing like the gowns I put together, and you have this darling print." Cooper leaned in close enough that Eden could smell his spiced cologne. "In fact, the only concern I would have is that AJ is going to demand to know why I didn't go with a design closer to this. She's fun, that girl. Where'd you find the print?"

Eden glanced down at the sequined blueberries, each tiny fruit winking up at her in the overhead light. "I stitched them," she said. "Blueberries are my favorite fruit. They're always a surprise. Sometimes sweet, sometimes sour." Cooper grinned.

"You don't need a job, do you? I'm envisioning a whole line of sequined fruits."

"I'm good, thanks," Eden smiled back, "But I'd consider designing some prints for special occasions."

"Like your own nuptials?" Cooper nodded out the back door, where Ted had joined the rest of the wedding party for photos overlooking the water. "You strike me as the non-traditional type, but I bet Ted is just itching to drag you down the aisle."

"Oh no," Eden shook her head. "We definitely aren't... I mean, we're not... it's not..."

"My mistake." Cooper raised his hands in apology. "Love on the brain, you know."

Out on the patio, Ted laughed at something Will said, and Eden felt her breath catch in her chest. He looked good out there, talking with his friends. Even in the short time she'd known him, it had become apparent that Ted didn't spend too much time having fun. In Eden's experience, those were the people most deserving of a little enjoyment. She could help with that.

But Cooper was right. Ted was looking for the perfect woman to follow him down the aisle. Someone who didn't need to be hog-tied and carried over his shoulder. That wasn't her. Eden had assumed they were on the same page. Their contract had lain things out in black-and-white and while she hadn't thought it necessary at first, even Eden had found comfort in knowing exactly what each of them expected.

And then last night happened, their chemistry overflowing like a steady stream of lava, and even she had to admit that they hadn't done enough talking as they peeled off their clothes. Definitely not as they'd slid skin-to-skin. She *could* assume that no talk meant no changes, but Eden had woken up to him pressed against the length of her back, cuddling into her like one half of a couple, and it had sent her running. So… conversation first. Fun after.

Ted met her eyes through the door. He didn't smile as he turned his body to face hers. Didn't tilt his head or acknowledge her as he slipped his hands onto his hips. Even from across the hardwood floor, out the open glass doors, and across the wide green lawn, she swore she could see his eyes darken with heat.

Attraction wasn't the issue. Even now, she could feel need tightening her belly. It was tempting to grab his collar and drag him up the main staircase, but they still had dinner and dancing and toasts. Still had cake. She needed to get a handle on her parts. Eden gripped the edges of her skirt, spreading the fabric wide as she bobbed a curtsy. The corners of Ted's mouth twitched up into a begrudging smile.

Eden chatted with Michael and Cooper. She made friends with AJ's old roommate and coworker. She kept one eye on the clock and another eye on the photographs. She helped walk AJ's grandfather into the dining room for dinner. She found her place card and table assignment. She and Michael took their seats and waited for the rest of their party.

There was a DJ for the reception, and as he announced the bridal party entrance, Eden wiped her sweaty palms along the edges of the table linens. There was no reason to be nervous. Except that Ted had blown off his duty as the best man to tell her to be herself. He'd cut through a crowded room to see her, and now she was waiting for his reaction again. She didn't do things for a reaction. She did things for herself. She didn't need anyone else's validation. Until tonight.

Tandy danced in with Cooper. Then Alex and Logan. They boogied across the dance floor in the center of the room and stopped along the edge of the open space. And then there was Ted. Chloe's arm looped through the crook of his elbow, and he looked serious and grumpy and hot and Eden's pulse kicked up. She sat straighter in her chair as his eyes focused on hers.

Chloe nudged him in the side, laughing as they stepped into the room. Decidedly not dancing. Actually, Chloe was dancing, shaking her shoulders in an exaggerated shimmy before stopping to wiggle her hips. Ted didn't join her, but he paused to give her time to have her moment. He didn't hurry her along, or roll his eyes, or sigh. Just stood and waited for her to keep moving.

Later, Eden wouldn't remember the first dance, the toasts, the food, or anything else about the reception. She would remember the way her heart pounded as Ted arrowed toward her, took her hand, and led her onto the dance floor. Barely waiting for the DJ to open the floor after Will and AJ danced with their parents and each other.

"Dance with me." Ted had held his hand out for her to take. His fingers closed around hers and he pulled her from her chair. He didn't step back, letting her body press up against the front of his as she got her feet underneath her.

"I'm not that steady in heels, Bear." He was already moving back towards the dance floor, holding her tight to the curve of his body.

"Then take them off," he said against the shell of her ear.

She tensed. It wasn't the suggestion that gave her pause—Eden preferred to be barefoot anyway—it was the brush of hot air over the sensitive skin usually hidden behind her hair. He'd unbuttoned his jacket and her breasts pressed against the crisp cotton of his shirt. In a heartbeat, Eden had kicked off the heels and let him tow her out to join the newlyweds on the dance floor. Ted wrapped his full arm around her waist, his hand cupping her far hip. His thumb rubbed the tulle as his nose traced her hairline. She was engulfed by him, completely and utterly surrounded. She couldn't seem to draw in a full breath. She didn't want to.

Eden was a competent dancer. Rhythm came with the instruments and singing. Graceful movement came from the yoga. Ted was another kind of dancer. He'd clearly had lessons in his life, and he twirled her around the floor with a firm pressure on her waist and a solid grip on the hand he held in his. The same hand that he'd pressed to the thudding beat of his pulse. His chin dropped to his chest as he stared down at her, pupils swallowing the dark irises. He was looking at her like he wanted to…

"You look good enough to eat." He plucked at some of the purple blue sequins Eden had spent hours hand stitching onto the fabric during the hottest week of last summer. "Blueberries are my favorite. Sweet."

Well, if she'd been worried that this dress was too much for him, she was clearly an idiot. This was a full court press. Full steam ahead. All hands on deck. And it was working. She felt loose and languid as he swung them around the dance floor. Eden pressed closer and felt Ted's groan vibrate through every point where they touched. He was hard against her belly and she was ready to drag him out the door, forget the rest of the evening, and give them both what they clearly needed. And there she went, forgetting her plan to clarify where they stood.

"Ted," he didn't respond, lips pressing to her temple instead of forming words. "Teddy." He drew her up onto her toes and his mouth slid down to her ear, down her jaw. "Bear." He hummed against her skin. "What are you doing?"

"Making my move," he said, and Eden's stomach did a free fall. The kind that happens when the roller coaster tips over the highest point and rushes toward the ground. "Yes or No Eden?"

She needed to tell him, needed to remind him that even if she said "yes" it was only for this moment, this night. She didn't have it in her to give more. It didn't matter that he'd seen into the heart of her, that he'd supported her; ultimately relationships let her down. Eden was the only person she could count on. That sounded cynical and awful and wrong, but even if she was looking to change that, even if she was interested in testing the waters, Ted wanted forever. She couldn't ask him to wait for her to figure things out, only to run when things went sour. She wouldn't ask him to waste that kind of time on her. On them.

"I want to say yes," Eden said, and that got through to him. Ted stopped moving, other couples flowing around them as they stood in the center of the dance floor. He pulled back just enough to meet her eyes.

"I'm not going to pressure you. You don't have to do or say anything you don't want to Eden. I promise you that." What a sweet blockhead.

"I want to say yes," Eden repeated, "but I can't say yes to more than one night."

"Technically," Ted dropped his voice until she had to lean in to hear him over the music, "we already had one night."

One night should have done it. She shouldn't have gotten her fill when she got her orgasms and she should now be coolly unaffected by him. It must have been that they didn't really have sex. That sounded a little too much like a former president. Oral sex was sex, the orgasms counted, but it had to be the lack of full horizontal mambo that was making her desperate for another round.

"I'm down for sex. You're hot, I'm interested, and we clearly work like magic when naked." Eden smoothed the lapel on his jacket with her free hand. Ted still clutched her right hand to his heartbeat. "But I'm not looking to start a relationship. I'm not looking for anything beyond today and tomorrow, Ted. I'm sorry." The changes had already started. Look at the way she'd dressed for him tonight?

His throat bobbed as he swallowed.

"I will not ask for more than you're willing to offer."

"Are you sure?" Eden asked, wondering when her voice got so breathy. "Because I can see the wedding bells in your eyes, Ted, and that scares me."

"I'm sure," he said. "You're safe from the bells. Think of this as a proposed addendum to our current contract, no escalation necessary."

"Get a room," Chloe yelled as Logan spun her past them.

"I'm trying," Ted called back with a grin, and Eden couldn't stop the laugh that bubbled free from her own chest. Every time she tried to put him neatly into a box, a tiny piece of rebel Ted popped back out and delighted her.

Eden looped her hand around the back of Ted's neck. She pushed up onto his toes, laying her lips across his. What was the saying? Seal it with a kiss? Eden drew her tongue along Ted's full bottom lip. The wiry hair from his beard scratched against the skin of her cheeks. She shivered, imagining it somewhere lower. Ted opened his mouth on a ragged exhale and Eden pressed into his mouth, her tongue the aggressor. In a heartbeat he was kissing her back. Deep, drugging kisses designed to make her lose her mind along with her panties.

"Is that a yes?" He asked against her mouth.

"Cut out early," Will said as he twirled his bride around the floor, spinning close enough to pass on his advice. "Seriously, no one will judge you two."

"Don't do anything we wouldn't do." AJ pressed a kiss to her husband's jaw. "Or maybe don't do anything we would."

Eden darted her eyes between Ted's. She nodded. "It's a yes, but not until the party's over."

"Okay," Ted said, and drew in a shaking breath. "We'll stay and play nice. For now. Later you're all mine."

Ted touched Eden like she was made of spun sugar, like if he pressed too hard she'd lose her shape and deflate under his hands, crumbling into nothing. It differed from the last time he'd touched her, nothing like the wild heat that had blazed to life like a match held to dry kindling. This was a slow burn. Standing too close to the fireplace while the warmth built and built and built until it was almost blistering, but by that point it required Herculean effort to get up and move.

Ted kicked their room door shut with his foot and framed her face in huge hands. He swept his thumbs along her cheekbones, down to her jaw, and tipped her chin up. Eden's lips parted on a sigh and Ted leaned down to swallow the sound. His lips were soft, sipping little suckling kisses as his hands traced the column of her throat. Ted angled her head, moving her where he wanted her before he pushed his tongue into her mouth and rubbed it down the length of hers.

"You taste so fucking sweet." Ted traced his mouth over her jaw and licked the skin behind her ear. "I knew you would. Even before I got my mouth on you the last time."

Eden's bones went liquid as she melted into his body. *She* tasted sweet? His mouth was a dream. It wasn't just the moves he had, although she definitely needed a repeat, it was the words he pressed to her skin. The way they heated her blood, pouring off his stoic tongue like lava. She'd never been with someone who spoke the way he did, blunt words describing her body, her taste, his need. Couple that with the firm way he moved her, and—Eden's inner feminist would deny it until her dying day—she'd never been so turned on in her life.

Strong teeth nibbled at her earlobe. Eden sagged even further into the wall of his chest and Ted spun them, pressing her body to the back of the door. The bevels in the wood bit into her shoulders, but Eden was fairly certain she would lie down on hot coals if she got to have the man in front of her. She'd already lain down in the frigid ocean water, and she'd come her brains out with no problem. He pressed a muscled thigh between her legs, and she fisted her hands, unsure what she wanted to touch first. Ted slid an arm behind her shoulders and his hand cupped the back of her head. He was holding her off the door. She hadn't even had to say anything.

Skin. She needed to get her hands on his skin. Eden skimmed her fingers down his shirt and gripped it in her fists, pulling it free from his suit pants. His belt needed to go too, and the pants. For now, she focused on touching whatever was closest. He had an undershirt on too, and she dug her hands under the cotton, flexing her fingers against the heat of his stomach. Ted's muscles contracted under her touch and he pushed his hips into hers, pinning her to the door with the full weight of his body. He rolled his hips into her once, twice, grinding the length of his erection against the sensitive, needy juncture of her thighs.

"Slow down." Ted's voice vibrated from his chest to hers.

Her nipples ached. He rubbed against her again and she lifted her thigh to wrap her leg around his waist. Anything to lock their bodies into the perfect position. Anything to prolong the contact and the tremors and the heat. Ted moved a hand to her thigh, skating his fingers up under the hem of her dress. Her hands were still trapped between their bodies. Sandwiched between the muscles of his abdomen and her own. He moved against her again and the pleasure popped, fizzing out along her nerve endings like a curling explosion of the finest champagne.

"It's you." Eden found the words as he dragged his lips along the tops of her breasts. "You're doing all the work." He moved his mouth to hers and she kissed him back. "You're setting the pace, Bear."

Ted pulled back enough to look into her face, hands stilled on her skin. The shift gave Eden just enough space to get her own hands moving again. She rucked up his shirts, pushing her fingers into the coarse hair along his belly and pectorals. The buttons needed to go. Both shirts needed to go, but she'd have to take her hands off him to do that. Not happening.

"You're wrong." Ted pulled his hand out from under her head and the other from off her thigh. He reached between them and worked the buttons at his throat. Eden spared exactly one millisecond, wondering why he was starting at the top and not the bottom before he'd reached over his shoulder and yanked both his dress shirt and undershirt off in one smooth motion.

Okay.

That was certainly faster.

What had he been saying?

Eden slid her hands up over the curve of his pectorals. The dark hair there was springy and rough under her fingertips. She spread her palms over the ink she knew swirled across his chest. His tattoos were all animals, photo realistic designs carefully laid into his skin. Eden pressed her mouth to the phoenix that hovered over the planes of his chest, wings stretching from collarbone to collarbone. His skin was a brand against hers. He could heat her entire apartment on a winter evening. Forget the ancient furnace and fighting with the fireplace flue. She'd just install Ted on her couch and stay toasty warm for all of eternity. She traced one hand up to curl her fingers into the hair at the nape of his neck.

"How am I wrong?" Her lips brushed his as she spoke.

Ted swallowed and took her mouth. Eden was plastered to the door again as Ted dragged his lips over hers. He had a hand on the length of her throat, not squeezing, just resting. His thumbs stroked the skin under her chin as he tipped her head back for his kiss.

"You're wrong about who's in control here." He fed the words directly into her mouth before kissing her again. "The minute you touch me, I'm so far out of control that it's laughable. You don't even have to be touching me. You step into the room, you look at me, and I'm gone. I can't think or breathe or focus on anything except getting near you. Putting my hand on some part of you. I know it's not appropriate. I know I have less than zero rights over any piece of you. But I forget, Eden. I keep forgetting. So no, I'm not the one in control of anything here. You are."

His words unraveled her. She was fraying at the edges like a scarf slipped off the knitting needles then tugged too tight. She wasn't in control either. This whole scenario was out of control, and she was a big dumb bunny for thinking that she knew what she was doing. As if saying the words "Only for tonight," really mattered when she was being pulled inexorably toward him like the moon pulled the tides. Her need for Ted consumed her. Consumed and terrified and maybe, just maybe, it was all too much.

Maybe she'd made a mistake. A mistake touching him, laughing with him, coming to the Cape. A mistake hunting him down in his office and kissing him that first time. A mistake because every moment she spent in Theodore Norman Hughes' presence just made her want extra moments. Eden was not a woman who did extra moments. She did short and sweet.

If marriage was a ten course feast, then Eden's preferred trysts were hors d'oeuvres. Something delicious and fun and a great way to sample new and interesting fare, but not something that would fill up a person expecting a full meal. Meal size wasn't something people could compromise on. People who were hungry wanted more after a brief taste. People who weren't, felt sick after too much. There was no winning for both sides, which is why Eden avoided anyone looking for more than a quick bite.

Until Ted.

She was terrified, and turned on. This could change everything. No matter what she said to him, she felt like she was standing on the edge of a cliff as a storm blew in, threatening to send her crashing into the ravine below. And yet nothing could make her step away.

"Hey," Ted cupped her cheeks in his hands, and his dark eyes darted between hers as he tipped her face up to his. "You okay?" Was she? Not in the slightest. "We don't have to do this." He dropped his forehead down to hers and she closed her eyes. "I'd never ask you for anything you weren't comfortable giving."

They stood there, minutes morphing into eons, as her heart raced. Ted pulled back, putting distance between them, and she felt cold. It was more than simply the loss of his body—the man radiated heat like a furnace—it was like the first dive under a cold ocean wave. Or like the mad dash to the outdoor bathroom during a surprise October snowstorm when she had been living in the little cabin in Maine.

Eden had loved that little retreat, and her art from those three months had been inspired. But just like now, that cold had clarified something for her. She was a creature of comfort. Warm beds, a handful of close friends, her favorite set of watercolors, her sense of self. So she'd hightailed it back to a lower altitude and indoor plumbing. Now she followed Ted as he stepped away.

"I want you," she told him, slipping her hands around the bulk of his naked waist. "I've wanted you since you barged into a police station to rescue me. I've been pretty upfront about it." Although the care he took to keep her comfortable was also a turn on. "But what you said… Ted, I'm worried about what happens after."

It was a magnet that guided her mouth to his chest, pressing her lips to the skin that covered the solid beat of his heart. Her kiss sliding over the red bloom of an inked flower. Ted inhaled a shaky breath, but he didn't step away again. His hand came up to tangle in the hair at the nape of her neck.

"You've been honest from the start. Don't worry about me. I can handle after."

Could she?

Maybe it wasn't only his heart she was worried about, but her own.

They had less than a day left together and even now, Eden kept finding herself thinking beyond the weekend. Her constant need to remind him of their lack of future, was proof enough that it was constantly tumbling through her lust-soaked brain. Her self-preservation had to be stronger. She knew what happened in relationships. She'd already started putting Ted's preferences ahead of her own by putting on that damn dress, and if a little voice reminded her that he'd told her she didn't have to be anyone but herself, well now she had to decide if she trusted that he'd meant it. Or if it didn't matter that he'd told her to change, because the idea that she'd needed to was dangerous enough. That was more than she wanted to dissect tonight. Eden didn't have the brain capacity to worry about tomorrow when she was so keyed up she thought she might come the minute her dress hit the floor.

"Are we going to have the same problem as last time?" She asked and Ted frowned at her, trying to parse her subject change. Then his mouth dropped open into an O of understanding and his eyes widened. Eden raised an eyebrow and pursed her lips to hold in her smile.

"No." A flush tinged his cheeks. "I have protection."

"Good," Eden said and turned her back to Ted, pulling her hair over her shoulder. "Unzip me?"

She heard his shallow intake of breath a fraction of a second before the warm pads of his fingers brushed the skin of her spine. He lowered the zipper at a crawl, the front of her dress loosening around her breasts. Eden lifted her arms to hold it in place. Ted dropped his hands and leaned forward to place a soft kiss on the back of her neck.

Was his heart pounding as hard as hers was? Ted stepped back and Eden spun to face him, letting her dress drop to her hips and then fall to the floor in a rustle of blue. His tongue poked out of his mouth, touching the center of his top lip. Now he was overdressed. His pants were still buttoned and belted while she stood there in her silk underwear.

Eden was a firm believer in wearing beautiful underthings as a confidence booster, but even she had to admit that she'd picked this simple blue ruffled panty set with Ted in mind. His reaction was everything she could have hoped for, pupils swallowing the dark brown of his irises as he reached for her with a trembling hand. She stepped out of his reach and walked around his body toward the bed. She could feel his eyes on her ass as she moved, and it took considerable willpower not to turn around and watch his over her shoulder.

She reached the mattress and crawled on top of the down comforter. Eden moved toward the center of the bed before she flipped over to lean back on her elbows. Ted's chest heaved as he stared at her body, his eyes traveling from her feet, up her legs, and to the tips of her aching nipples. He met her eyes, and she lifted one hand to crook her finger at him. He moved faster than she could have imagined, pressing her down into the bed with his mouth fastened to her neck, and Eden reached between them to fumble open his belt buckle.

Her legs went up around his waist and she used her feet to help push his pants down muscular thighs. His boxer briefs went next. She lost track of where they went after they reached his mid-thigh. Ted dropped his hips down to hers and rubbed his thick erection against the ruined silk of her underwear. She was so wet that it was almost embarrassing. Nothing this man did was a turnoff.

Eden tossed her head back and moaned. Ted kissed her again. This kiss wasn't smooth or full of finesse. It was all teeth and tongues and panted breaths. A hand shoved down the front of her panties and cupped her between her legs, blunt fingers spreading her wide.

"Don't make me wait," Eden said, rocking up into his touch. "Please Bear."

"Foreplay." he kissed the word into the skin between her breasts. His body was sliding down hers and Eden knew exactly where he was headed. He pressed open-mouthed kisses to her belly, the top of her panties. Ted kneeled on the floor as he snagged the silk with his teeth.

"The foreplay has lasted all weekend." Eden said as he pulled the underwear down her thighs. Then he was back, breathing hot over her core as she squirmed on the coverlet. "I need you inside me."

"And I need to make you come." He licked into her then, groaning against the deepest part of her as his nose bumped her clit. And Eden decided she'd give him a few minutes.

That was all the time he needed. Her body shook as he speared her with his tongue, a thumb circling the tight bundle of nerves until her back bowed, arching her off the bed with a whine. Her hands gripped strands of his hair, his beard tickled the sensitive skin of her thighs. The tension was so intense that she almost wanted to wriggle right out of his grip. Almost.

"I'm going to come." She was about to take his head off with the tension in her thighs. Each one of her muscles was locking down as the pressure came to a head.

Ted looked up at her from his spot between her thighs. "So do it," he said and thrust two fingers inside her just in time for her to detonate. She opened her eyes as he pulled his fingers free, muscles loose, and a dopey smile spreading across her face.

"You're good at that." She said as he worked his way back up her body. His lips were shiny, and she tasted herself when he pressed them to hers.

"You say that like we're done," he said as he ripped open a foil packet with his teeth and rolled the condom down his length. The vague thought crossed Eden's mind that she wanted to do that for him, but she was too relaxed to care. She blinked sleepily up at Ted's gorgeous face, smiling as he lined his cock up at her entrance. "We're not done, Sweetness," he said and slid into her in one push.

Eden's eyes rolled back into her head and her back arched under his weight. She hadn't expected the pressure to build again so quickly. He stretched her to the limit and then some, but it wasn't the fit that was doing her in, it was the harsh curse words he panted into her skin. His hips rolled and hers rose to meet them. The smooth motion devolved into a stuttering, jerky rhythm, his words unintelligible, and Eden thought she might die as she sat right there on the edge of something powerful.

Ted took her mouth with his. Not even kissing, just devouring her lips as he licked his tongue along hers. Her muscles were tightening almost to the point of pain, her thighs ached, her arms shook, she clutched at his back... It was right there, she could taste the edge of glory. Eden had never been known for multiple orgasms, especially not back-to-back ones, but it looked like Ted was the holy grail of sexual partners. At least it had looked that way until he stopped moving and groaned into her neck.

Eden whimpered, shifting her own hips to get him moving again. He was still rock hard inside of her. She slid her hands down his back and dug her fingers into the firm globes of his ass. She tried to rock him back into rhythm and he resisted, instead pushing a hand down between their bodies to circle her clit.

"Hold on," Ted grunted against her neck. "Let me get you there first, Eden. I need a minute… let's get you there."

But he didn't get it. All that lovely tension was bleeding out of her, and she couldn't complain. Couldn't complain because he'd already pushed her over the edge once, and the sex until this point had been lovely. No, that sounded lame, and naked Ted was far from lame, but… but… she needed…

"Please." She rocked under him again.

Eden pulled on the ends of her hand and then fisted her hands in the sheets. His fingers felt good. Better than good, but without the friction, the movement, she wasn't going to get there. He'd been hitting a good spot on the inside and now… now he wasn't and this wasn't going to work, which was fine. It was all fine. He'd already gotten her off, but if this was over for her, then he could at least follow through for himself.

Ted pulled his hand away from her core and gripped her wrists, holding them down above her head. The thrill of that move almost made up for the lack of anything else.

"I'm about to lose my mind inside you, Eden. I've given you about two minutes of action and I need to redeem myself somehow, but clearly I picked the wrong way. Tell me what you need, baby. I'll give you anything that you need. If I get one chance to be inside you, then I'm going to do it right.

Dammit." His chest heaved over hers. "You need my hands? Anywhere. My mouth? It's yours."

She shifted her hips again, and he squeezed her wrists. Eyes blazing down at her.

"You need me to move." He rolled his hips, his breath sawing out of his lungs as Eden threw her head back. Yes. There. She needed that. Her muscles clenched and Ted spit a harsh curse out as his spine locked. "Is that it, Sweetness?" He moved again and Eden moaned "yes" as she writhed under him.

"You need the friction," Ted said and gave her a long, slow thrust.

She moaned as the head of his cock dragged over that spot. God. Slow was even more devastating. In the most delicious way possible.

"I've got you," he said and pushed his pubic bone against her clit.

Her abs contracted.

"I've got you." He rolled his hips again, and the tension built. "I've got you. I've got you. I've got you." He panted each word, punctuating them with thrusts of his cock until Eden was shaking under him, staring down at the monster of all orgasms.

"Fuck Eden." Ted slid his lips over hers. "Anything you need. I'm your guy. I'm the one, Eden. Anything."

She came screaming his name, and he followed her right over the edge.

"This is exactly what I imagined," Eden said as they walked to the foot of the white and red building. "If someone asked me to paint a picture, this is what I'd have come up with. That's crazy."

"Crazy?" Ted asked. "Is it what you actually imagined? Or have you just seen it before since it's the lighthouse on Cape Cod chips?"

"Is it?" She tilted her head as she took in the structure. The curved white base and the bright red top, the gray shingled building just behind it, and the cliffs overlooking the beach and the water. "Show me."

Ted frowned. "Yes, Eden. I have potato chips stashed in my pockets."

Her grin was blinding and his heart kicked hard in his chest.

"And some people think you have no sense of humor." She leaned forward, her dark ponytail brushing the underside of his jaw as she dipped her hand into the pocket of his shorts. Ted took a deep breath, willing his body not to react. Not in public and not ten feet from a family with roughly a million children under the age of seven. Her fingers wiggled and Ted gritted his teeth. "Where's your phone?"

Ted reached into his back pocket and pulled the device free, pressing it into her hands. "Where's yours?" Even as he asked, he was expecting her to shrug. He hadn't seen the woman pull out her old model phone more than once a day. She usually left it on the nightstand in the blue bedroom, not even charging, just thrown on the wood table, gathering dust. Eden shrugged and held the phone up to his face to unlock it.

"In your car. It's dead."

Even when she did pull out her phone, it rarely had a charge. Ted couldn't even fault her for that. He'd seen the number of notifications she had on her email, text messages, and social media. If that many little red bubbles showed up on his phone, he'd probably hurl the device off the nearest cliff and into the waves.

Eden tapped at the screen and then held his phone up to the lighthouse. She took a few steps back and waved her hand at him as though she wanted him in the shot. With her head tipped to the side and her ponytail swinging, she was probably the sweetest thing he'd ever seen. Her hair had been down the night before, and sliding his fingers into the strands had been like dipping into heaven, but today he wanted that tail wrapped around his fist.

"Look at that," Eden laughed. The sound was brighter than the summer sun as she tapped at his phone screen again, no doubt googling the chip bags. "You were right."

"I was what?" He couldn't have fought the smile if he wanted to. "Can you repeat that?"

"Oh, did your hearing fail you, Bear?" She slid his phone into his back pocket and smiled up from under her thick lashes. "Did you know that keeping your phone there is asking to have it pickpocketed?"

Ted looked around at the families and couples soaking in the view. "Where would you suggest I keep it?"

"The front, of course." Eden dipped her hand back into the pocket and wiggled her fingers. She looked up at him, green eyes smiling and playful. Then they widened and dropped to his zipper with alarming speed. "Oh," she said. "Are you worried about your..."

"My what?" He fought the urge to cup himself.

"Some preliminary studies show cell phone radiation can affect—" Eden darted a glance around at all the kids before she sent an exaggerated look to his crotch.

Ted slid a fist around her ponytail and dragged her head back. Her throat worked on a swallow as he bared it to the sun and Ted seriously considered working the delicate skin with his teeth. He dropped his mouth to the shell of her ear, tugging on her hair and eliciting a gasp from her parted lips. If he thought he could kiss her and still stay appropriate, then he'd have already dropped his mouth to hers.

"My dick," he crowded into her body and let her feel the swelling against her belly, "is in perfect working order and you know it." Three rounds of sex after a full night of revelry should have proven that.

Red streaked across Eden's cheeks. Ted needed to back off. This was just a normal day visiting a tourist destination with a friend. A friend he'd slept with, but still a friend. She'd been up front about her needs for the future. His decision to bring her out to the lighthouse was just to prove that they could spend time around each other. To prove that they could actually *be* friends, even without the benefits, because he wasn't ready to let her go yet. Not completely.

Her giggle drew his attention back to see Eden shaking her head. "Not the hardware." She shifted against him and Ted clenched his jaw until it ached. "The swimmers, Ted." He must have looked horrified because she pressed on. "It's only one study, so take that with a grain of whatever, but I assume you want to keep those puppies pristine for your future progeny." He definitely was horrified now. "Or we can stop talking about it altogether. I didn't really think through how uncomfortable this conversation might get."

It was only uncomfortable because she was considering his future orgasms. And since they probably—most likely—would not have sex again, then at some point that would happen with someone else. But the idea of being with another woman, or Eden with another partner... that was disconcerting. It grated against his skin like the itching of a sunburn. It wouldn't kill him, but it was decidedly not something he wanted to dwell on.

"I'm not having kids," he told her instead, trying to derail his runaway thoughts before any actual damage could be done.

"You're not?"

He shook his head. "I've spent too much of my life with negative family experiences. I'd be a horrible father. I have nothing to give to a kid."

It was Eden's turn to frown. With a shake of her head, she pushed up on her toes and smacked a kiss across the curve of his cheek. "You have a lot more to give than you realize, but I'm not going to try to talk you out of your choices. It's obnoxious when people try to do that. Like we haven't spent years knowing that parenthood isn't the right path for us."

"You don't want a dozen little artists of your own?"

"Nope." Eden shook her head. "I like being selfish. For a long time, my choices were made for me or influenced by everyone around me, but I'm done with that. I'm not interested in changing myself or doing things that don't directly benefit myself."

"Not selfish." Ted said because Eden was the opposite of selfish. He'd watched her put everyone else at ease all weekend. "It takes a lot of strength and courage to be yourself unapologetically."

Ted had never felt shame over his choices before. He'd been angry when his stepfather decided things for him. Furious when he felt like he was receiving special privileges. And okay, that was a lie. He had felt shame over the teenage rebellions and the legal troubles. He hadn't felt shame over trying to find his own way to fit into the life his mother and stepfather wanted for him. He'd gone to law school the way they wanted, but he'd pursued his own specialty.

Instead of relying on nepotism to get a job, he'd started his own firm with his best friends. When he'd wanted tattoos, he'd gotten them. In places that were covered by a dress shirt and sport coat, sure, but the ink and the art were still his. He still took his mother's calls and if he avoided his stepfather as much as possible, he hadn't formally cut the man off. Yet.

All of that had felt like a suitable compromise. A way to keep the peace. Not just for his mom and stepfather, but for himself, too. And yet it wasn't until meeting Eden. It wasn't until he saw exactly how she stayed true to herself, no matter what. That's when the shame set in, because he should do the same thing. Right? Martin was categorically a bully, and everyone knew bullies weren't supposed to win. But every single day that he buried pieces of himself to avoid angering his family, he let his stepfather win.

"I chose to look at every single person who didn't like me and give them the middle finger, but you can cut down a bully with more subtlety than I did." Eden took his hand and linked their fingers. "As long as you're happy, then they didn't win, Ted. You did."

How did she always know exactly what to say? She studied him with those grassy green eyes flecked with brown and she saw right to the innermost core of him. She stripped him down with one knowing look as effectively as she'd removed his clothes the night before. It was a heady feeling, to have someone know you that deeply. Especially for a man who'd always felt like he wasn't enough. Good enough, strong enough, successful enough.

It didn't escape Ted's attention that Eden had been raised in a very similar environment and her reaction had been the polar opposite of his. While Ted hadn't felt like he could waste the second chance that he'd never asked for, Eden had waved goodbye to all the things her stepdad tried to give to her in favor of being true to herself. Even then, she didn't have an expunged juvenile record to show for her rebellion. She had a catalog of illustrated children's books to her name, a handful of private music students, and the knowledge that she was the sole party responsible for her creativity and drive.

"Do we get to go inside?" Eden asked, walking backward toward the lighthouse, pulling him along with her.

She wore the same minuscule shorts from the start of their road trip, and Ted was having a hard time keeping his eyes off the smooth length of her thighs. He had tried to keep his gaze firmly planted on the rainbow dyed shirt that was short enough to show skin above the waistband of the denim, but loose enough to offer the illusion of coverage.

At least until she turned around and the whole shirt looked like it had twisted in on itself, until the skin of her back gleamed in the June heat. If Eden had any sort of support for her breasts, it was a string bikini at most. One he could untie just by looking at the knots the right way. It couldn't be more than that because he'd have undoubtedly seen the strap of a bra.

This wasn't the time to tell her he'd go anywhere with her. With this woman, there would never be a time to do that. This was the time to nod and follow her into the sandy-colored cement block interior, up the curving red staircase winding its way to the top. Inside, the building was stifling hot, each breath a solid weight in Ted's lungs. It was probably why most visitors were outside enjoying the ocean breeze. Not about to hike up forty some-odd metal stairs.

"We going to the top?" Ted asked. He already knew Eden's answer, but maybe she'd want to walk back out into the sunshine. Where he could put a few feet between them and not feel overwhelmed by her presence. Where he could breathe without tasting the sunshine and vanilla of her scent.

"Isn't that why people visit lighthouses?"

"I'm sure the view factors in, yes."

Ted couldn't speak for other people, but he'd brought Eden here because it was something to do while they waited for the bulk of the weekend traffic to die down. Who didn't think of Cape Cod and lighthouses? The potato chip bag was proof enough. And yes, they could have driven a few minutes down the road to the Chatham lighthouse, but it was on a National Guard base and didn't have the same old-fashioned feel. He'd thought Eden would like the history.

"We aren't going to comment on how red my face is about to get, or how hard I'm going to be breathing by the time we make it to the top."

"It's only forty-four stairs, Sweetness."

"Cardio, Bear." Eden smiled at him. "I do yoga. It's strength training. Totally different."

"When your legs give out, I'll carry you."

"You think you're making a joke." Eden pushed a finger into his chest and he curled his hand around hers, holding it to the heat of his body. "But you grossly overestimate my stamina. Lucky for you, I'm not the damsel-in-distress type." Ted raised a single brow and Eden tossed her hair over her shoulder. "There is a difference between you offering and me asking. The fact that I benefitted from your help that first day doesn't change the fact that I didn't ask for it."

Eden turned and started up the steps, her sandals clacking on the metal treads. Ted following right behind her. She stopped halfway up the staircase, peering through a small arched window. Ted's footfalls echoed on the steps as he moved. Eden didn't turn away from the view, but she did motion toward the small opening, inviting him to look out at the ocean in the distance.

The stairs were narrow, and he had to squeeze in behind her until her back nestled against his chest. It was instinct to wrap an arm low on her waist and rest his chin on her shoulder. Beyond the window, he could see the green tops of trees and past that was the glittering shine of the ocean. Eden leaned back into his touch, the back of her head resting on his chest. She smelled delicious. The heat diffused her scent over his entire body.

"I've always loved lighthouses." Her voice flowed over him like honey. Ted was on sensory overload. Eden overload.

"I loved the idea of living here alone. My only job to tend the lamps and warn the ships away from impending doom." She rolled her head, turning toward him so that her breath wafted over the tender skin of his neck. "How did you know I'd love to come here?"

Could she hear his heart pounding in his chest? Could she feel the tremble in his muscles?

"Don't punk out on me now, Sweetness," Ted said, because he needed to let go of her. He needed that more than he needed his next breath. "Only twenty steps to go."

Eden turned in the cradle of his arm and gave him a playful push. Not enough to off-balance him, but enough to make him smile. She started up the second half of the steps, up toward the roof deck and the famous light.

"I'm not punking out," she threw over her shoulder. "I want to see the famous light."

"Jokes on you," Ted said. "They swapped out the original Fresnal lens for aerobeacons in '81."

"Look at you, Mr. Ivy League Education," Eden grinned. "What else do you know?"

"All this information is on the sign out front," Ted said as she cleared the top of the stairs and stepped out onto the observation deck. The large black lights spinning in the center.

"You're ruining the fairytale. Here I thought you were a learned scholar."

"This lighthouse was originally the second tower over in Chatham. They moved it here around 1920 and dismantled the Three Sisters, the trio of buildings just down the road."

"There we go, Bear. You're sexy when you're having fun."

He was having fun. She was fun.

Ted lied. There was a second reason he'd brought her out here today. It wasn't just to avoid the afternoon traffic. Bringing her here had been a last ditch effort. Not a date. A last chance to see if they could be friends beyond the wedding. He wasn't ready to lose her yet, but sex changed things. Especially amazing sex and the kind of chemistry that meant his body was pulled to hers like the tide.

It was a chance to show them both that spending time together was possible. Spending time together was enjoyable. Spending time together was worth it. Even when it was platonic. Or, more accurately, when he lied to himself and said that their time together was platonic.

"Did you ever think that maybe the lighthouse worker's job wasn't just warning ships away and screaming out potential dangers? But that the actual task, the real role, was bringing the ships and the sailors safely home?"

Eden turned to look at him. "That was a very squishy, marshmallow sweet thing to say." Her tone made it clear it had also been unexpected. "Which part of you is the hopeless romantic? The suits? Or the tattoos?"

"Can't it be both?" He asked. "Not everything is exactly what it seems."

"I think it would be worse." Her voice dropped to a whisper, "to bring all those people home to their parents and lovers and babies and then still end up alone in the tower. Better to send them on their way. It's easier to be alone when you choose it."

Her cheeks flooded with color and she dropped her chin until she was staring down at her shoes. Her hands twisted in the hem of her shirt and Ted wanted to haul her close and bend her back over his forearm as he feasted on her mouth. He wanted to lose himself in her, swallow down her nerves and self-doubt and reward her vulnerability with love and warmth and pleasure.

"The last lighthouse keeper, Eugene Coleman, lived here with his wife." Ted said. "They weren't alone. They bought groceries in town, they had friends. They weren't alone."

Eden looked up at him, eyes shining with unshed tears, and Ted felt his heart stutter and turn over in his chest. The problem *now* wasn't that Ted was dangerously close to falling in love with an unavailable woman. He'd already gone and done it. And she had no intention of falling down with him.

"Are you sure you don't want a ride?" Ted's hands curled and uncurled as he stood on the sidewalk. He'd parked his car in a miraculously open spot in front of the HMP building, and opened her door. Ted helped her out of the passenger seat, but didn't move to get her bag. Not something he *had* to do, except that he'd loaded and unloaded her bag from the minute they met on this very sidewalk.

The drive back into Boston had been quicker than the drive out, and Eden had been tempted to take Ted up on his offer to drive her all the way to her front door. But ending their time together at his office would also bring her full-circle. She'd met him at the office, he presented her with a contract for the terms of their weekend, she fulfilled her end of the deal, and then they would part ways at his office too. A date would drop her off at her door, at least a good one would, but Ted wasn't her date.

"Are you hungry?" He asked like it wasn't almost eight o'clock at night. Like he hadn't taken her to a tiny seafood place off the beach before they got into the car. Like he hadn't then handed over her favorite chocolate in the car because he remembered her mentioning how much she loved peanut butter and chocolate.

Eden shook her head and Ted dropped his head and rubbed one large palm over the back of his neck. She swore she could hear the scrape of his skin over the short strands of hair at his nape. She shivered.

"You're cold," Ted said, like it wasn't a balmy seventy-five and she wasn't wearing a sweater over her tie-dyed shirt.

"I'm fine."

Ted took a tiny step toward her, then seemed to catch himself before taking a larger step back.

"I know we agreed about what comes next," Ted said, and Eden braced herself for the inevitable moment when she'd have to actually reject this man standing in front of her. The purpose of talking about their lack of a future *before* any declarations or requests was to avoid actually rejecting someone she genuinely liked. She didn't want to hurt Ted. She couldn't date him because she didn't want to hurt him. Or herself.

If there was one person who might tempt her into a relationship, it was him, but what came next when she wanted out? When she lost herself being part of a couple? When he wanted to take the next steps and she wanted to backpedal back to single life? Not only would she have hurt him, but he'd have wasted who knows how long waiting for something she wasn't ever going to give.

Eden had yet to find a single relationship that didn't involve either giving pieces of herself until there was nothing left or changing herself until she was unrecognizable. Flings she could handle, temporary interludes of fun and pleasure. She often ended up friendly with her partners for years. Friendships, committed relationships, were equally difficult to maintain.

Eden had a sizable group of surface friends. Ones who she could smile and laugh with, stretch with, create with. But her inner circle of confidants? The people she trusted above all else and with all else? That circle included Romy and her mother. When she'd briefly tried to widen the circle to include Justin, she'd ended up apprehended by the authorities. If that wasn't some sort of sign from the universe, then Eden didn't know what was.

"I like you Eden," Ted said. The way he formed the words had her swinging her head up to look him directly in the eyes. "Yeah," he said when their gazes locked. "I like *you*. I'm not going to ask you for anything you don't want to give, and I'm not going to sit on the sidelines and try to change your mind. You were clear and I respect that. But if there ever comes a time when you change your mind and think maybe you'd like to give me a shot—give *us* a real shot—then you have my number."

"I wouldn't mind being your friend, Bear, but you have to know I will not call you." He opened his mouth to protest, and she pushed on before he could speak. "You said you won't hang around hoping, but waiting for a phone call *is* hanging around. That's not fair to either of us. Not when I know you want it all."

And the fact that she might have considered *all* with Ted was completely irrelevant, especially when she knew she wasn't going to do anything about it.

Ted shoved his hands into the pockets of his shorts and dropped his chin to his chest. He rocked on the balls of his feet.

"I understand." he stepped back and opened the back door of his car to pull out her weekend bag. The strap looked dainty and small in his hands as he squeezed his fingers around the cloth. "You sure I can't drive you home?"

"I'm sure. Clean break and all that." Eden took her bag, looping it over her shoulder. She pushed up onto her toes and pressed a kiss to the scratch of his cheek. As she settled back onto her heels, Eden realized she probably shouldn't have done that. She was giving a submarine sized heap of mixed signals. "Sorry."

"Don't." Ted rubbed the back of his neck again. "You don't have to apologize for being you. Not to me, Eden."

Ted's fingers flexed and his hand raised an inch, like maybe he wanted to reach for her, before he dropped it back to his side. He got in his car and started the engine, but he didn't pull away from the curb. Eden smiled and waved at him through the car window, and he waved back, but continued to stay right where he was. Taking the T seemed like a monumental effort this late, not to mention the quarter mile she'd still have to walk to get to and from the stations.

Eden pulled out her phone and keyed in a request for a ride, grateful Ted had plugged the device in to charge after she admitted she'd drained the battery. She frowned at his car, still idling at the curb. What was he waiting for? Eden tapped out a message and watched as Ted picked up his phone from inside his car.

What are you doing?

Waiting for you.

Go home stalker ♥

You first

Not wanting to explain why she hadn't needed a ride from *him*, but was perfectly willing to hire an Uber—that was a vulnerability that showed maybe a little too much—Eden waved through the car at Ted one more time and then stalked her way down the sidewalk. She'd get just out of sight and then, once he'd left, she'd go back. Her phone buzzed again.

Hey Sweetness, the T is the other way

It took five full minutes of peering around the old stone building for Ted to put his car in drive and pull away. Eden hurried back to the HMP entrance just in time for a tiny red sedan to pull up. The driver was a probably mid-forties and sported a nose ring and a Patriots sweatshirt. Eden slid into the small but clean backseat and waited for her driver to merge back into traffic.

No matter the time of day, driving in the city made her dizzy. Lanes started and stopped without warning, there were a million tunnels where GPS signal was spotty at best, and drivers liked to see how fast they could go from zero to sixty even with only a single car length between them and the vehicle in front of them. Eden's driver, Susan, was clearly more comfortable than Eden could ever hope to be. That's probably why Eden wasn't super concerned with getting her car back from the BPD.

"Hey, you okay?" The driver asked, flinging them around a curve like the slingshot rides at the Big E.

Honestly, Eden would probably feel better if the car slowed down a little. Or a lot. And while she appreciated Susan's concern, she could also do with her driver keeping their eyes and their concentration on the road. She wasn't nauseated—Eden rarely got carsick—but she had a weird, heavy feeling sinking into her gut. She pressed her fist into her stomach, trying to ease the discomfort. It felt like something tugging on her insides, pulling them back out of the car and towards the ocean.

"I'm fine," she told the driver. Susan nodded and flipped on her blinker to make another turn. "Have you ever met someone who made you question everything about yourself? Not because they're judgmental or rude, but because they make you wonder if you've made the right decisions? I don't like relationships. I like being on my own. I can call my own Ubers and make my own dinner. I like being able to walk through my apartment naked or fly to Idaho on a whim."

"Idaho?" Susan asked.

"Just picked somewhere random. I like not having to worry about anyone else. You know?" Susan turned the car onto Eden's street and the leaden feeling intensified. "Just because he's hot and kind and likes me for me does not mean that I should date him. Right? It doesn't mean that I'm making a stupid decision because the possibility of being with him and destroying all the good parts of us is worse than never having it. Right?"

Susan pulled the car to the side of the road and let the engine run. "Listen, kid—"

"I can't let myself worry about the what ifs, right? I just have to make the decision that's best for me and that's okay. It's not selfish. I was honest. He understood that. No use bringing it up over and over and over. It's just been a long weekend with insanely good food. That's the reason I feel like I might throw up or pass out or both."

"Hey," Susan said, and Eden barely heard her.

"Ted might be unique and supportive and good, but chances are that he'd end up like all the others. And even if I wanted to give this relationship thing a shot, I'm *not* ready to be a wife, so I'd ruin that for us anyway—"

"Kid!" That time there was an actual sense of urgency and Eden stopped staring down into her lap and met her driver's eyes in the rear-view mirror.

"What?"

"Are you going to be okay getting out here?"

"Oh, I'm fine," Eden said. "I promise I'm not having a mental breakdown in your car. Or at least not one that will get you stuck with me."

"I meant, are you going to be okay with the circus?"

Eden looked out the window at the four cop cars parked in front of her building. Red and blue lights flashing like fireworks, blinding her as they flickered in separate rhythms. What was going on? The strobe effect was giving her a headache to match the pitching of her stomach.

"I can take you somewhere else. Off the record." Susan turned to look at her this time. "I'm all for avoiding the cops."

Eden had to admit that her initial reaction was to bail. Her last run in with the Boston PD had set her on edge. But she hadn't done anything wrong. Not when she was dating Justin-the-drug-dealer—and wasn't that still bizarre to think about—or after her last conversation with the officers. Even if they had found a reason that they thought warranted talking to her again, Romy had been left with detailed contact information, and she lived right across the hall. Hell, the officers had her contact information. She'd given it to them on her driver's license before they asked her to come to the station.

It was more likely that something had happened, either to one of the neighbors or to the gas main, or something along those lines. Either let her into her space or she could grab a few essentials before being back out on the sidewalk.

"I'll be fine," Eden wasn't entirely sure she believed her own words, but what else was she supposed to do? She then tipped Susan an easy one hundred percent and stepped out of the car.

When no one swarmed her, Eden's chest loosened. She walked up the front steps and let herself into the building. There was a single officer just inside the main door. He stopped her as she walked by and asked her for some identification, which of course meant Eden's wallet was buried at the bottom of her crochet bag and then that her license itself was stuck inside the plastic sleeve. She prided herself on her cool, calm, confidence, but it had to be human nature that tripped her nerves as she talked to the cops. Even for something this innocuous.

She could take some deep breaths, try to calm down. They had to make sure that whoever came and went was an actual building resident. That's all. Just while they dealt with whatever had happened.

Except when she was allowed past the man, her front door was wide open. And uniformed officers stood on either side of the doorjamb with more milling around inside her apartment. Everyone stopped to look at her, and Eden had a sinking feeling in her gut that she'd been a dumb baby all over again. The feeling grew even stronger when she recognized Keith. He wasn't in uniform, but in dark slacks and an ill-fitting button-down shirt. He smiled when he saw her at the door and her stomach heaved.

"Miss Yates," he called across the small living room. "We were just wondering if you were going to show up."

"I live here," she said.

Ted had told her not to speak to the cops without a lawyer, but that statement was so bland and easily checked that she was pretty sure it was okay. Should she ask them what they wanted with her? Had they found Justin? If he'd lied to them about her, she was going to beat him to death with her Casio keyboard. Maybe stab him with the handle of a paintbrush. One of the travel ones. She wasn't wasting one of her Winsor & Newton brushes on him. Those were thirty bucks a piece.

"What are you doing here?" She figured that was a safe enough question.

"Oh Miss Yates," Keith's smile grew even wider. Why was he smiling? "Did you think the Boston PD wouldn't investigate a crime just because it happened in your home?"

Crime? What crime? Had Justin been selling drugs out her front door? She was seriously going to murder him.

"We can do this the easy way or the hard way." He stepped toward her with a glint of something silver in his fists. Cuffs. He was holding handcuffs.

"What?" The word barely made a sound as she choked it out.

"You need to come down to the precinct and answer some questions."

"About what?" She asked, feeling the nervous itch to back toward her door. That would probably be a terrible idea. Running away from the cops could never end well.

"We have questions about Mr. Fredecker," Keith said, and too late Eden noticed the white sheet laid across her hardwood floor. She'd taken enough anatomy art classes, painted enough people to recognize the shape underneath.

"Oh god." Eden pressed a hand to her mouth and willed back the acid that crawled up her throat.

Think Eden, think. This wasn't like the last time they'd chatted. There was a dead body in her living room. When was the last time she'd heard from Romy? Her best friend lived next door, but she'd been away for the weekend, staying with two of their mutual friends. Given the questions the body was probably Justin's. She hadn't been serious when she said she'd want to kill him. That had been a typical human reaction to being dragged through the criminal system. Right? Didn't most people say and think stupid shit like that? Except he was actually dead. Probably. Someone was. There was no blinking this one away.

"Is that—" the words stuck in her throat, acid burning its way into her mouth. She was not going to throw up now. She wasn't.

"Why don't you tell us?" Keith asked, hands on his hips. "We found a man dead on your floor, one who doesn't live here, beaten and bruised to hell and back. I think we're going to be asking the questions from here on out."

Could she refuse to go to the precinct? Was that an option? Was she under arrest? Could they do that? Didn't they need to think she'd committed a crime? They couldn't actually think she'd *done* something, right?

Eden took a shaky breath and laced her hands together. She squeezed her fingers until they ached and her wrists began to tremble. She hadn't even been in her apartment in the last three and a half days. That should be easy to prove, right? Was she supposed to tell them where she'd been? Now? Ted would know. Would they let her call him?

"Miss Yates," Keith had stepped closer. He'd tucked the cuffs out of sight, and Eden fought the urge to step back out of his reach. "This is a time sensitive situation."

Lawyer-up. That's what Ted said. Ask for a lawyer and if you don't need one then you aren't under arrest. Never talk to them without representation.

"I think I'd like to call my lawyer," she said.

Keith smiled again. "Of course."

Ted's phone rang as he wiped drops of sweat from his forehead. He'd been hopped up on weird energy after watching Eden try to fake him out before getting into a small red car and drive away from his building. He'd had an almost overwhelming urge to follow the car to her house— it would have been merely for safety reasons—but decided it would probably give her the wrong impression.

Yes, he'd driven her home before and technically had her address, but she should be able to trust that he wouldn't use that information without her explicit consent.

So he'd driven home to West Roxbury, parked his car in his one-car garage, and walked up through his unfinished basement to his tiny slice of private heaven. Was Ted's home the grand showpiece that he'd grown up in? Not even close.

At barely a thousand square feet sometimes it felt more like an apartment without neighbors, but he had a private backyard complete with picket fence, an extra bedroom for his treadmill and home office, original kitchen with red-oak cabinets, and beautiful textured ceilings he kept meaning to remove someday.

The icing on the cake? It had horrified his stepfather when he'd closed on the property. Martin had offered additional funds for a "decent" home, but Ted loved his house. It was exactly what he needed. The commute wasn't awful, and he hadn't borrowed a cent for the down payment.

He left his overnight bag by the washing machine, changed into running shorts, and hopped on his treadmill for a workout. He cranked his speed and pushed himself as hard and fast as he could. It had nothing to do with the fact that he was avoiding going to bed. As much as he probably needed a solid eight hours after the weekend—hell, the week—he'd had, Ted was stuck on the idea that if he stayed awake, then technically the weekend wasn't over.

He was in his own house, with his dark green bedroom and king-sized bed instead of baby blue walls and an overstuffed queen. His windows looked directly into the neighbor's house, instead of out over the ocean waves. But everyone knew a trip didn't end until after bedtime.

It also had nothing to do with the heaviness weighing down his body. Like the feeling that accompanied too much thanksgiving turkey, where every limb felt swollen and tired. He felt like he was moving through thick soup. That was the product of too much relaxation. Too much alcohol and orgasms and not enough of his everyday life. Each thud of his feet against the machine's belt both brought him back to his normal routine.

Ted was breathing hard, his lungs aching on each inhale, by the time he stopped the treadmill and stepped off. He glanced down at the screen of his phone, expecting an update on work, or the happy couple, or hell, maybe even his mother. He normally called her on Sunday evening, but she'd known not to expect a call this weekend because of the wedding. Eden's name flashed across his screen and for a moment Ted forgot to breathe. His pulse pounded in his chest, a faint ringing in his ears as he watched her name scroll across the black background.

Had something happened?

Was she okay?

Ted took a deep breath as the phone rang again. The most likely scenario was that everything was fine. She'd simply forgotten something at the Cape house and was checking to see if Ted had scooped it up by mistake. Or she cared enough to see if he got home okay. He would not be the idiot who got his hopes up, not after the conversation they'd just had. This was exactly what he'd promised her he wouldn't do.

A tiny piece of his brain told him to let the call go to voicemail, but Ted couldn't do that. He sent very few people to voicemail, and doing that to her, because of his own haywire emotions, was the definition of unfair.

Ted swiped to accept the call, brought the phone to his ear, and his relative calm shattered almost immediately.

"Ted?" There was a waver to her words, like she was fighting hard to keep them steady and even. Like someone was standing next to her, threatening her.

His heart kicked painfully in his chest and that seemed to unstick his feet long enough to have him striding to his bedroom and throwing open his closet door. He needed a shirt, never mind the sweat and odor, and then he'd be in his car and on his way to wherever she was. He should never have left her alone, he should have pushed harder, because now something was obviously wrong and he wasn't there to fucking fix it.

"Yeah Sweetness, I'm here." Ted yanked open the top drawer of his dresser and fumbled over the neatly folded piles of shirts. He grabbed the top one and two more fell out of the heap and tumbled to the ground. At least he sounded calm, even though his hands were shaking.

"What do you need?" He'd break the land-speed record getting to her.

"I—" her voice broke, and she cleared her throat before soldiering on. "I think I need a lawyer."

"Okay," Ted said, trying to sound calm and collected. They'd been apart for less than an hour. What the fuck could have happened in less than an hour? "I'm going to take care of this. I'm going to take care of you." He pressed the speaker button and yanked his shirt over his head, unwilling to risk missing even a moment of her needing him. "Where are you?"

"I'm at my apartment," A shuddering breath, "but they want me to go down to the station. I'm pretty sure I can't stay here."

"If you aren't under arrest, they can't make you go anywhere." Ted told her. He looked around for his shoes but couldn't see them. He needed shoes. He couldn't drive without shoes.

"No," was it possible to hear someone frowning through a phone? Because Eden was definitely frowning. "I don't mean I'm under arrest, but my apartment's a crime scene and—"

"Are you admitting there *was* a crime committed here?" Ted didn't recognize the voice, but he did recognize the attitude. The same condescension he faced from the firm's wealthier clients.

Not all of their clients with money were devious, loophole-demanding assholes out to take advantage of their clients or workers, but in Ted's experience the companies that did all of that tended to have healthy bank balances. The stranger's voice held the same self-assurance he'd heard time and time again when the biggest of dickwads thought they'd done something clever. Something that was usually less than legal and definitely immoral. It was the same attitude the two cops at the precinct had thrown about the day he met Eden. So sure they had something on her or that she was about to give them something of value.

"Don't say anything else." Because Eden could ask for a lawyer before answering questions. She could call him for legal counsel, but until they arrested and mirandized her, then anything she said in front of the cops could be used in whatever case they thought they were building.

"I don't think a trip to the station is going to be optional anymore." Her voice shook.

"That's okay," Ted said, even though it wasn't. There was absolutely no need to scare her any more than she already was. "Go with them and tell them your lawyer will meet you there. Do not say anything else to them. It's probably nothing, you were with me all weekend and we should be able to clear everything up fast, but Justin put you on their radar before and they're probably going to make it difficult. Don't say anything to them until your lawyer okays it."

"Okay." He imagined her squaring her shoulders, and he heard the deep breath she pulled into her lungs. "I can do that."

God, she was brave. And she'd reached out to him. He would not let her regret it.

"Thank you Ted. I—" Ted didn't breathe during that pause. "Thank you."

"You don't need to thank me. I'm glad you called." The thought of her handling anything like this alone made him want to throw things. Large things. Large breakable things.

"Right." Eden laughed, but the sound was strained. "At least I learned something from last time. You said to call a lawyer. You're a lawyer."

Of course she was calling because he was the lawyer she knew. Or the first one whose number she had handy. It wasn't because… It had nothing to do with… Nope. He was probably wrong, but he was going to clarify this right the fuck now.

"You did good, Sweetness." He was gripping his phone so tight that the case was protesting. "But you didn't call just because I'm a lawyer, and not because you learned something from the time I yelled at you about legal representation. I'm sorry I did that, by the way. I'm glad you called because you need help. And I want to be the one you turn to. I'm the best man for the job, not because of my law degree and my credentials, but because I am deeply invested in your well-being Eden. I care about your future and your happiness. If there is even a chance I can make something better for you, I am going to do it. I want you to call me. Every fucking time."

There was silence on the other end of the phone, and then she had to go. Eden promised to text him the address of the precinct she was headed to, and Ted was eternally grateful that he'd had the foresight to charge her phone. He didn't want to think about what she'd have done with a dead battery. Then the call went dead, and Ted was alone in his bedroom.

His t-shirt on inside out and backward—now that he wasn't one hundred percent focused on Eden he could feel the tag tickling the sensitive skin of his neck—and he was freezing as the sweat on his skin cooled in the AC. Ted pulled his shirt back over his head and flipped it the right way around. He took the extra moment to grab a pair of clean sweatpants, mostly because the shorts were going to smell. Not that it mattered since he was forgoing a shower and all of him was going to smell, anyway, but those few extra minutes felt important. His shoes were exactly where he'd left them, as were his car keys. Ted opened the garage, started his car, and slammed his hands against the steering wheel.

He wasn't a criminal attorney. He didn't have the skills or the experience to be exactly what Eden needed right now. Something had happened in her apartment, most likely while they were gone, but the treatment she was receiving was tied to the last time the police had questioned her. Either they still thought she was guilty or they had something on her now. He could barge down to the station and give her an alibi for the weekend and they might let her walk out the door with him, but if they needed more than her weekend whereabouts then Ted vouching for her wasn't going to cut it.

The first time they had brought her in for questioning, he'd told her to call him because he had contacts in the criminal defense world. Now panic was pushing him to call the one person he went out of his way to avoid asking for favors. This could be nothing more than a misunderstanding, or power-bloated officers flexing their muscles over a terrified woman, but if it was wrong…

The case against Eden's ex had been big. She could be in real trouble. He needed someone who would destroy the opposition. Someone who would fight tooth and nail for the woman who meant everything to Ted. There was absolutely no use denying it. The words had been right there in his throat, ready to burst their way out into the world. Three little words that he had no business saying. Not to the woman who asked him to let her go. So he did the only thing he could do and keyed in the one number he swore he'd never again use for legal help.

"Martin James."

"Hello Sir."

"Theodore, are you aware of the hour?"

"Yes, Sir." Ted barely stopped the sorry from slipping through.

"I can only assume you have a reason for disrupting your mother and me this late at night. I must also assume that this is a matter you deem of highest importance."

"Yes Sir," Ted said again. His knuckles were white, bone pushing against thick skin as he squeezed the leather steering wheel as tightly as he could. Anything to stop him from saying what he really wanted. Anything to stop him from burning a bridge right before he took a flying leap off a cliff.

"Well, out with it, boy."

It didn't matter that Ted stood five inches taller than his stepfather's five foot eight. It didn't matter that they held bachelor and legal degrees from the same alma mater. It didn't matter that Ted was successful in his own right, that he owned a home and a nice car, plus a bike he loved. It didn't matter that he was a founding partner of a legal firm that was fast making a name for itself in the community. He was always going to be "boy."

Not even Martin's boy, just "boy." He would never live up to his stepfather's ideals. He would never be enough. For a long time, he'd done what he needed to do to keep the peace. And as soon as he got Martin out of his cushy armchair and into Boston to meet with Eden, he was going to be making some big changes. Keeping the peace hadn't kept him happy, but the shell he'd adopted to survive the war had been slowly suffocating him.

"I need you to meet me at the police station on Sudbury."

There was a wheezy laugh on the other end of the phone.

"No, Theodore. I won't be doing that tonight. If you've made a mistake, you're old enough to fix it on your own."

Fuck him.

Fuck Martin James and his fucking superiority complex.

Fuck him and his impossibly high standards.

Fuck him and his icy disdain for everyone and everything, including the members of a family that he fucking chose to join.

Fuck.

Him.

Ted took a deep breath and counted backward from ten.

"It's not for me, Sir."

"So one of your delinquent friends, then?" A long-suffering sigh, "Do you have any idea what my going rate is? The people I defend? And you want me to offer my services pro bono?"

Ted wanted to scream. Yes, his stepfather defended the uber wealthy and—usually—probably guilty. That was why he needed Martin for this. Because although Eden was staring down the police gauntlet, although she needed an attorney, there was not a doubt in Ted's head that Eden hadn't broken a single law. He doubted she'd ever even toed the line.

Ted had seen the look on her face as they sat in the pounding surf under the light of the moon, but he'd known before that. He'd known the minute he'd seen her sitting on the ugliest couch imaginable, agreeing to walk to the guillotine because she didn't see the blade.

"I'm prepared to cover the cost of your fee."

"Don't be ridiculous," Martin sighed. "Imagine the scandal if I took payment for a family member or a close family friend." The sound of paper shuffling drifted through the phone. "I can fit her in on Tuesday. Have her call my office."

"No," Ted said and Martin said, "I beg your pardon?"

"She can't wait until Tuesday. She needs you now. At the A-1 precinct."

"What are the charges?"

Ted didn't know. He hadn't wanted Eden to say anything on the phone that would cause problems, but he did know what they'd been questioning her about the first time they met.

"She hasn't been arrested," that he knew of. "She's being questioned about her connection with a known drug dealer."

Martin clicked his tongue the way Ted remembered. The same noise his stepfather made every single time that Ted managed to purposefully—or accidentally—break the family rules. "Clearly you haven't upgraded the company you keep. Barring William, of course, your taste in friends is less than ideal. Alright, I suppose I can come down and help your questionable little girlfriend. We can add it to your tab. I can be there in forty minutes. Tell her to keep her goddamn mouth shut until I get there."

"Eleanor loves her," Ted said, knowing even as he shared the information that Eden would have told him it didn't matter. She wouldn't have cared what Martin thought of her. She wouldn't have asked him to do anything more than believe in her himself, but he couldn't stand listening to Martin degrade her without having met her. "Her name is Eden Yates. She is kind and smart. Eleanor loves her. Will and AJ love her. She sang at their wedding. She paints. She teaches music to small children. She is scared and alone and she's trusting me to do the best for her."

Ted sat up in his seat and rolled his shoulders. He unfurled his fingers from the steering wheel and clicked his seatbelt into place.

"You can put anything you want on my goddamn tab, Martin, because you're a fucking bastard, but you're also the best. I promised her I'd do everything I could. I promised I'd get her the best, and that's you, so yes, I'll owe you. I'll see you at the station in forty minutes and you are going to be a fucking bastard *for* her. Not to her. Got it?"

He pulled his car out of the driveway and backed onto the street.

"You said she sang at the Masters' kid's wedding?" Martin said, conveniently ignoring Ted's words.

"Yeah," Ted said, "We went together."

"Good, get me any proof you have of her whereabouts for the last few days you spent together and anything else you can find since you first learned of her legal troubles."

"Thank you," Ted said and then he hung up the phone so he could call his best friend and get the name of his wedding photographer.

Theoretically, Eden hadn't expected Ted to be the lawyer who showed up at the police station. He'd told her as much the first time this had happened—how embarrassing that there had been a "first time"—but after the phone call that somehow talked her off the edge of panic, some part of her still expected to see him slamming open the heavy wood door and striding toward the small table where she once again sat with Keith and another officer.

Eden would go on record saying that she'd rather see Ted's glowering face than a check made out to her for a million dollars. And yes, she wasn't someone who cared about wealth as a measure of success, but a million dollars was a million dollars.

The man who came in Ted's stead was handsome—if you liked them older—polished, and colder than a deep freezer. He breezed into the interrogation room with the disgusted disdain she'd expect from a chef walking into a rat-infested kitchen. He didn't say anything to her, didn't introduce himself or shake her hand. She'd have thought he was with the DA's office, except the looks he'd sent towards Keith and the other cop in the room were definitely worse than the one he'd sent her way. Legal trouble or not, she would not want to switch places with them. No, thank you.

And despite the down-turned mouth and the icy stare, Eden was still happy to see him, because anything was better than sitting in frosty silence with two men who clearly thought she was a drug dealer and possibly a murderer. Her stomach heaved.

"Martin James," Keith said, leaning back in his chair with a sick grin. "Called in the big guns, huh?"
Keith narrowed his eyes and just like that, Eden wished she was back in the stagnant silence, because Ted hadn't just sent her a defense attorney. He'd sent her his stepfather. And Eden didn't know whether to be grateful for the legal shark in the water beside her, or to be heartbroken that he'd felt he needed to contact someone he clearly despised for help. From all accounts, Martin James would not have come quietly, and steady, loyal, honorable Ted had probably had to endure pointed comments meant to rattle his self-esteem just to get his stepfather to agree. All for her sake.

"I wouldn't need to be here if you two weren't trying to intimidate my client. Is she being charged?" Her attorney said, with a look that could have flash-frozen even oil paint.

"Intimidate? We just wanted to have a friendly chat." Keith folded his arms across his chest. "A dead man was found in Ms. Yates's apartment. He was left beaten and naked on Miss Yates' floor. Seeing as how we were under the impression that she lived alone, we'd like her to shed some light on the situation. Standard practice." The look on Keith's face said that was a lie.

Martin took the offered chair next to Eden and still didn't introduce himself. How ridiculous was it to focus on his manners instead of the fact that someone had possibly killed her ex in her apartment. Or the police definitely thought she'd done something to her ex. Martin might be a dick, and under normal circumstances Eden had no desire to spend even a moment in Ted's stepfather's presence, but in this instance she'd take him. She felt a little disloyal thinking that, but Ted wouldn't blame her. He was the one who'd sent him.

"I don't have any light to shed," she said, and Martin shushed her. Like a child.

"I think we'll be the judge of that, don't you, Eden?"

She wanted to tell Keith not to use her first name, but she'd told him the opposite last time they'd met. He'd seemed nice then. His questions came with a smile, offers of comfort. Then Ted had told her it was an act, and now… it was ridiculous to think he was out to get her. Right? They'd let her go the first time they'd pulled her in. They would this time too. They had to. Ted was being overly cautious sending his stepfather. That was all.

"Miss Yates is willing to cooperate in your investigation," Martin said, and Eden wondered if there was an option to do this another day. Or month. Or year. "There is no need for scare tactics."

Another time when she hadn't just received the news that a man she might not have loved, but used to sleep with regularly, was now sleeping with the fishes. Not actual fishes. He was on her living room floor. Someone would move the body, right? God, was she that callous that she was more concerned with a body on her floor than with his actual life?

Hopefully, Justin had had someone in his life who loved him. No one should die and only be remembered by people who only felt annoyance or dislike for them. He still deserved to have someone to think of him fondly. Someone to miss him.

Keith shuffled through some papers he had on the desk in front of him, although he didn't appear to be looking at them.

"Eden—" he started, and Martin cleared his throat. "Miss Yates. You used to date Mr. Fredecker?"

They already had this information, so Eden didn't see the harm in answering. "Yes, but I ended things almost two months ago."

This time Martin aimed his throat clearing at her.

"Messy breakup?" Keith asked, and Eden opened her mouth to respond, only to feel Martin's fancy leather shoe dig into the top of her foot. She shook her head instead.

"Did you live together?"

"You already know she lives alone," Martin said, and Eden wanted to stick her tongue out at Keith. She didn't. "My client already answered this question just last week."

"Funny how she had a different lawyer then," Keith said.

"And now she has me." Martin folded his hands on the top of the chipped Formica. "Either ask the right questions or Ms. Yates and I will be leaving."

Keith straightened his shoulders as if squaring off for battle.

"Ms. Yates. Can you account for your whereabouts over the last forty-eight hours?"

Eden had an airtight alibi. That's what they were asking for, right? Not only had she been out of the city for the last three and a half days, but she'd been constantly surrounded by other people. Trustworthy people. Wealthy established-members-of-society people.

And yes, the prospect of explaining to AJ and Will, or Eleanor, why she'd need them to vouch for her was deeply embarrassing, but Eden had focused a lot of time and energy on not letting embarrassment get to her. Embarrassment wasn't even real. Only Eden could decide if Eden was embarrassed.

The information could embarrass Ted though, and that thought made her recoil like she'd touched an open flame. That ship had definitely already sailed. He'd had to call his *stepfather*. Eden knew what that would have meant for her sweet darling man. To ask for help from the one person he spent so much time and energy trying to… impress wasn't the right word. Ted wasn't trying to impress Martin, Ted was trying not to piss Martin off, trying not to ruffle his stepfather's feathers.

"I spent the weekend on the Cape," Eden said. "For a wedding."

"That should be easy to verify. What hotel did you stay at?" Keith motioned to the other officer, who lifted what looked like a tiny yellow steno pad and a neon blue pen. Didn't they usually record these things? She couldn't take her eyes off the brightly contrasting colors. They were making her think of the gouache paints she preferred for vibrant flowers and high contrast scenes.

"I didn't stay in a hotel," she said and instantly regretted her words as Martin cleared his throat and Keith sat up straighter. There was a gleam in his eyes, like someone had just offered him Sox tickets behind home plate.

"We'll need to know where you stayed, Ms. Yates, along with the names of anyone who can corroborate your stay."

There went that pen, scratching over the yellow notepad. Was that sound deafening to anyone else? What was he even writing? She hadn't said anything of value. Except clearly she had or he wouldn't be writing. She'd unwittingly given them some information, and she did not know what that information could be.

"Ms. Yates attended the Masters/Mulligan wedding this weekend. She stayed at their home. Eden and her date drove down Thursday afternoon and had only just returned when she found you at her residence."

Eden had to admit that it was gratifying to see Keith's eyes go wide and his scribe's hands still. Apparently, the Masters' name carried some weight. Of course she knew who they were. Most people at least recognized the name, but how interesting that name-dropping a senator—or his son—was a fast way to rattle the police. Weren't they supposed to help her, no matter what? Even without wealthy connections? The first time she'd met these cops, they'd been nice, even if it was an act. Now she got the distinct impression that they, one, thought she was lying, and two, hated her for it. Which was a fucking lot to deal with at the end of a long day.

"We have professional photographs from the day itself, personal photographs with time stamps. Witnesses who can corroborate Ms. Yates's whereabouts, and we can access security footage from both the HMP building showing a return to Boston and a gas station on the drive back, and she has a record of the Uber that picked her up downtown and brought her back to her apartment." Martin's cheeks creased in what might have been a smile. "I'm certain that will suffice."

"That should do it," said the officer with the notebook.

"If that's all, then Miss Yates and I will be leaving now. You can contact me if you have any further questions. Have a pleasant evening." And then Martin pushed his chair back from the table and stood. He smoothed the front of his sport coat as if the screeching grind of the metal chair legs against the scuffed linoleum hadn't sent a shudder down his spine.

"I didn't kill Justin." Eden realized the words were a mistake the minute they came out of her mouth. "I mean—" she hadn't liked him, but she hadn't hated him either. She also hadn't been thinking when she opened her mouth.

"Outside, Miss Yates." Martin held his hand out to her for the first time, but Eden would rather chew shards of glass off the sidewalk than take it.

She pushed her own chair back, wincing at the squeal, and smiled stiffly at the officers. She would not thank them.

"Ms. Yates." Keith stood too. "We never mentioned that the deceased was Mr. Fredecker."

That couldn't be right. It couldn't be. The implication behind every question was that she'd known Justin was dead. That she'd been the one to make him that way. And she hadn't. She really, truly hadn't done that. Oh god. Eden pressed her fist to her stomach. She would not throw up. Not here. Not now.

Knowing her luck, if she did, they'd somehow grab DNA from the wreckage and Martin would read her the riot act. She swallowed past the thickness in her throat.

"You've been asking questions about Justin. *You* pointed out the body," she tripped over the word because oh my god this still could not be happening.

Any minute now, Eden was going to wake up with her face pressed to the passenger window of Ted's car. There'd probably be drool and unflattering snoring involved. And the best part was that he'd do that little half smile, the one that tipped the corner of his full lips as he shook his head back and forth. He did it when she said something particularly out of left field. Especially when he thought she wasn't looking at him.

But she wasn't sleeping. This wasn't some horrible, twisted dream dragged up from the depths of her creative psyche. This was real.

"I assumed—"

"A little callous," Keith said, "assuming someone's death? Perhaps you did more than just assume it?"

"That's enough," Martin stepped forward, putting his own body between Eden and the officer. This close, he was smaller than she expected. Nowhere near Ted's height or width. It wasn't surprising that they didn't share the same height. They weren't biologically related after all, but he was a gently rolling hill compared to his stepson's mountain. "Ms. Yates made a pretty obvious inference, given the information at hand. We both know if you had enough evidence to make the claim you just did, that she wouldn't be leaving because she'd be under arrest."

Arrest.

Oh god.

"Have a good night," Martin said, then leaned into Eden and mouthed the words, "Walk. Out. The. Door."

Eden left the room on autopilot. Even late at night, there were people everywhere. Martin had stepped around her the minute the door to the interrogation room closed behind them, and she followed his heavy stride toward the exit. She needed to get out of here. She needed a breeze. Fresh air. Something.

Martin didn't hold the door and Eden scrambled to push it open. She jogged down the cement steps, marveling at how quickly he moved. He stopped next to the street, slipping a sleek phone from his pocket and thumbing through the contacts.

Okay. So he wasn't warm and cuddly. Eden had known that even before she'd met him. He wasn't friendly, or even vaguely polite. Martin James was definitely a man judging the ketchup stain on the front of her shirt and the length of her shorts. She wasn't wearing makeup, but she could feel the oil from the day sitting on her face like some sort of perverted sheet mask. Martin was probably judging that too.

"Either you're willfully stupid or painfully naïve, but either way, you need to toughen up fast, Miss Yates." He hadn't even looked up from his phone as he said the cutting words. "I'm helping you as a favor to my boy, and it's clear why they're eager to pin everything on you. You're dumb enough to almost give them exactly what they want while dancing around the one piece of evidence they need. You can't even do them the courtesy of closing their case for them. No wonder Ted begged me to take you on. You, my dear, are an absolute train wreck."

Eden couldn't explain why the words hurt so much. She'd been hearing variations of them for years, although her stepdad usually focused on how weird she was and left her intelligence out of it. Actually, he usually lamented her decision to waste her brain on arts and crafts. She knew she wasn't stupid. Naïve? Sure, especially about the legal system. Her personal experience with cops involved *Law & Order*. But the thought that Martin may have said some or any of his thoughts to Ted? That couldn't be why she imagined the sidewalk splitting and swallowing her whole. Not at all.

"I'll have my assistant contact you about a meeting this week." He tapped a few buttons on his phone before finally glancing at her.

"Do you think this will drag out? I really didn't do anything. Won't they just check my alibi and move on?" Eden said, aware that she sounded whiny. Aware that her hands were shaking. Aware that she wanted to be anywhere but on this sidewalk in the dark talking to a man who thought she was a stupid possible-murderer.

"That will depend entirely on what killed that man. You might not have been here but they could try to prove you lured him to your home and had someone do him in while you conveniently were out of town. We'll need to wait on the autopsy for more information. But whether it does or doesn't drag out, it would serve you well to receive some lessons in etiquette before you destroy your case with another ill-timed outburst. I have a reputation in this city and I won't allow an ill-mannered idiot to ruin this for me."

Well, wasn't that charming. Eden wanted to tell him to fuck off. Ted hadn't been exaggerating when he said Martin was a piece of work. He made her own stepdad look almost cuddly. She wanted to tell him to go away and never come back and if she wasn't half terrified that the Boston PD was about to arrest her, innocent or not, then that's exactly what she would have done.

"Her manners are fucking fine, Martin. Yours could use some work."

Eden whipped around to find Ted closing the last few feet between them as his long legs ate up the distance. It was instinct to step into the circle of his arms, to press her cheek against the solid beat of his heart. Her pulse slowed to match his as she clutched the hem of his t-shirt and he rubbed a circle into the spot between her shoulder blades. Martin studied them, eyes cataloging all the places they touched. Ted dug his fingers into the knots as tension stiffened her muscles.

"Excuse me?" Martin coughed the words out, as if he'd been as surprised to hear his stepson speak that way as Ted was to have said the words.

"Your job is to help her, not to bully her."

"You led me to believe my *job* was doing a favor for a friend of Eleanor Masters, not for your criminally connected girlfriend." Martin's focus locked on his stepson. "Not together. Right."

"I'm not his girlfriend." It was important to create a sense of distance here. Ted didn't need to be tied to all of her perceived inadequacies. She knew he had already dealt with enough as it was.

"Is that supposed to make this better?" Martin dropped his gaze to Eden. "You roped me in for your most recent piece of tail."

"We're not doing that—" any more. They weren't doing that any more. She supposed that technically Martin was right about this one. Ted had gotten his stepfather to help his most recent fuck. She'd laugh if the tears weren't already bubbling up inside her like a geyser about to explode.

"I asked you to help her because she is fucking innocent, Martin. You knew it after two seconds in there. I don't know what hard-on they have for her, but Eden did nothing wrong."

And there went her heart galloping through her chest again. A herd of wild horses stampeding.

"I will not be spoken to this way." Martin looked distinctly less put together with anger ruffling his feathers.

"*You* don't speak to me this way. You were a disappointing kid, but I thought we'd finally gotten you ironed out."

Eden's spine stiffened at that. She wanted to say something, was itching to say something, but Ted might not thank her for getting involved. This interaction was decidedly different than the relationship Ted had painted for her. He wasn't standing quietly on the sidewalk, letting a grown man talk down to him.

"And you don't get to be an ass just because you think you're better than everyone else." Ted's arm tightened around Eden's body. One of his hands dropped to her hip, his thumb pressing into the curve above the waistband of her shorts. It swept back and forth over her skin and she shivered. "You're going to stay on Eden's case because she deserves it and because your ego won't let you do anything but win. I'm going to cover your fee and then we won't need to consider each other family anymore. Case closed. Chapter ended."

"After everything I've done for you—" Martin pointed a shaking finger at Ted's chest.

"I never asked for any of it," Ted said. "And I've paid over and over again. I'm done." He brushed his bearded cheek over the top of Eden's head and she felt her curls snag on his facial hair. "You take care of Eden, and then we're done. No more phone calls, no more holidays, no more disappointments. We aren't family anymore."

He had paid. Years and years of pretending to be someone he wasn't. Hiding away behind button-down shirts and fancy ties. Making the right career and social moves. And here he was, standing up to it all. Telling his stepfather to go fuck himself.

Metaphorically.

For her.

Eden was pressed tight to his chest, the comforting weight of her keeping his muscles from shattering under the strain of facing down his stepfather. Ted had spent a lot of time forcing his temper under wraps, a temper that had, in his youth, often led him to use his fists.

There had been a point in his life when he was quick to anger and quicker to hit. It had been years—Logan notwithstanding—since he'd felt the urge to curl his fingers and strike someone. But hearing the poisonous judgment dropping words from Martin's mouth as he tried to darken an actual ray of sunshine, well, that was fucking unacceptable.

For a heartbeat, Ted pulled Eden in tighter. He could feel her breath through the thin cotton of his shirt. She smelled good, even after a full day in the summer heat, and then in his car, and then in that station reeking of stale cigarettes and burned coffee. Ice cream and sunshine and the sweet thrum of the white and yellow bell-shaped flowers his mother used to grow in her garden. He should ask Chloe what they were called. He remembered sucking on them as a kid, a honey drop on the tongue.

"Come on. My car is this way." Ted pressed the words into the top of her head, her hair flooding his mouth.

Eden followed him the two blocks to where he'd parked, and it didn't escape Ted's notice that only a few hours ago he'd been offering her the same ride. He wasn't sure if she wanted to say yes now, or if she felt like she had no choice and he'd backed her into a corner. She could have been so overwhelmed that she'd followed him on autopilot. At least if this were true, some part of her trusted him. He wanted to be worthy of that trust.

Ted opened the passenger door and Eden climbed in. She propped her feet up on the dashboard almost immediately and hugged her knees. Ted jogged around the back of his car and folded himself into the front seat. Visible goosebumps spread across the tanned length of her arms. Ted didn't have a sweatshirt to offer her, or a blanket, so he cranked the heat and turned the vents her way.

Eden rolled her head against the headrest, her brows furrowed as he started the car.

"Did you skip ahead a few months? Because I usually make it to December before turning my heat all the way up." She leaned forward and moved the knob from the max setting down to the lowest, but she didn't turn it off.

"You were cold." Ted pulled away from the curb. "I didn't have anything to give you, so I thought—" he shook his head, "I'm sorry for what Martin said."

"You don't have to apologize for him," Eden said. "Although I'm definitely sorry for what your childhood must have been like."

"Of course I'm apologizing. Why are you apologizing?" Ted turned down a side street, partially to buy more time together in the car, partially because he didn't know where he was taking her. His house wasn't too far. He was already heading in that direction, so he'd just carry on, making as many extra turns as possible. "I'm the one who called him, which makes his gross personality my responsibility."

Eden shook her head.

"Nope." She popped the P sound at the end of the word. Ted fought a smile, but lost. "Before we walked outside, he was an even bigger ass to the jerks in the building, so I'll keep him for now. Besides, you told him to heave-ho. He's officially not your anything anymore. Remember?"

"Eden." She gutted him. How did she do that?

"Anyway, *I'm* sorry because you had to call him for me. I know you don't get along, but I had no idea how poisonous he was. Was he like that your whole life? Because that's abusive Ted. That's wrong—" she turned her body towards his and dropped her hand to the top of his thigh. "I really appreciate you helping me. I swear I'm not always a train wreck."

"You're not a train wreck." Ted felt the urge to say sorry again, because hearing Martin talk must have taken Eden right back to her own warped childhood.

"Ted." Her hand on his leg was a brand, even through the fabric of his sweatpants. "The first time we met, you had to rescue me from the cops because I was in over my head and didn't even realize it."

"You couldn't have known." He wanted to drop his hand over the top of hers, squeeze her fingers tight. Both to show her he was there and that he was supportive, but also so that her hand wouldn't travel any higher. Her call changed nothing between them. She wasn't asking for more from him. Letting his body react right now was going to be uncomfortable for both of them.

"That's definitely not what you said last time." Her laugh wrapped around him and he took another steadying breath, pleading with his dick to behave. "And here you are rescuing me again."

Ted started to tell her she hadn't needed a rescue; she was smart and resourceful and if she hadn't called him she'd have called someone—her best friend, Romy, maybe—but she cut him off.

"You can't help yourself, can you? Damsel in distress and every part of you springs into action."

That was categorically false.

Okay, maybe not.

Ted did like to help people. He'd received so many chances, without ever asking for them, that he felt he owed other people a fraction of the same. Teenaged Ted hadn't wanted any special treatment. Adult Ted recognized how privileged it was to think that way. But it wasn't just his need to protect and help that sent him to Eden's side again. That was Eden herself. He was physically incapable of standing by while she floundered. She could stand in an inch of water and he'd still splash his way in to make sure she was okay. Every time.

"I'll admit," Eden said, pulling her hand back from his leg. Ted felt cold down to his marrow. "I could have taken the T, but I appreciate the ride."

A dark part of Ted wanted to point out that if she'd accepted his ride the first time, then she wouldn't have been alone and ambushed at her apartment. She wouldn't have had to call him because he'd have been there to take her hand in his and lend her his strength. He wouldn't have needed to hear the broken sound of her voice through the phone. She'd taken possible years off his life with the dejected way she spoke.

"I just realized I don't know where I'm supposed to go." There was the dejected tone again, and the laugh she forced out didn't change it. "I'm not sure if I can go back to my apartment." Her eyes were wide when she turned to him. "How long will it take to remove—" a swallow.

Ted could explain that the medical examiner would collect the body and take it for an autopsy. The actual issue was if they'd open the scene back up for her or keep it closed during the investigation, but since it wouldn't tell her if she could go back home, the information would not be helpful. He already knew she could stay with him. And okay, his guest room was a study and home gym, but they'd just spent a weekend in the same room. What was a little longer? He'd keep his hands to himself or set himself up on his living room couch.

"I can probably stay at Romy's," Eden's voice was quiet, as if she were talking to herself rather than him. She pulled out an old phone and was scrolling across the screen. "She won't be home for a few more days. She's dog sitting this weekend at Graham and Garret's. They went up to Maine for a wedding." A hollow laugh, "Small world, huh? They're at a wedding, we were at a wedding—"

"Do you have a key to her place?" Ted asked, even though it was a moot point. He wasn't letting her stay in an empty apartment across from where her ex's body had been found. He'd have to die too before that happened.

Eden nodded. "But I don't really want to go back into the building. You can take me to Garret and Graham's. They have a studio in Southie...but that's completely out of your way. You can drop me off at the T."

If she really wanted to go stay with her friend in a South End studio apartment, then he'd fucking drive her there.

"Or you can stay at my place."

Eden studied him for a long moment, the radio burbling out an entire song before she looked away again. The tips of her ears tinged red, and she wrapped her arms around her knees again.

"Is this another rescue thing?" She asked, her gaze trained out the window at the dark street. "Because I really appreciate everything you've done for me, and I know you wouldn't offer if you weren't serious, but I don't want to be difficult or a burden. I really don't like having to rely on people."

Ted's heart turned over in his chest. This sweet woman. She was trying so hard to stay strong and brave, and she was dealing with something unthinkable. Her thoughts must be pinging around her brain like a runaway bouncy ball, leaving her uncertain, and uncomfortable, and utterly alone.

"I'm offering," Ted paused, tasting his words before releasing them, "because I want to. You're someone I care about. We've already been over that once today and don't need to go there right now, but you're someone I care about and you went through something awful tonight. You scared me when you called and if you're in my home, at least I know you're okay. I know you're safe. I'm willing to help with anything and everything, Eden. Let me do that. Okay? It's not you relying on me; it's you doing me a favor."

"Okay," she said. "Okay, take me home."

Eden didn't say anything else until he pulled the car into his driveway. Ted thought she might have fallen asleep against the window. Her temple pressed to the glass and her long dark hair covered most of her face. She sat up as he turned off the car and she was standing next to the passenger door by the time he made it around the car.

No sudden moves. He would not betray the fact that his heart was pounding. He would not scoop her up into his arms and carry her into the house. He was going to keep this as relaxed and normal for her as possible. Ted unlocked his front door, and she followed him in, slowly, quietly. It was late. She had to be exhausted.

He showed her around fast. It wasn't like his home was huge. She wouldn't get lost on the way to the bathroom, or stumble over how to work his kitchen appliances, but he wanted her to know she could make herself at home. She'd been robbed of that moment after a trip, when settling back into a familiar space and routine was welcome and comforting. No matter how good the getaway, everyone liked to be back in their own space when it was over.

"Do you want anything to eat?" Ted felt like a parrot. They'd had this same conversation hours ago. But that was before…everything. He could whip something up if it would put her at ease.

Eden shook her head. "I'm good." Her arms banded across her chest as she looked around his space. "I like your house." A smile. "It feels like you."

Ted looked around his living room, trying to see it through her eyes.

"It's solid, and comfortable, and real. It's exactly what I thought it would be," she said, and then, as if she hadn't just reached into his chest and branded her name across his heart, robbing him of breath and thought, she said "Do you mind if I grab a shower?"

Ted had already known he was half-way to falling in love with Eden Yates. He'd probably known that from the moment she looked up at him and smiled in a dirty police station. He'd definitely suspected it when she'd straddled his hips in the cool ocean surf. Known it when he'd tucked her close and whirled her around the dance floor while wishing he could make each song last forever. But as he sat on the edge of his bed, listening to the shower run in his small bathroom, he realized he was down for the count.

No last chances, no take backs, no substitutions. Theodore Norman Hughes loved Eden Mary Yates, and would until the day some poor soul had to collect his ashes. If there was a lead weight sitting in his stomach, it was because it didn't matter if Eden felt the same way. It didn't matter if there was a possibility that someday she might. It wouldn't change the way he felt.

Dammit, he was pretty sure he'd just won AJ a bet. Will would never let him hear the end of this.

The water turned off and Ted's heart pounded. He'd seen her naked. They'd had sex. Wildly athletic and deeply gratifying sex. Multiple times. And he was more nervous for her to walk out of his bathroom, put on his clothes, and climb into his bed than he'd ever been about anything in his entire life. He'd grabbed one of his t-shirts and a pair of boxers he'd shrunk once in the wash but had never gotten rid of.

Tomorrow he'd call Martin and see if they could collect some of her things, and if they couldn't, he'd take her to buy new essentials. Eden was proud, but practical. He wondered if she'd argue with him about financing a new wardrobe. Well, this would have to be the one argument between them she'd lose.

Ted heard the bathroom door open, and the light padding of Eden's feet as she moved down the hall to the bedroom. He stood up as she walked in. She'd wrapped a dark gray towel around her head, covering her hair and defying gravity. Another towel was wrapped around her chest. Ted took a shaky breath, resisting the urge to dry his palms on his shorts. She approached the bed, and he held out the clean clothes. Eden smiled as she took them and then dropped the towel with zero thought and pulled on the shorts. Ted turned his head away and studied the framed photo above his dresser.

"It's nothing you haven't seen before," Eden said, and he could hear the goddamn smile in her words.

"I'm trying to be respectful." Was that his voice? That growl that sounded a lot like the engine on his bike?

"Right." She pulled the shirt over her head and Ted called himself several names because he could still see her out of the corner of his eye. He hadn't actually given her privacy at all. An asshole. He was an asshole. "The contract. We were only a thing for the weekend and the weekend is up, even if I followed you home."

The contract had also said that either of them could amend it. It was on the tip of his tongue to point that out, but he didn't want to sound like a coercive asshole. He turned back to face her as she unwound the towel from her head and used the fabric to squeeze the water out of her hair.

"You need microfiber towels." Eden said as she scrunched. "Terry causes frizz."

"What frizz?" He asked, and the smile she sent him was heart-stopping.

"I could kiss you for that," she said, and Ted was tempted to pull her close and let her. The urge was a drum line pounding through his veins. "I spend more time than I care to admit trying to get my hair to behave." She tipped her head, her eyes sliding over his face. "Just so you know, I don't mind you looking."

And just like that, his body seized up and his dick tried to punch a hole through the front of his pants. The change was enough to make him light-headed as all his blood rushed south.

"Eden," he was definitely begging. The problem was that Ted didn't know what he was begging for.

She stepped into him, dropping the second towel on top of the first. Her hands came up to his chest and then slid around the back of his neck. Her tongue swiped across her bottom lip and Ted brought his own hands to her hips, powerless to step back. Powerless to break the connection. Powerless with her so close and looking at him with so much heat. She tugged his head down and their lips barely slid together. They both let out heavy breaths and then their mouths fused again and Ted couldn't remember why he'd been looking away. Why he'd been holding himself back.

She sucked his tongue, bit at his lips, rolled the length of her body against his, and Ted lost himself. He groaned into her mouth and then her shirt was on the floor, his hands running up the smooth heat of her back to fist in her wet hair.

He tipped her head back and fed her hot, wet kisses, his tongue pressing deep as he claimed her the only way he could. Eden's hands yanked on the neckline of his shirt until he broke the kiss long enough to pull the cotton over his head and drop it to the floor. Her breasts pressed to his chest, her nipples firm points that he wanted to taste.

He kissed her again, swallowing her breathy sound of need. Ted's brain was misfiring. Small thoughts bleeding through the fire and threatening to melt his frontal lobe out of his ears. She pressed up on her toes, her stomach rubbing the length of his erection, and he rolled his hips into hers, sucking her gasp into his own lungs.

One of her hands trailed down the front of his chest and he sucked in his stomach as her fingertips brushed his waistband. She closed her fist around his cock and his hips stuttered in her grip, and for one desperate minute he rutted into her hand before he pulled back in one last-ditch effort to do the right thing here.

"Eden, wait."

She stopped her movements, but didn't release his dick. "You don't want to?" Her words were low, husky, almost impossible to understand through the haze of heat covering both of them. Her fingers flexed and her grip loosened.

"I want to," he said, because she had to know that. "God, do I want to, but I need to make sure you're okay."

"It's okay Ted," she pressed her mouth to the spot right above his left nipple, or his heart. "This wasn't the first time I've been questioned by the police." She was trying for flippant, but he saw right through her.

"I'll give you whatever you need, Eden. Trust me on that one. But I wasn't asking about the police. Today you learned that someone you used to care about," he refused to say love, "died and that's a lot to take in. You're allowed to have powerful feelings about all of this, and I don't want to anything you're uncomfortable with. I can't hurt you more, Eden. I can't do that because I think it's fairly obvious that I more than care about you. I—" he stopped himself.

"I'm being selfish," she said, and she ducked her head to avoid looking directly at him, but she didn't disentangle from him.

"You aren't selfish." He said, but she was already shaking her head.

"I am. I'm selfish and greedy and horrible because I don't know how I feel about Justin's death. I'm numb to it maybe, but I should probably feel sad, or horrible about it, or something, but—"

"That's probably normal," Ted said.

"But I'm selfish because I know you want more from me. You've been up front about it. I know you want a girlfriend turned fiancée turned wife. And that terrifies me Ted. I'll lose myself and then I'll mess that up for you, or be unable to commit to the job, and I'll ruin everything. I shouldn't be doing any of this with you, except that I need—"

Anything. He'd give her anything.

"What do you need?"

"I need you," Eden said. "You're the only person who can make me feel okay. Like I'm not about to vibrate right out of my skin. You're the only person who I can think about being around right now. The only person I want to be around. And I need you. I need you to make me forget the last six hours. You're the only one who can. The only place I feel safe. The only place I still feel like me. So Please, I know it's not fair, but I'm begging you to be with me tonight and not read more into it than that."

Except he'd already read into it because she'd made a mistake. She hadn't said she needed a release. She hadn't said she needed just sex or an orgasm or even just random human contact after the night she'd been through. And honestly, he'd have given it to her, anyway. She said she'd needed *him*. Ted. She just hadn't figured it out yet. And he could work with that. He absolutely could. Because she'd given him a gift and hadn't even realized it. He was the only one.

"Take your pants off and get on the bed, Eden. I'm going to take care of everything."

She sucked in a breath, her eyes glassy and unfocused, but she scrambled onto his comforter and laid back. Topless in a pair of his boxer shorts. God, he hoped this would work. For both of their sakes.

"I'm going to take care of you." He said, and then he climbed up after her.

"Get in the car, Eden," Ted pinched the bridge of his nose and held open the passenger door of his SUV.

"I really don't need you to do this." She insisted, "I can just—" just what? She didn't have anything at his house. Not a toothbrush, not her phone charger, not pajamas. She'd dropped her overnight bag just inside the door to her own apartment and it had completely slipped her mind to pick it back up when the officers had shepherded her to the back of a police vehicle.

Ted had washed her clothes from the night before, so even if she was an outfitter repeater, she was a clean one, but the jean shorts and the crop top weren't exactly conducive to teaching her yoga classes. He'd offered her a t-shirt of his, but it had come down below the hem of her shorts and she'd looked nearly naked.

Ted's eyes had lingered on the skin of her thighs before he'd wrenched them away, leaving blistering heat in their wake. Heat that only intensified when he tracked the movements of her arms as she pulled his shirt back over her head and swapped it with her own.

"I can take the T," Eden said even as she slid into the warm front seat. This was a couple thing right? Having your boyfriend take you shopping? "Or order things online."

"You teach a class tomorrow morning," Ted said, sliding behind the wheel and starting the car. "Nothing would get here in time. I'm available. Let me help so you don't have to lug everything home on the train."

"Ted," Eden put her hand over his on the gearshift. He flipped his palm up and tangled his fingers with hers, squeezing once before pulling away.

"Relax Eden. I'd do it for Will or Logan, too."

"You would?" A laugh bubbled in her chest, picturing any of the tall, dark, and suited men carrying each other's shopping bags.

"I'd probably complain more and make them feed me, but yes."

Okay, it was her. She needed to stop making this weird.

"That I can work with," she said as she propped her feet up on the dashboard. "You complain and I'll buy lunch. Maybe even a beer." Ted grunted as he leaned over the console to hand her a white cord. "Oh, my phone's charged. You plugged it in for me last night."

He had. Sliding the device onto the smooth, clear top of his nightstand before turning out the overhead lights and sliding under the covers.

"Pick the music, Eden."

"Right."

Three songs later, Ted parked his car in an empty spot and jogged around her car to hand her out as if they weren't at a department store to buy her a six-pack of cotton panties and a hairbrush. That feeling was back. The overwhelming rush that whispered this was more than just two friends walking into America's favorite store. As if he could read her mind, Ted bumped his shoulder into hers, mouth flattening into the tiny smile he liked to send her way.

"You brought me to Target," Eden said as they stepped through the sliding red-framed doors.

"If you'd rather go somewhere else, we can," Ted took the basket from her hand and looped it over his forearm.

"Ted, you brought me to nirvana. Target is my personal version of heaven. And I don't get here nearly as often as I'd like. It's dangerous to my wallet."

"Your wallet is safe today, Eden. I've got this. Get some stretchy pants and the shampoo you like."

"Actually, *your* wallet is safe," Eden looped her arm through his free one. "But I am going to pick your brain with options the whole time we waltz through this wonderland of fluorescent lighting."

Eden navigated to the athletic section and browsed the rack of bright colors. She held up two pairs of spandex shorts, trying to judge the length of the inseams. Pants would be a more practical choice, since she could use them even when the weather got cooler, eventually, but it had just been so damn hot recently. The idea of sliding long pants on when she'd already be a sweaty mess was simply unbearable, but go too short, and her students would get an eyeful in downward dog.

"Get the pockets Eden."

She held up the green pair. "Are you sure? The purple might be a little longer. I don't want to give Rodney a heart attack when I bend over."

"Rodney?"

"One of my regulars. He's eighty and a sweetheart. He's never missed a class," but she couldn't help the flush of pleasure at the grumpy way he'd spit the name.

"He's shouldn't be looking," Ted said, "Get the green ones."

Eden held the shorts up. "Are you sure?"

"What's in your pocket today?"

She dipped her hand into the denim and pulled out her items. The smooth gray surface of her favorite worry stone, her cellphone, a crumpled blue sticky note with the name of a book she was supposed to check out, and two hair ties that were just tight enough to not wear on her wrists.

"Right. I need pockets. I'll get the green ones," she said, looking down at the collection sitting in her palm. "Just need to try them on and do a squat test."

"Squat test?"

"Make sure they aren't see-through when I squat. Or bend. Come on, you can help with that."

Ted followed her to the changing rooms at the back of the store. It was the middle of the morning on a weekday and the only people Eden had seen so far were the red-shirted workers and a handful of solo women pushing toddlers and babies through the aisles in the bright red carts. She turned to tell Ted he didn't have to wait for her—she'd been joking about checking her panties—but he was right there. His body a wall of solid heat.

No one stopped them when he followed her back into the bank of dressing rooms or into the biggest stall at the very end. Eden had a moment of guilt for stepping into the accessible room, but they were the only ones there and Ted definitely wouldn't fit in the smaller ones. Not *with* her, at any rate. And okay, she didn't really need him to come into the room with her. Even if she was itching to touch him again, the point of trying these on was to make sure she wasn't about to flash any of her regular students. She couldn't exactly stretch out into a wide leg forward fold in one of the smaller spaces.

Ted followed her in and pulled the door behind them. At least it was a door, and not one of the thick shower curtains so many stores had, but it ended a good two feet off the ground. On the plus side, Eden doubted any of the moms walking around the store would find their way back here. Their kids would escape in about 2 seconds flat.

Eden kept her back to Ted as she unsnapped her shorts and pushed them over her hips. It was one thing to tease, another to be cruel. The denim hit the floor and Eden used her foot to move the clothes further away before grabbing the green spandex shorts and stepping into them. At least she had on bikini cut panties printed with neon pink flowers. She'd definitely know if they showed through the fabric.

Eden pulled the new shorts up and spun, sticking her ass out towards the mirror. So far, so good. She spread her feet wide and bent at the waist, and let her hands drop to the rough gray carpet. She felt her spine relax as she let gravity weigh her down. Was it her imagination or had Ted's feet stepped closer?

Warm hands closed around her hips. Yes, he'd gotten closer. She rolled up slowly, one vertebra at a time, until her back pressed to the muscles in his chest. Ted's fingers twisted in the fabric, brushing against the smooth skin there, and she felt his exhalation against her neck.

"I can't help you with this, Sweetness," his lips teased the sensitive column of her throat.

"You didn't get a good look?" She was teasing him. It felt good to tease, to feel the smile he pressed to her skin. Almost normal. "I can bend over again." Eden cupped the back of his nape with one hand and let the other cover his fingers.

"You are burned into my brain, Eden. I see you when I close my eyes. I could have waited in the hallway and I'd still know what you look like in your flowery underwear. It doesn't matter what you put on over the top, I still see you. All I can do right now is try to get myself under control because we're in a public place and I swore—"

Ted's fingers flexed as he pulled her a fraction closer before suddenly releasing her and stepping back. Eden shivered in the store's heavy AC.

"The shorts look great. I'll meet you at the car." He slid his fingers and a credit card into the pocket of the shorts, and then he was gone. The door to the changing room slammed closed as he left her standing there, feeling like he had taken all the air with him when he left.

Eden changed back into her jean shorts, carefully storing the card he'd left with her, and headed back into the aisles. She grabbed a generic yoga mat, splurged on the nicer pack of undies, a sports bra, and two t-shirts. She debated an insulated water bottle for about three seconds before putting it back on the shelf. Ted kept his fridge stocked with bottled water and he'd been adamant that she make herself at home.

She shouldn't miss him. They'd spent almost every minute—when she wasn't in an interrogation room and facing down the cops—together since before Will and AJ's wedding. Eden was a strong, independent woman. She valued her privacy and her ability to take care of herself. She shouldn't miss Ted just because he hadn't wanted to watch her try on athletic wear. She should be grateful for the time to hear herself think, to revel in a modicum of privacy. Instead she rushed through the aisles, trying to get out of the store in record time. It wasn't even so that she wouldn't keep him waiting. She missed him. He'd been gone two minutes and she already wanted him back. That could not be a good sign.

Eden used the self-check-out and walked into the parking lot. Ted was standing by the car. He had his arms crossed over the bulk of his chest, a deep furrow between his brows as he watched her approach. It was instinct to push up onto her toes and wind her hand around his neck. Instinct to press her mouth to his and suck on the fullness of his lower lip. Instinct to smile when he leaned into her to kiss her back.

Ted set her back on her feet before she could climb her way up his body, which was fine. They were in a parking lot—this couldn't go anywhere now even if she wanted to—but she still felt cold as his hands dropped from her body. She walked around the car and pulled open the passenger door. There was a plastic grocery bag sitting on the seat. Ted had taken all the other bags and stashed them in the trunk. Maybe he'd grabbed something for himself.

Eden lifted it up, intent on putting it in the backseat, when Ted slid into the driver's seat next to her. He pulled the bag from her hands and Eden buckled her seatbelt.

Ted opened the bag and put it in her lap. It held a collection of paints, brushes, pencils, and sketch pads. Eden checked the front of the bag and saw the name of an art supply store. He hadn't waited in the car at all. Ted pulled the car out of the lot as Eden stared down at her art supplies. The ones she hadn't asked for. She hadn't even considered replacing them, figuring she could go a few days without drawing something, without painting. Except Ted had made sure she didn't have to. He hadn't just left her in the store. He'd gone to buy her paints and brushes.

He needed to stop doing these kinds of things for her. Driving her all over the city, financing her shopping trips, thinking of what she needed before she could ask for it. Because she already knew that her feelings for him were beyond appropriate for two friends. She knew it was a slippery and easy slope to the point of no return. She should ask him to be colder. Ask him to be a borderline jerk. Anything to save her sanity.

"Thank you, Bear." Eden said instead, and she held the bag to her chest.

Ted had kept his hands to himself for two days. Two days of brushing kisses on her cheeks and forehead, but not her mouth. Tucking a blanket over her lap as she watched television on his couch, but not tucking her into his side. If he'd thought stepping out of the dressing room was tough, it was nothing compared to waking up next to her each morning—her hair mussed, and her face sleep swollen—and slowly remove the arm he'd thrown across her waist.

Ted supposed he could buy a bed for the guest room. It would make sense, and with a little rejigging he could still keep his office space in there and move his gym to the three-season porch. Of course Eden loved sitting on the old wicker lounge out there, but he could keep a sitting area, give her a spot to do yoga, replace the furniture there too. Was that too much? He wanted her here. He wanted her comfortable. He wanted her to recognize that they could be everything together. Right now, his job was to give her a safe place to stay. He was being a good fucking friend. And yes, he had an end goal, but rushing into things wouldn't win her over. She'd dissolve their partnership before he could plead his case. Again.

As hard as this exercise in restraint was proving to be, Ted knew it was important. He and Eden had chemistry—undeniable, clothes-melting chemistry—but she was already aware of that. Eden wasn't shying away from intimacy, she was scared of being in a relationship. Of being someone's girlfriend, or wife, or partner. Ted could understand that. By all accounts her stepdad hadn't been hard just on her, but also on her mother.

They'd basically had the same upbringing and reacted in opposite ways. Eden had conformed while under her stepdad's roof and then left without a backward glance. Ted had rebelled at every opportunity as a child and fallen into line as an adult. So no, Ted wouldn't blame Eden for protecting herself, but if he wanted a chance to show her that he would *never* be like her stepdad, then he had to take sex out of the equation. He had to make sure she knew that they shared more than chemistry and heat.

Ted wiped down the kitchen counter with a white dish towel and resolutely refused to look out the window. Eden was in his tiny backyard, her yoga mat rolled out under the big oak tree. The same one he loved to curse every year when it dropped all its leaves the week after leaf pick up. She sat cross-legged in the evening shade, her hands palm up on her knees, wearing those heart-attack-inducing green shorts.

They'd fallen into a simple rhythm over the last few days. He started coffee each morning and scrambled eggs while she made toast. She'd have dinner going when he'd walked in the door. Tonight she'd had tomatoes and garlic roasting in the oven while she boiled water for pasta. He'd set the table, sliced some crusty bread, and pressed a soft kiss to her temple. They'd sat side by side as they ate. Then Ted cleared the table, and Eden headed outside to take advantage of the waning sunlight. Now here he was watching her through the windows like some pervert.

Ted would not touch. He wouldn't, but he was going to go out there and spend every minute that he could with her. He was going to change into his basketball shorts and sneakers and go let her boss him through a yoga session because one day soon she was going to go back home. That was okay. He was prepared for it.

Even if his plan worked, even if she recognized what they meant to each other, recognized that he was worth the risk and that he'd never ask her to change herself, it would still be too soon to move in together. That would rush things, and the last thing he wanted to do was rush Eden. There was no need to when his goal was forever. So, no matter what happened over the next few days, she was going to move out, and he was going to miss spending every second with her.

Eden's eyes were closed, but she turned her face toward him with a smile as he sat beside her. The evening was hot and dry. Ted could smell the charcoal of someone's barbecue and hear the laughter of a backyard party. And over all of that, he heard her soft sigh as he settled in next to her.

"Need something?" Eden asked, tipping her head back so that the sun poured over the smooth lines of her face.

"Put me through my paces, Sweetness." Ted grinned at her as her eyes popped open.

"I thought you were going for a run."

Eden had pulled her dark hair up into a long ponytail, but a tendril whipped across her face and stuck to the curve of her lips. Ted's fingers twitched. He wanted to reach out and push back that piece of hair. He wanted to trace the fine shell of her ear as he did. He wanted to duck his mouth and kiss her. He shrugged.

"I can run anytime. Today I have a yoga teacher in my backyard and I might not get that chance again."

"Have you ever taken a class before?"

"No, but I can touch my toes, so I don't think I'm a totally lost cause." Ted reached his arms across his chest, stretching the tightness in his shoulders.

"I've seen the way you move," Eden watched him, her eyes dark with heat. "You aren't a lost cause, but I'll go easy on you, just in case." She winked, and it was like a waterfall of heat pouring straight down over the top of his head. He turned away to get his body back under control.

"So," he cleared his throat. "Are we doing a sun salutation?"

"Sun salutations are for greeting the morning," Eden rolled her head to crack her neck as she stretched her legs in front of her. "We're going to be stretching our hips, hamstrings, and shoulders because those are the spots that hold tension from the day. Then we're going to focus on our breathing, and our awareness of our bodies, until our minds relax."

Ted stretched his legs out, too. He didn't have a yoga mat for himself and the grass tickled his calves and feet. He made a note to pick one up.

"You don't have to talk me through anything," Ted said as Eden leaned back on her mat. Ted lay back, too. "I don't want to get in your way. I'll just copy what you do."

"We'll hold each pose for 5-10 breaths, repeat on the opposite side, and then we'll go through the flow as many times as we feel like it, okay?" She raised one long leg up above her body, flexing her foot until she could reach up and grasp her toes with the same side hand. She held there as Ted tried to lift his leg, too. His knee bent automatically as he tried to pull his foot higher. "Don't lock your knee, but try not to bend it," Eden said. "Just do what you're comfortable with." She let her leg slowly drop to the mat and lifted the other one. Ted followed suit.

Ten poses later, Ted's arms were shaking as he stepped his leg forward and moved from downward dog to lizard. His balance was off, his body too bulky to move the way she did, but the moments in between each movement—where they breathed together for long, slow seconds—was enough to calm the thoughts ricocheting around his brain.

He wouldn't trade that intimacy for anything. She talked him through resting on the flat top of his foot instead of balancing on his instep, and that helped with some of the pitching fight with gravity. It made him brave enough to drop his leg to the ground and attempt the pigeon pose she was showing him.

"You're a great teacher," Ted said, his muscles burning in the best way. Her hair covered most of her face, but Eden's smile could have lit a pitch black basement. There was no missing the sweet curve of her lips.

Four poses later, as Eden lifted her right leg to restart the whole flow, she turned her head to the side and let her eyes roam his face. "Thanks for giving it a shot," she said.

Ted lifted his leg too, keeping his knee straight and pulling on his toes until he felt the stretch. "I'm not sure I'm meant to be a yogi, but this is fun. I can stretch with you any night you want me to, but if I'm expected at classes, I'm picking up another yoga mat."

Eden rolled onto her side—not the next movement—and reached her hand out to rest on his chest.

"No, thank you. You don't have to come to classes, this is enough. Justin never—"

He covered her hand with his, feeling the long tapered fingers twist in his shirt. He wished he'd taken the damn thing off. He wished that her hand was flexing against his skin, tangling in his chest hair, fingers tracing the lines of his tattoos, but this was better. Safer.

"It's important to you, Eden." Ted said, because that's all there was to it. Of course, he'd join her. Of course, he'd support her. Only a fool wouldn't cherish everything about this woman, and Ted Hughes was not a fool.

And an hour later, they both sat on the couch as she tucked her feet under the meaty part of his thigh. Eden covered them both with a fuzzy blue blanket. Her hands cradled a large ceramic mug and her phone was in her lap. Ted reached down and squeezed her ankle with his free hand, using the pen in his other hand to make a note in the margins of the document he was re-reading.

Eden opened her phone and pulled up her most recent book, flicking through pages a lot faster than he would have. She smiled, shook her head at something she read, and Ted flipped the page on the contract he was looking through. He'd thought he could never beat the quiet intimacy from earlier… he'd been wrong.

"I like having you here," Ted said, turning back to his work so she wouldn't feel like she had to reply. "Doing yoga, and sketching, and sitting with me while I work. I just wanted you to know that."

Eden rested her head against his shoulder.

"I like you too, Bear," She said, and went back to her book.

"So you go to a wedding, and I go dog sit, and the next time I see you, you're a person of interest in a murder with a hot live-in boyfriend?" Romy handed half of her sandwich across the table to Eden and clacked her fingers open and shut like a crab claw. Sal's was cheap and fast and had the absolute best paninis in the North End, but neither Eden nor Romy could ever decide on what to order, so they always split two.

"He's not my boyfriend," Eden said, putting Romy's offering onto her plate and sectioning out half of her own sandwich to hand over.

"Are you sleeping together?" Romy snagged a fry from Eden's plate and popped it into her mouth.

Eden didn't answer.

Mostly because she actually wasn't sure of the answer. She and Ted had had sex the first night. He'd taken her down to the sheets and obliterated every single worry that had bounced through her head. He coaxed her to orgasm after orgasm until she was a boneless mess of quivering jelly.

When she'd woken up in the middle of the night, gasping in breath after breath that left her lungs empty and screaming, he'd wrapped powerful arms around her and pressed her head into his neck. Holding her and letting her match her breathing and heart rate to his. So yes? But then they hadn't done anything since.

"Okay, but you are living in his house." Romy grinned as she said the words, and Eden tried not to roll her eyes.

"Only until I'm allowed back into my apartment."

Martin's office hadn't contacted her yet. Sure, it had been just over a week, but according to the internet, it could be days, weeks, or even months before the BPD decided they'd gotten all the evidence they needed to get and no longer needed to preserve her apartment as a crime scene.

Eden assumed Ted's stepfather would call her with any important updates, but she was also comfortable enough at Ted's house that she hadn't pushed beyond the three messages he'd left with her lawyer's assistant. It was embarrassing to think about. Eden did not sit and wait for someone else to take care of her. She took care of herself. She was going to figure out her living situation today. Well, first thing Monday morning.

"You guys eat meals together." Romy sipped her Dr. Pepper.

"You're reaching," Eden said. "It makes more sense to cook one meal for two than two meals for one. And you and I eat meals together. We aren't dating."

"Fine, fair enough. Does he drive you to work?"

Right, she'd see about her apartment *and* her car.

"Stop." Eden rubbed a hand over her eyes and leaned back in the booth. It was a beautiful sunny day, but they'd opted to eat inside because of the humidity and Eden's hair was definitely happy with the choice. "He bought me a hair dryer."

"A what?"

"I told him my hair frizzes and the next day there was a hair dryer in his bathroom. One of those flat ones meant for curly hair and it wasn't there the night before because I looked." Not necessarily for the hairdryer, but it was common to snoop when you were in someone else's bathroom alone.

Romy took Eden's hand in hers. She squeezed and only then did Eden notice her fingers were shaking.

"What's the point you're trying to prove here, babe? Because—don't freak out—that sounds like a point in *my* favor."

"I know," Eden thunked her head down on the scarred wooden table. "It doesn't matter. It doesn't matter because I don't date. Not anymore."

Romy came around the side of the booth and put her arm around Eden's shoulder. "Look, I love you, Eden, and I know that being in a relationship scares the shit out of you given your stepdad and your ex. I know you are so worried about having to change for someone else that you've decided your safest option is to never be a wife or girlfriend again. I'd never tell you not to protect yourself. We all have the right to protect ourselves."

"I'm sensing a but," Eden said into the table, voice muffled.

"But," Romy pressed a kiss to the back of Eden's head. "You have relationships. Maybe not romantic ones, and maybe not a ton of them, and maybe only with the right people. People who give you the space and support to be exactly who you are. Like me. Just maybe, it's possible you can find that in a romantic partner too. Maybe Ted." Eden groaned, "Or not Ted, but someone. Someday. Okay?"

This was the moment for Eden to make a snarky comment. To say something about how she didn't need anyone, but she was starting to suspect that wasn't true. She needed people. She needed this green-haired bitch across the table. She needed her mama, even if it was mostly through phone calls recently. She'd needed Chloe over the weekend, just to be an additional friendly face in a sea of strangers. And yes, she needed Ted, needed his strength and his support and just him.

"You're right," Eden said into the table, not wanting to see the smug satisfaction on Romy's face. "And Ted is my friend. We do have some form of something."

Romy pumped her fist in the air and whooped. See? Smug. Eden rolled her eyes and lifted her head.

"He's still not my boyfriend," she said. Her best friend shrugged.

"Baby steps. Even on the Cape, you barely referred to him as your friend. 'Business Associate' is the term I'm pretty sure you used when you texted. Now at least you can recognize that he's your friend. A sexy friend. With sexy benefits."

Eden looked around for the waitress. Was it too late to ask for her meal to go? Romy slid her plate across the table and grabbed her sandwich, taking a huge bite. Okay, it was too late. Romy was blocking her exit, anyway.

"Yeah, benefits like letting me stay with him. Hey are there still officers posted at my door?" Ted had mentioned that they'd keep her apartment cordoned off as long as they were investigating, or more accurately as long as the city was willing to pay shifts of uniformed cops to guard the door and make sure no one walked in.

Romy shrugged. "I didn't see anyone this morning, but I'm not the most observant when I leave in the morning."

Romy taught music classes at a magnet school in the city, but she also played her own compositions at just about every open mic night she could find and then stayed up until all hours writing more. The woman just did not sleep.

"Can I come stay with you?" It was time to let Ted have his space back. She couldn't just move in. It was giving people the wrong idea. Like Romy. Or Ted. Or herself. "I'm not sure how I feel about going back into my place, even if I'm allowed, but my lease is up next month anyway and I need to get out of Ted's space."

"I'm sure he doesn't mind," Romy said, "But yea, you're always welcome. You really want to leave a cushy guest room to sleep on my couch?"

"I'm not staying in Ted's guest room," Eden pushed some of her food around her plate. "I'm, uh, staying in his room."

"There's no way that man can fit on a couch, so you're giving up sex to come stay with me? I'm flattered, but I thought you said he knew what he was doing in bed." Romy shook her head. "That ruins all my hot fantasies."

"We're not having sex. Or we haven't been. Not since he took me home."

"So you've just been—"

"Sharing a bed. Platonically."

"Cuddling?"

Eden nodded. "For the past week."

"And neither one of you moved to the guest room."

Eden shook her head. Ted's guest room was a home gym with a desk. And sure, she could have moved to the couch, but it had been nice having someone there. They didn't start snuggling—in fact most nights they started facing away from each other—but every single morning she woke with him curled along the line of her back, his thick arm thrown over her waist and his mouth pressed to the skin of her neck.

Every morning he slowly disentangled them, moving with a sleepy slowness that made parts of her ache. Not just to be naked, but to pull him back around her like a thick, weighted blanket.

And yet every single morning he bussed a kiss to her temple and then rolled out of bed and shuffled to the bathroom as if he wasn't packing heat in his pajama pants. And Eden pretended she didn't hear the shower turn on as he flushed the toilet. Or that she didn't sit surrounded by his covers, breathing in the leather and man scent of him, and imagine him stroking himself under the spray. He had to be doing that, right? To thoughts of her, maybe? That's where she was taking care of her business.

"He told me we could go bed shopping," Eden admitted, and busied herself with her straw wrapper. "Set up an actual room and space for me to sleep, but I can't have him dismantle his treadmill or his office space. Not for a temporary situation. Beds aren't exactly cheap."

"I need you to rewind a million steps and explain in more detail," Romy said. "So you aren't sleeping together but you share a bed every single night and he cooks you meals and drives you to your jobs and now he's going to furnish an entire room in his home just for you? But you're not having sex and you're not dating?"

"That's why I need to get out of there," Eden said. "I'm starting to get ideas, but I don't know if I'm ready for that,"

Romy narrowed her eyes and Eden added, "yet. So let me stay with you before I ruin his life, anyway."

Romy frowned. "How are you ruining his life?"

"He wants a wife and a marriage and forever, Rome." Eden's stomach twisted. "And I'm so scared that I'll try because he's wonderful and then six months, a year, three years from now look in the mirror and see my mother again, and it will be so much worse because I would have wasted his time. So no. We aren't having any more sex and we aren't dating and I can't let him redecorate his house for me when I'm nothing more than a girl he once saved from the cops and took to a wedding."

Romy put her arm around Eden's shoulder and pulled her into a half hug. Warm, comforting, familiar. Eden took a shuddering breath and was surprised when her eyes watered.

"Sometimes you're the stupidest person on the planet Eden, and I want to shake you." Romy nudged her shoulders to punctuate her statement. "Every single relationship either lasts forever or ends. No one knows which unless they try, and the fact that you're less concerned about your normal relationship worries and more concerned about hurting a good guy, tells me you already know he'd be safe. That he wouldn't ask you to be anyone but yourself. Have you asked that darling hunk of man if he'd rather have you try now and risk losing you in the future than have you walk from day one? Maybe marriage is negotiable even for Ted. Didn't you say wanting to get married had something to do with his parents? And he just cut those bastards right off."

"I don't know." Eden admitted. "Being questioned by the police has definitely added more doubts about my ability to pick romantic partners. But staying there is giving us both the wrong impression. If I can't make up my mind then I need to move out."

Romy ran her fingers through her shoulder-length bob. "I was planning on changing up the green and I could use your expert hair dying skills."

"Thank you," Eden pressed a kiss to her friend's smooth cheek. "I'll be over after my classes this afternoon."

"That's right," Romy said, "Eat up bitch. You have to go teach people how to hoist their legs up in the air at 2."

"It's yoga," Eden pointed out. "Stop making it sound dirty."

Eden's afternoon class was small because of the heat, but she still rolled out her mat in her favorite spot in Christopher Columbus Waterfront Park. Most of her attendees were older women looking for a relaxing way to pass some time outside as opposed to strength training or weight loss. Eden had taught classes at fancy studios before, but she'd always preferred the quiet outdoor practices that attracted participants of all abilities. Participants who showed up in sweatpants with battered mats as often as matching yoga fits. She'd once had someone show up with a beach towel for a mat. It hadn't stopped them from enjoying each pose and the summer breeze.

Eden loved yoga. She'd started practicing it as a toddler, clumsily copying the movements her mama did in the living room, but Greg had put a kibosh on all the "hippie crap" as he liked to call it, so she'd taken an extended hiatus from asanas until a Saturday morning class during her brief stint in community college. Yoga helped her think, even when she was supposed to clear her mind during each flow. By the end of a session, her muscles ached, a sheen of sweat covered her from head to toe, and she usually had answers to some of the impossible questions that had been plaguing her.

Sometimes she had answers for questions she hadn't even asked yet. Eden looked out at the five women—and Rodney—setting up their mats and wondered what her brain was going to give her today. Probably something about Ted. She hoped it would be something about Ted. Anything. Because Eden suspected that when she told him she was leaving his house... well, it was going to be the beginning of the end. Everything between them was going to change.

"Eden!"

She looked up from her mat at the two women crossing the grass, mats strapped to their shoulders. AJ had tied her curls up with a big flowered headband, she was impossible to look away from even before the hot pink bike shorts and lime green tank, and there was Chloe with feathers in her hair, wearing honest-to-god leather shorts and a sports bra.

"Aren't you supposed to be on your honeymoon?" Eden asked, standing up to hug both women.

"We did a pre-honeymoon." AJ said, a flushing creeping up her chest and over her cheeks.

"That's not a thing," Chloe said. She rolled her eyes, but she was smiling. "The pre-honeymoon is everyone else's honeymoon." She turned to Eden. "They just spent the whole week in a fancy B&B in the cutest little postcard town in Maine, and they didn't leave their bed once. Ask her where she's going next month." Eden didn't ask fast enough, so Chloe kept going. "He's taking her to Paris, of course, and I'd accuse the man of having less than zero imagination, but they're going to the UK first, and hitting every quaint fairytale bookstore her heart can handle. And you know he's going to buy her a metric ton of books."

"Sometimes I forget Will has money," AJ said.

Chloe laughed. "Not me. I had to sign paperwork about it on the show. Also, it's yours now too. He's the only rich person we aren't eating since all he wants to do is buy you novels and give the rest away to orphaned animals."

AJ shoved Chloe's shoulder and Chloe shoved right back. They were laughing and grinning and… Eden was late to start her class.

"Are you guys staying?" She motioned to their mats.

AJ rifled through her bag before coming up with Ted's water bottle. The giant insulated one that she stole every chance she got.

"Of course we are. Ted may have mentioned your class a time or two, and he asked us to drop this off." AJ handed the bottle over and Eden took it, ice cubes clinking as it moved.

"By time or two, she means all the time." Chloe stretched her arms across the front of her chest.

"We're not here to be creepy," AJ said. "Just supportive. We'll go set up at the back."

"You can set up anywhere," Eden said, but they were already moving to the rear of the small group and unfurling their mats.

Eden unscrewed the water bottle cap. A small sip before the start of class. She wrapped her hand around the cool aluminum and her finger brushed the edge of something raised. Eden looked down at her thumb and brushed it over the front of a sticker. Ted wasn't the sticker type. She knew this because she'd teased him about it while threatening to commandeer this very bottle.

"I'll cover it with stickers," she'd told him. "You won't even know it's yours."

"Please do," he'd said "Every time I take a sip I'll think of you."

Right there, underneath the pad of her thumb, was a sticker. She recognized the character from one of her favorite childhood stories. It was a tiny baby bear with a bucket full of freshly picked blueberries.

"I think it's time," Eden said as Ted sat on the couch to pull off his dress shoes. "I can't stay here forever."

It wasn't a surprising request, Ted had been expecting it for almost a week now, but the idea of her gathering her things and closing the door behind her made his heart stutter. It hurt. Even knowing that it wasn't the end of anything but sharing a milk carton and his physical space, they'd definitely stay friends…right? It still hurt. To buy some time for a response he wouldn't choke on, Ted carefully arranged his shoes in a neat row and slid wooden shoe trees into the supple leather.

It couldn't be considered a breakup if they weren't together. Right?

"Have you heard anything else?" Ted asked. He hadn't heard anything from Martin, but maybe the man had been in touch with Eden.

Eden shook her head. "No news is probably good news."

Not necessarily. If there had been no case, then the investigation would have likely been wrapped up by now. Eden had a solid alibi for the weekend, but that didn't mean her apartment was cleared or that they'd dropped the questions about Justin's extracurricular. Ted was holding onto the hope that other cases had taken the forefront. The state had a month to file an autopsy report, perhaps no news before the thirty-day time limit was good news.

"You're frowning." Eden stepped into Ted's space and touched a finger to the corner of his mouth. "Don't tell me if I'm wrong, okay? It won't change anything, other than making me panic."

Ted pressed his lips into a firm line.

"There's nothing to panic about." He said instead, and when she dropped her head to the center of his chest, he wrapped his arms around the curve of her shoulders and held on. She wasn't crying, wasn't shaking, but if she needed to borrow some strength, then she could take anything she needed from him. Anything at all.

"I still need to get out of your hair," Eden said into the cotton of his dress shirt. Even through two layers, he could feel the heat of her words.

"You're not in my hair," Ted said, but he was being supportive, dammit, "I can understand wanting to get back to normal. How can I help?"

He brushed his hand over the wave of her hair, tucking thick strands behind the curve of her ear. Eden relaxed into him, her body liquid against his own. One hand cupped the nape of his neck over the thick collar of his dress shirt, the other curved around his waist, fingers twisting in the material. Ted wished he'd stripped to his undershirt before walking in the door. This was probably their last evening together, and he wanted to feel her hands on his skin or at least with one fewer layer. Eden took a deep breath and then pulled back, dropping her hands from his shirt. She suddenly felt miles away.

"I'm not packed or anything," Eden said with a laugh. "I'm not even sure I have a suitcase."

Did he offer her one? Make a joke about how she couldn't leave? Help her pack? If she took a suitcase, he'd have a reason to collect it, right? Was that too pathetic? Normally he'd say yes, but faced with her walking out his door he was seriously considering doing just about anything to keep her there. Even when he'd planned for this.

"There's no rush. We can talk about all of it after dinner."

"Yeah, sure." She turned to lead him into the kitchen. "I have some veggies and chicken roasting in the oven. Rice is on the stove. Hope that's okay?"

Ted smiled. She wasn't rushing to leave either. She'd started dinner. He grabbed plates from the high cabinet that she couldn't reach unless she pushed up on her tiptoes and took them to his round kitchen table. There was a small glass jar full of fresh flowers, bright yellow and red-orange daisies. There was a woman who sold them right around the corner from where Eden taught her morning yoga classes, and Ted was getting used to seeing the sunny blooms in every corner of the house.

She'd been sketching, her notebook open in front of the only pulled out chair. The flowers looked almost real, their petals curling on the page as if she'd pressed a real bloom down instead of painstakingly choosing colors to blend into the perfect shade. This was one of her favorite spots to draw. She'd perch in his wooden dining chair, one knee pulled up to her chest, tongue tucked into the corner of her mouth. He could practically see it now. Ted knew she liked the light in the kitchen. He'd felt a burst of pride when she'd gushed over the wide windows he had in each room.

He put the plates in front of two empty chairs, leaving her art right where it was. Never would he move or touch the images she poured her soul into. She could take over every fucking square inch of the damn house. She made his house into a home. He'd never, ever want to change that, but if she needed a bit of space to realize that they belonged together, then he could work with that. And if not? If she never figured it out? Well, he'd deal with that later. Much later.

Eden pulled a baking tray out of his oven and shook it gently. She was humming under her breath as she set the tray on the stove and turned off the heat. She checked the rice, fluffing the white grains with the tines of her fork, and Ted took a deep breath through his nose. He wasn't a horrible cook, he couldn't be when he usually lived alone, but Eden had definitely brightened up the meal choices. The room smelled tangy and spicy and delicious, but he could eat unseasoned, raw potatoes for every single meal and he'd still think it was incredible if he had the chance to share the meal with her.

"If you're worried about sleeping arrangements," Ted said between bites of the bell pepper, pineapple, and chicken, "then don't be. I have a bed coming for the guest room tomorrow."

He'd pulled some strings to get the furniture and mattress delivered in less than forty-eight hours, but she didn't need to know that. A flush heated her cheeks and Ted bit down on his lips to stop himself from smiling. Their entire relationship had involved a single bed, and he wasn't necessarily in a rush to change that, but he wanted her comfortable. And it was getting harder and harder—pun absolutely intended—to keep his hands to himself when he woke up wrapped around her.

"It's not—" Eden chewed a bite of her own dinner, "Okay, so it is the bed thing."

Ted's stomach swooped in a free fall and he looked at a spot over her shoulder. He commanded himself to play it cool. He should have been sleeping on the couch. He'd known that, but she'd said it was fine. Even after their weekend with the Masterses. He knew he was a big guy with a scary growl. One who'd told her he was into her. Maybe she'd felt pressured. Maybe she'd felt like she didn't have another choice. Maybe he'd read the entire situation entirely wrong and she…

Eden's hand covered his. She was frowning as she tried to catch his eye.

"Hey," her voice was soft, her fingers smoothing over the back of his fists. "I think you misunderstood me." Ted dropped his head a fraction of a fraction and her eyes flicked back and forth between his. "It's the *new* bed that's the problem."

Ted's brain needed a moment to reboot.

"Do you want me to cancel the order?" He asked, pressing his free hand to his mouth. The store would definitely charge him an arm and a leg, but he'd bet he could get them to turn around without ever unloading a single bolt.

Eden shook her head. "That's just it. I don't want you to do that either. I don't know what I want." she let go of his hand and he flexed his fingers on the tabletop, missing the loss of her touch. "I like you a lot Ted. I like being around you, spending time with you. You've been nothing but supportive since the day we met. It doesn't faze you that I wear loud colors, and paint for children's books, and don't have a 401k or a retirement plan. I trust you as much as I trust just about anyone, you've never let me down, but things change when you're in a relationship. I'm terrified of what it will mean if things change for us, because I already feel invested with you. The longer I stay, the more I blur the lines of what we are and I don't know if or when I'll be ready to take that next step. The longer I stay the more leaving is going to hurt."

"Going to hurt who, Sweetness?" He'd said he would not push, but this moment felt too important to ignore, like standing on that one wobbling stone in the middle of the river, knowing that you couldn't sit there forever as the water rushed by. "Me? I always knew you weren't going to stay, whether or not we were together. Jumping into a joint living situation is a lot for any couple, and if I have you, I'm playing for keeps, Eden. I'm not playing a short game. Is it going to hurt *you*? If leaving me is going to hurt you, then you haven't been paying attention. Stay."

"Paying attention," she said, her tone sliding into pissy as her guard went up. She sat back in her chair, putting distance between them. "You say we're just friends and then you change your entire home for me? We sleep in the same bed, but it's literally just sleeping. At one point we were having sex, but that changed too. I've been paying attention just fine. It's you who can't clarify your message. If I can't figure out what I want it's because I don't know what's being offered. I don't know what you want."

"I'd have bought a bed for any of my friends who stayed here. I'd open up my home for any of them."

"Right, you'd fuck Will if he needed a place to stay? Rearrange your schedule and drive Logan all over the city?

Buy him art supplies and clothes and things and then pretend you couldn't hear when he offered to reimburse you?"

"Maybe the last part. I've never been into either Will or Logan, but it would be practical to share the bed if they had to crash here. None of us would fit comfortably on my couch."

Eden let out a short bark of a scream and pushed back from the table, her chair legs scraping against the tile floor. "See? You offered to sleep on the couch when it was me. Admit it. You haven't been treating me at all like a regular friend. You're treating this like it's something more," she held up her hand to stop him from speaking, "no matter what you say."

Sweet darling girl. She was running smack into the point and still missing it. Missing one crucial piece of the puzzle. Which meant she probably wasn't ready for it.

"Do you think I cook for just anyone? Share my art with just anyone? Do you think I would have *called* just anyone? I—"

Eden spun away from him to dump her plate in the sink, but it was too late. Because there it was. The piece she was missing. Except the tears in her eyes meant she wasn't ready. She wasn't ready for him or this. Not yet. Ted took a deep breath and let the fresh oxygen chase the frustration from his bloodstream.

"Eden," he took a step toward her, palms outstretched, and trying not to corner her like a scared animal. He'd never seen her this way, not even at the police station. She seemed to shimmer with tension and he felt like an ass for pushing her.

"You want to get married, Ted. You told me you wanted to get married and I don't know if I'll ever be able to commit to you. No matter how much I might want to." a ragged inhale. "We're the wrong fit, Ted. We knew it the minute we met. Wanting that to be different just hurts."

Ted closed the space between them and pulled her in close, tucking her head under his chin. He slowly rocked them back and forth as if they were dancing while the cabinets watched and she slowly relaxed in his arms. Now was not the time to tell her that his goals had changed. She cared. She wanted to be with him, but she was still scared. He'd stay the course.

"I've got you Sweetness." He rubbed his hand down the length of her spin. "You're welcome to stay, always welcome, but if you need to go, you can go. Do you want me to drive you over tonight? Or in the morning?"

This would not change a thing. Deep down, where even she didn't want to admit it was true, she knew. Ted knew this was her Hail Mary pass. Her last ditch effort to stop the fall and protect herself from regret and heartache and pain. The only problem was that there was no stopping this. It was too late. They were both in it. Tumbling down that everlasting chasm, hoping the crash landing wouldn't break them wide open. Ted had already hit the bottom and now if she'd just open her eyes—if she'd just *pay attention*—she'd see him standing there with open arms. Ready to catch her and keep her whole.

That was why he packed her into his car with no argument, lending her a suitcase with no talk of how she'd return it. He'd driven her to Romy's and stayed in the car only because she'd begged him to. The sheen of tears in her eyes doing more to convince him than anything else. That was why he pulled away from her building and used his voice commands to open a new message and then he sent it off before he'd turned off her street.

I'm in over my head. What time are you getting here?

Isn't this your party? It can't be that hard to entertain your friends.

It's Will's party, and I don't entertain.

Isn't it at your house?

What time does he say they're coming?

You've always entertained me just fine.

Will's on phase two of his honeymoon.

You're different.

Eden's phone screen went dark as her battery gave up the good fight and she shoved it deep into her tote bag. Ted was ridiculous. He knew what time people were coming. He was the one who'd invited her. The annual party was usually hosted at Will and AJ's but with the happy couple off to parts unknown, Ted had stepped into the lurch and invited everyone over to his house. As far as Eden could tell, he'd seemed suitably horrified that he'd done so. Of course, it was easy to step in to help.

"Did you at least tell him we were here before your phone died?" Romy said, hefting the insulated bag she was carrying higher up her shoulder. The little containers inside clinked together.

"How did you know I was texting Ted?"

"You never text anyone else. Don't make that face. You're as bad a liar as you are a texter. Plus, you get that goofy grin when your phone buzzes and it's him." Romy gestured to the doorbell. "Now, I'm going to need you to ring the damn doorbell. Thanks."

Eden took a moment to smooth her hands down her front, before remembering that the mesh dress wouldn't do much for the sticky sweat coating her palms. Gold and completely see-through, except for the scattered spray of tiny gold stars, usually Eden paired the piece with a plain black dress that hit her mid-thigh. Today she'd gone for a bright blue tank top, a pair of red spandex shorts, and her white Keds. Cute, festive, not conducive to hiding nervous sweat.

Romy was wearing a much more standard red gingham sundress and a pair of bright blue high tops. She looked like a teenager from the fifties, if teenagers back then had tattoos, bright pink hair, and a nose ring glinting in the sun. With a frown and a mouthed "you okay," Romy reached past Eden to press the bell and then it was too late to turn back. Through the door, Eden heard the chimes and the

"Hey, thought you'd come in through the garage—" Ted was larger than life in the doorway. He was larger than life anywhere, but especially framed there in his navy shorts and linen shirt. He rested his hands on the top of the doorjamb and let his body lean into hers, eyes dark as he perused her from top to toe. "Woah."

"Her phone died," Romy said as Ted stepped back into his home. Eden paused on the front step, her eyes glued to his as his pupils expanded, and the telltale heat built in her belly. Romy grabbed her elbow and shouldered her through the door. "I'm Romy Fernandes, you're Ted. I have goodies that need a refrigerator."

There was a single moment of silence, Ted's eyes glued to Eden, before he seemed to shake off the stupor and respond.

"I've heard a lot about you, Romy. You're welcome anytime. The kitchen is just through that door." He pointed behind him and Eden's friend gave him a thumbs up before detouring around both of them to head to the other room.

"She brought shot glass cheesecakes," Eden said as her friend moved out of sight. The front door was still wide open, and she stepped to the side to close it, and Ted stepped even closer. "Hi," she tipped her head back to look up into his handsome face.

"Hi," he said. He was close enough now that a deep breath would press their chests together. "You look beautiful, Eden. Stunning."

"I wasn't sure how all-out your friends went for the Fourth of July," she admitted with a small smile. "I figured, given Will's family, that they probably went all out, but now I'm not so sure."

"They can do whatever the fuck they want." His words were low, gritty, meant for her alone. "This is you and it's perfect."

He dropped his forehead to hers, and then his arms were around her, pulling her into the heat of his body. Eden's eyes closed as she savored the feel of him. He smelled the same, like sunshine and leather, and she tucked her nose into his chest. Her things had smelled like him until a few days ago, when everything finally faded. She'd never thought of scent as something she could miss, but she had. So much.

"How are you?" Ted asked, the words rumbling through his chest and into her own body.

He asked like he genuinely wanted to know, despite the fact that they talked at least once a day. Sometimes it was a phone call in the evening, sharing details on his day and asking about hers. Sometimes it was a text message with a picture of something he said reminded him of her. Sometimes it was a meal delivered to her when he knew she was rushing from gig to gig. This time, the question felt different.

How was she? Well, she was still staying with Romy. The police hadn't been standing outside her door anymore, but she also hadn't heard from Martin. At all. She'd called him, once, and left a message with a surly assistant who probably made more in a day than she did in a full week and wanted her to know it.

So she was sleeping on the pull-out couch, still cycling through the clothes Ted had replaced for her—and an old Harley t-shirt she'd commandeered from his dresser—and wondering if she even wanted to go back to living in a space where someone had died. Honestly, she wasn't sure she did, even after all the legal stuff died down. And only half of that was because she missed him.

She'd left Ted's home to regain her sense of normal, and she felt like she was even more lost than before. So how was she doing? She had no idea.

"I miss you," she said into Ted's shirt, and his arms tightened around her. Solid, comforting, and she wanted to stay right there.

"I'm right here," he said and pressed a kiss to the top of her head. "I didn't go anywhere."

Eden wanted to argue, but he let go of her and shut the door, ending the line of conversation.

"Come on, everyone's out back," he said and Eden followed him into the kitchen, where Romy was closing the refrigerator.

Her best friend in the universe raised an eyebrow at her, clear curiosity on her face, but Eden shook her head. Whatever Romy wanted to know, there was nothing to tell. Romy cleared her throat and tipped her head to the side. She wanted Eden to look at something. Ted walked out into the sunroom and Eden stepped closer to her friend. There on the fridge was his calendar. Still open to June, her drawings in the corner.

Eden remembered putting them there. They'd been sitting together eating dinner, and she'd been trying to explain the kid and puppy she'd seen in the park that morning. She hadn't drawn them, her sketch pad already filled to bursting, but she'd watched them for eons, running in and out of the frog pond, ducking around trees, the tiny puppy tripping over his paws every third minute, the kid stopping to ask his companion if he was okay.

Ted handed her the calendar off the fridge and told her to draw them. "Like a comic strip," he'd said, and she'd filled in the squares as individual frames, smiling as she remembered watching them.

Ted had wanted to tear the strip right off the calendar to keep it forever—"A real Yates original," he'd said—and she'd stopped him, insisting he could always do it once the month was over. No use destroying the calendar just for something she'd drawn on a whim and could redo anytime. The next day he'd had Devin, HMP's receptionist, deliver a stack of fresh sketchbooks right to her. The smaller man had handed the stack over right there on the Harborwalk and given her the biggest grin.

And now it was July, and he hadn't switched the month, or removed the piece she'd drawn. It was still there, where he'd see it every morning as he grabbed orange juice or eggs.

"He probably just forgot to change the month," Eden said to Romy and her friend rolled her eyes so hard Eden worried they'd get stuck. "It's only the fourth. Still pretty early. It doesn't have to mean something." She just hoped it did.

Which was bad. She wasn't supposed to want it to mean something. They were friends. Just friends. Friends who were attracted to each other but were not involved enough to want to see signs in everything they did. Friends who absolutely would not be heartbroken and lost without each other.

Eden walked out into the sunroom, intent on moving right into the backyard and into the heart of the party. She pulled up short as she almost walked directly into the back of one of the wicker lounges. Ted had rearranged all the furniture in the light-drenched space. The seating now circled a small table, a vase of fresh flowers set in the center. His treadmill and weight machine took up half the room. And there, by the treadmill, was an unfurled yoga mat. Two blocks stacked neatly against the wall.

"I wish I had a home gym," Romy said. "He even has a yoga set-up. I bet this room gets the best light."

It did.

But Ted didn't practice yoga.

"He made that spot for you," Romy said, slipping her hand around Eden's neck in a half hug. "Didn't he? Cute that it's still up even though you haven't been here."

Eden didn't answer because she didn't know what to say. Technically, she didn't know the spot was for her. Ted hadn't owned a yoga mat when she left, practicing on the grass or hardwood floor whenever he'd joined her. It was possible he'd grown to like it, had started practicing for himself, but that didn't seem likely. She knew the spot was for her. The question was, why?

"Tell me again that you aren't dating." Romy said and Eden shook her head in self-preservation.

"We're not Romy, you know that. Nothing has changed."

But the words felt like a lie, because the yoga setup hadn't been here when she *had* been here. He'd set it up after she left. He'd kept her drawings up. There were still flowers sitting on his kitchen and coffee tables. Fresh ones. He'd had to have picked them up since she'd left. The house still looked like she lived here, and that meant something. It also meant something that staying with Romy felt like visiting a friend, but when she thought about going home, she thought of this house, this home, and this man.

Well, she just had to put more distance between them. With time, this feeling would fade. It had to. Right? Otherwise, she'd protected herself too late. Protected Ted too late.

"Hey," Romy tugged on the end of her ponytail. "Take a deep breath. Relax. You don't have to think about it now. You do have to introduce me to all the people here."

Right, the party. Eden could focus on that. Ted had been sweet to invite her. She opened the back door and stepped out into the yard with Romy right behind her.

"I don't know everyone," Eden said. "I pretty much know Ted and Logan." And maybe Devin. He was probably here if it was a work event.

"Well, introduce me to Logan and then we can make more friends," Romy said.

Eden looked around the grassy yard to see if she could spot Logan's curls. He was standing by the grill, head thrown back in a laugh as Ted said something to him. Eden started for the two of them but was waylaid by a smaller man in a flag printed tank top and star-shaped sunglasses. Devin threw his arms around her and squeezed her hard enough to steal her breath.

"Eden," he crowed, clearly drunk and happy. "I'm so glad you're here. You always make Grumpy a lot less grumpy."

Romy choked out a laugh. "Grumpy?"

"Ted," Devin said before hugging Romy, too. "I'm Devin. I work at HMP."

"Please tell me all the partners have nicknames." Romy said, "and then tell me everything you know about Grumpy."

"We all have nicknames," Ted pressed a cold bottle of bright red Cheerwine into her hands. He'd left Logan manning the grill and crossed the lawn to meet them. "Logan is Happy and Will is Doc, although he was Dopey for a while before AJ screwed his head back on straight."

"The seven dwarves?" Romy turned back to Devin. "Who does that make you?"

"Obviously Snow White. I clean up all their messes and take care of them while they think they're in charge." Devin winked at Ted, who just shrugged in response.

"Come on," Ted said, his hand resting lightly on the small of Eden's back. "I want to introduce you to my family."

"Go," Romy said, "I'm fine right here with Snow White."

"Your family?" Eden said, looking around the gathering to see if she could spot Martin and Ted's mother somewhere in the small crowd. There weren't many people, maybe a dozen total. She saw Eleanor and George, Alex and Michael, Chloe, and some faces she didn't recognize. She hadn't expected that Ted's family would be a part of a social event that he hosted, but she could be wrong. Will's parents were here talking with another older couple. The man looked like Logan in another thirty years.

"Sometimes we need to pick our own family, Sweetness." Ted said, tucking her further into his side as they neared Logan at the grill. "Everyone at this party? They're who I consider my family. Understand?"

Eden nodded. She did understand. She'd chosen Romy, Romy's parents, and Romy's cousin Shay for her family. That had been an easy decision. Now she looked up at Ted and her breath hitched. He'd said, "everyone at this party," but that didn't mean her too, did it? Yes, she thought. It definitely did. Because she considered him part of hers, no matter what else happened between them. Ted had earned the right to be part of her family.

"I have something for you," Ted said. He slipped his hand into the front pocket of his shorts and pulled out a small brown square. It had smooth, rounded corners and a tiny cartoon face printed on the front. Eden held it up for a better look. "It's an external battery. You plug your phone into it to get a boosted charge."

Eden looked up at him, tightening her fingers around the device.

"You gave me something extra to plug in every night?" She tried to swallow around the thick lump in her throat.

"I didn't think of that." Ted frowned and reached for the battery. "Never mind."

Eden pulled it into her chest. "No, it's mine. You were thinking about me."

His frown deepened. "Yeah." The *duh* was implied. "I don't like the thought of your phone going dead and you being stuck in an emergency." And he'd plugged her phone in every single night when she'd stayed at his house. Eden hadn't even had to ask.

She looked down at the battery in her hand.

The face was a bear.

Three days later Ted glanced at the daily calendar on his desk. He had thirty minutes before his next meeting, although it was probably closer to an hour. Mrs. Levin always ran late. Almost late enough that he'd started telling her earlier meeting times. Almost.

There was something inherently condescending about lying to a client, even about something this mundane. Instead, Ted usually took it for a bathroom break, or a chance to stretch his legs. Today, that extra time was going to come in handy, since police stations often put him on hold. Knowing his luck, today would be the one out of fifty times that Mrs. Levin showed up early, but Devin could get her some water and entertain her for a few minutes.

It had been just over a week since Ted had dropped Eden off at her old apartment building, and he wasn't nearly as calm as he was pretending to be. Ten days, sixteen hours, and twenty-eight minutes. Not that he was counting. They hadn't known each other long enough for him to miss her in his space but tell that to his bruised heart. He missed the way she hummed all the time—she never repeated songs, just seamlessly blended snippets together into her own melody—the way she talked to the silverware as she loaded the dishwasher, the way she curled up in the sunniest windows with a sketch pad open on her lap.

There were little things that helped, too. His missing Harley t-shirt. Eden had slept in it almost every night, even after he'd offered to buy her silky pajama sets. It was possible his washer or dryer had eaten the faded shirt, but he preferred to think that she was wearing it at her friend's house, the worn fabric rubbing over pebbled nipples.

There was the extra toothbrush that she'd left in his bathroom. Of course, he'd given her a toothbrush, but she'd left it behind in the little plastic cup right next to his. As if she were coming back for it. There were also the doodles on his kitchen calendar. Fireworks for the Fourth of July, lotus flowers for her yoga class days, suns and lighthouses and waves along the blank edges. Little reminders of the Cape. Like maybe she was thinking about each minute of their time together, too.

Ted dialed the number for the Suffolk County district attorney's office and listened to the automated options on the answering service. This might be construed as crossing a line, Ted thought as he navigated his way through the robot voice that tried so hard to sound like a real person, but no more so than the first time they'd met. In theory, he was doing exactly the same thing as before. A little gray morality for the right reason. Eden was always the right reason. It was just a little harmless nudging. No information that would affect any investigations or proceedings. He was just calling to get the status on whether or not she could collect her car.

Now that Eden was back in her own building, or at least not his house, he didn't have the option to drive her where she needed to go. He still tried, but it wasn't always possible. Even if she never drove it, having her vehicle back was at least something he could do for her. That made the guilt negligible as he gave his stepfather's name and allowed the women on the other end of the line to assume that he worked in the old man's office. That he was tasked with collecting the information he was asking about. For once in his life, that thought didn't turn his stomach. Not because he had any designs on joining Martin's practice, but because he knew he never would. Knew he never needed to, and allowing someone else to think it was helping Eden.

Eden.

Being near her felt like standing in the sun after too long under a blasting air conditioner. The kind of warmth that sent a shudder through his entire body. Warmth that pooled in his gut and popped through his blood like those candies that explode on the tongue.

"I'm sorry. Can you repeat that?" He said into the phone as the woman's words sunk into his consciousness.

"Of course, dear," the woman said, but she clucked her tongue like he was an errant child late to class. "I said she's free to pick up the vehicle whenever she'd like. She just needs to present her voucher at the precinct."

"How would she have known to go present her voucher?" Ted heard himself ask. They'd been together every single day since her car was seized. Okay, not the past ten days, sixteen hours and forty-seven minutes, but she'd have said something.

"Mr. Fredecker's death ended the investigation. I have a note here saying that a courtesy call went to Mr. James's office about collecting her personal effects. Typically we don't send those, it's up to the involved party to request updates." The woman dropped her voice to a conspiratorial whisper, "We know that with no charges, Ms. Yates no longer needs Mr. James's services, but he'd said to call about any updates."

No charges. Did she mean about the original questioning? Or about Justin's death? Goddamit.

He couldn't ask the woman on the phone because one, they were both crossing some ethical boundaries here—she wasn't exactly supposed to be handing this information to him over the phone. He could be lying about anything—and two, now he'd have to call Martin again. It was mostly likely the drug investigation. If Eden was free to pick up her car then they no longer thought it held any evidence of Justin's whereabouts or supplier. Technically his whereabouts were the city morgue.

"Thank you for your time, Ma'am," Ted said, his finger already hovering over the end button on his desk phone. "Apologies for the mix-up on our end."

Ted kept the phone pressed to his ear as he dialed his stepfather's office. The direct line. It was the number to the phone on Martin's over-bulked, hand-carved desk. The number that would bypass the assistants and junior partners. Almost no one had the direct line, but Ted had been given it the first time the cops had caught him tagging the side of a parked freight train at sixteen. It was the number he was supposed to use when he got himself into a jam. The number Martin told him to call, with the tone of voice that made clear Ted should never actually be in a position to need it.

"Martin James,"

"Have they dropped all the charges against Eden Yates?" He had less than ten minutes to complete this call. No time for pleasantries that did nothing more than soothe his stepfather's ego.

"Hello to you too, Theodore."

Ted could hear the scratch of a pen over a piece of paper. Martin still took long-hand notes in a yellow steno pad. Ted wondered what those notes would say about him right now.

Rude

No greeting

He didn't fucking care.

"Did they drop the charges?"

"You know I can't discuss the details of a case with you. Attorney client privilege is an important tenet of our legal system." More scratching. Ted eyed the respectable cup full of black and blue BIC pens on his desk. Martin was most definitely using a custom fountain pen. Probably engraved with his name. Everything in Martin's office was engraved with his name. That was at least half the reason HMP wasn't. Ted let his gaze rest on the painting Eden had given him. Just three meaningful initials.

"I'm paying the bill." Ted argued, even though he knew it didn't matter. Attorney client privilege still protected Eden no matter who signed the checks. "Please," he said, the word tasting like acid on his tongue. "I already know that the drug investigation is over. Did they drop the charges surrounding Fredecker's death?"

"I'm only telling you this because there were no charges to drop, so technically Miss Yates does not require my services at all. I'll send you the bill for my initial consultation." Martin said and the pen scratching stopped as the older man sighed. "No evidence in her vehicle or her apartment to tie her to Mr. Fredecker's past dealings. No evidence at all other than the suspicion that she might know something. That investigation passed along with the late Mr. Fredecker. Death was an accidental overdose. The beating he took appears to be from approximately twenty-four hours prior to his death, another local dealer has already confessed to that, and we have time stamped photos showing Ms. Yates was in attendance at the Masters-Mulligan nuptials. Aside from a severe lack of judgment that led her to warn him about his wanted status, she hasn't heard from or talked to him since they split a few months ago. No crime. No charges."

She hadn't just been at the wedding. She'd been with him. Ted had seen the photos. Almost every picture of Eden showed him as well. Even when this thing between them had been going nowhere, he'd been possessive. He'd wanted her time. Wanted her attention. Wanted her.

"When did you find out?" Ted asked. Autopsy reports were required within ninety days, so this could have been anytime in the last ten days, sixteen hours, and fifty-six minutes. Which, shit, meant he had two minutes before his meeting.

"Fredecker was a key component in a larger case. Results aren't official yet, but I got the call at the end of the month."

The end of the month. Eden had still been staying in his house then. If she'd been told that her home was safe, and she was in the clear, she'd have told him.

"Did anyone tell Eden?" The silence on the other end of the line said more than anything else. "You didn't tell her."

"I don't have time to baby your latest liaison, Theodore. I have actual cases I'm working on. This case is closed and you are now wasting my valuable time."

"She is your client. It's your job to inform her of changes in her case," Ted said as the clocked ticked through another minute.

"There was no case, Theodore. That girl consorts with known drug dealers and felons."

"They are people too. You're a defense attorney. You defend people accused of the most heinous crimes every single day. Don't act pompous now."

"I don't need to like my clients to do my job," Martin said. "My personal feelings don't affect my work in the courtroom, they do however, affect what I think of her consorting with my boy. I'm sure you think she's wonderful now, but don't become distracted from your own future because of a pretty face. I worked too hard to get you a clean slate."

"Distracted." Ted laughed, a dry grating sound.

He was distracted by Eden. He thought of her constantly, missed her with each pulse of his heart. She lived in his every breath now, but it wasn't a bad thing. It was beautiful, and it was rich, and his life was significantly better because of it. Because of her. He'd been so focused on the future he'd forgotten how to live. Eden...she gave his dreams back to him. That future Martin wanted him to focus on? It wasn't him. And it was never something they'd both worked for. Martin had made some phone calls, and written a huge check, and then Ted had done all the heavy lifting ever since. And now he was done.

"I love that girl," Ted said, and he already felt lighter. "She *is* my future."

"Now really Theodore, the company—"

"Stop. Your opinion here does not matter." It didn't. "I'm going to call Eden. You're off the hook." And this was going to be the last phone call he made to his stepfather. If Ted wanted to think seriously about his future, then removing Martin was probably the best first step. "And I'm not your boy. I never was. This will be our last correspondence. Goodbye Mr. James," Ted said into the phone. "I hope you have a fulfilling future."

Slamming the phone down felt good, the shock of it vibrating up his arm, and Ted smiled. And then he laughed. It had been ten days and seventeen hours since Eden had moved out of his house. Ten days and seventeen hours since he'd decided that he was going to give her the space to figure out what he already knew. They were in a relationship. Had been since she'd walked into this very office and pressed her mouth to his.

He'd been putty in her hands. Hers to direct as he would, even if he hadn't known, not then. Inviting her to the wedding hadn't been random. His heart had made a choice before his brain could catch up. Every single second they'd spent together, sitting in the ocean as the surf pounded over them, pressed back to front on the plush queen bed, spinning in dizzying circles around a square dance floor, every moment had been them finding each other. They'd been building bonds, forging those tiny strands that pulled people together, wrapping around each loose piece of each other until there was no way free.

So Martin had given Ted a gift. He'd been waiting for the legal troubles to pass. He'd been waiting for her to be ready. The case was closed. She was free. And no one had done the decent thing of telling her she didn't have to worry anymore. No one had bothered to treat her like a human being, No one thought she might be anxious to know what was happening beyond her control.

"Logan!" Ted called out as he jogged around the corner of his desk. "Take Mrs. Levin for me."

"Everything okay?" Logan met him out in the hall, slurping an iced coffee from the Dunkin' a block over.

"I need the afternoon." Ted was already halfway to the lobby. He shoved one hand deep into the pocket of his dress pants and closed his fingers around his keys.

"Will's on one of his post-marriage vacations." Logan said, rattling the ice in the base of his cup. "You sure you need the whole afternoon?"

"Yes." Ted said as he strode through the lobby. Devin barely looked up from the front desk. "Reschedule everyone after Mrs. Levin," he told the younger man, and he took the finger wave he received as agreement.

"Don't worry," Logan called after him. "I won't call you even if I need you."

Eden slipped her tongue between her teeth and used her finger to smudge out the line she'd sketched. She was working on a design option for a children's book about ducks, so coming to the frog pond in the center of the Common had seemed like a great opportunity to get some inspiration.

The only problem was that there was an adorable couple sitting on a bench a few feet away, and Eden kept getting distracted. There were no couples in the story—definitely not a sweet older couple, hands entwined on the bench between them—but creativity had its own roots, and fighting against the impulse to draw the sweet scene in front of her was next to impossible.

She tried to catch the curve of the man's cheek as he tipped his head toward his partner, his smile wrinkling his skin. The woman dipped her free hand into a bag of what looked like oats and corn kernels, tossing handfuls down onto the ground as a small band of mallards darted forward to steal bites. Ducks! See? This totally counted as doing her job. She'd just draw a duck into the portrait once she was done capturing their likeness.

Except something in her drawing was off and Eden couldn't put her finger on why. She'd drawn the man's newsboy hat, and the woman's short-sleeved dress. She'd captured the bob of curls and the curved fingers. There was something missing in the way they angled toward each other, as if drawn together by a string. Except a string was breakable. Whatever drew these two together was anchored deep down in their souls. It just didn't look right. Eden smudged out the line again and tried one more time.

The back of her eyes burned, and she blew out a breath while straightening her shoulders. It had been a long time since she'd looked at a scene like the one in front of her and ached with a sort of jealousy. Surely before Justin. She sketched in a little duck body, trying to push down the weird, choking feeling, but it didn't help. Someday Eden wanted to be old and happy and sitting on a bench with someone who knew and loved her inside and out. It was the same feeling that had convinced her to take a chance on Justin. To see if he was the right one.

Except… she'd felt it more recently. She'd felt it at the wedding, staring up the aisle at Ted's larger-than-life body, his dark eyes cataloging each part of her face. She'd felt it when he tucked her close as they danced, when they sat together on his couch—her reading and him working, and she'd felt it at his holiday party when he'd tucked her into his side and smiled down at her like she was the only person he wanted to see.

A break. She needed a break. That's all.

She put her pencil down and stretched out her fingers, feeling the joints pop the way they always did when she tensed up while working.

For the first time in a long time, it wasn't Romy's voice—or her mother's or Chloe's or any of her other friends'—she heard in her head, but her own. A voice reminding her that if she wanted *that*—love, devotion, tenderness, care—then she needed to take a chance.

She'd had all that, hadn't she? Or at least half of it. She'd had tenderness and care with Ted. He'd held onto her when she thought her legs couldn't hold her another minute. He'd listened when she spoke and heard even more when she was silent. He'd put her first over and over and over again, even when she'd made it clear she had nothing else to give. He'd given her tenderness and care, and all she'd had to do was give it in return. Maybe he'd give her love and devotion too, for the same reward. She already loved him. Staying at Romy's hadn't changed that.

For the first time in a long time, the bigger risk was ignoring all the squirmy, warm feelings. Eden wanted that partnership more than she feared the possible future fall out. She knew how he felt. He'd told her that he cared, shown her it was even more than that. He might love her. She was pretty sure she loved him.

Eden fumbled with her phone. Ted was working, but she might catch him between meetings. If not, she'd leave him a message. She'd ask to see him tonight. She'd beg, because now that she wanted to take the chance every single second apart was torture. She swiped the screen and saw the Nauset Lighthouse for less than two seconds before the screen went black. It was the photo he'd allowed her to take on his phone. The one she'd wanted to compare to the chip bags.

Eden hadn't needed a photo, not after she'd googled the comparison, but he'd handed over his sleek phone without question and she'd backed up and aimed at the red and white building, catching his broad frame in the shot. Tattoos winding down his tanned arms, sedate classic cape cod clothes over a body she knew was straight out of an alpha hero romance. He'd ducked his head down, chin to chest, but his eyes were on the camera, a corner of his mouth tipped into a sly smile.

Devastating because she knew it was for her, because of her, it was *her* smile. It had been second nature to send the photo to herself and she'd set it as her background the minute she'd collected her own phone from his car. What an idiot she'd been. Even then, she'd been orbiting him. Centered on him. And now, when she needed to tell him she finally figured it out, her phone was dead. She'd forgotten to charge it again. She dug into her bag for the extra charger and plugged that in. Nothing happened. She'd forgotten to charge that too. Dammit.

Eden shoved her phone back into her bag. She couldn't call a ride without it, but she wasn't too far from Ted's office building. Fifteen minutes on foot, maybe. She pulled the headphones off her ears and looked around at the other Bostonians enjoying the sun. From her shady spot on the grass she couldn't see the road, but she could hear the faint roar of the traffic on Beacon Street. The sweet older couple was still sitting right where she'd left them. The woman's head pillowed on the man's shoulder and Eden swallowed past the lump in her throat. She needed to go. Right now.

"Did you know this is where Will and AJ fell in love?"

She hadn't heard him walk up, maybe because of the music, but probably because she'd been lost in thought.

Either way, her heart seized at the sight of dark-headed Ted settling himself onto the grass next to her.

"Here?" she asked, and he nodded.

"Maybe a few trees over, but she was reading. His dog may have bowled her over, but he's the one who fell."

Eden smiled. Will and AJ. Another couple tied together by those unbreakable strands woven through every part of their being. Eden couldn't lift her gaze away from the smile that twisted Ted's mouth. He felt both too close and too far away. He wasn't looking at her, so she soaked him in. Why was he here? When he dipped his head down to meet her gaze, she realized she'd asked out loud.

"I'm here for you," Ted said, as though his words didn't just filet her right on the lawn.

"Me?"

"Yes, Sweetness. Of course you. Always you." His smile this time was softer, fuller. Hers. She had to smile back. "How is Romy?" Ted asked.

"She's—" not you, Eden wanted to say, but that wasn't fair to the friend who was more like a sister. "She's good. Her hair is blue now. Electric blue. I don't know how it hasn't fallen out from all the times she's changed colors. Did she tell you where to find me?"

Ted shook his head. "I know you're working on that book. The one with the ducks. Figured you'd find some ducks to sketch."

"You know me so well." Her words were meant to be teasing, complete with a nudge to the shoulder, but his response was soft. Not teasing at all.

"Yes." He dropped his forehead to hers. "But I want to know even more."

Eden didn't breathe, didn't think, didn't move. Then Ted leaned back and the humid air rushed into the space between them and smacked her in the face.

"Have you talked to your attorney recently?"

His stepfather? She hadn't. Figured no news was good news. There was no use worrying about hypotheticals.

"I figured he'd call me if something came up. There haven't been any officers outside my apartment, but I left a message and never heard, so I just stayed at Romy's."

Ted muttered something under his breath that included a lot of curse words. He cupped a hand around the back of his neck, closed his eyes against the sun.

"It's over, Eden," Ted said, and for two horrible minutes Eden thought he meant the slippery strands winding between their very souls. Then she understood and relief swamped her, rushing over her limbs like a dip in the clear water of the frog pond. "No charges. No investigation. It's over. They know you did nothing wrong."

"Oh," Eden said. Ted took her hand and squeezed her fingers between his.

"I'm sorry no one told you before now. I came over as soon as I heard."

"Oh," Eden said again. For a moment there she'd thought... "Thanks for letting me know."

"Hey," a big finger curled under her chin, tipping her face until she closed her eyes against the bright sunlight. A dark shadow passed over her eyes and when she blinked open, there he was, looking down at her. "What just went through that pretty head of yours?"

"I, um," Eden licked her lips and Ted's eyes dropped to her mouth. She flushed hot. "I didn't realize you found me for that. I thought—"

She thought he'd been meeting her halfway. She'd been headed to his office, ready to leap into the unknown, and hope like hell that he was waiting with his arms out to catch her. Then she'd turned around, and he'd been sitting right there. Of course, her heart hoped he was there for a grand gesture. Of course, her brain agreed. Like this was some big screen movie when the hero and the heroine both get their heads screwed on right at the same time.

She'd jump in a cab just as he went running across town, converging on a beautiful spot with some deeper meaning for both of them. He'd take her into his arms, pulling her up tight against his body, slotting his hips against her. A promise, nothing indecent. Her eyes would flutter closed, she would tip her head back, and they'd admit to the feelings that the audience had seen coming in the first ten minutes.

Except he hadn't come for any of that. Ted had shown up in the park to tell her she wasn't being indicted on murder or drug charges, and while that was a relief, Eden couldn't help but feel disappointed it hadn't been a declaration of another kind.

It was okay that this wasn't their romantic comedy happy ending. Until recently, Eden hadn't even considered herself part of a love story. And just because Ted hadn't figuratively run through the pouring rain, calling her name while holding his bloody, beating heart in his cupped hands, didn't mean that this wouldn't be a happily ever after.

"I thought," Eden cleared her throat as she tried again, "that you found me for personal reasons. Not professional ones. I was hoping, at least."

Ted's mouth was on hers before she finished pushing the words from her burning lungs. His tongue slid past her parted lips and slicked over hers. The kiss was hot, wet, deep, and Eden melted into the heat of Ted's body, letting his muscles prop her up as she angled her head for a better fit. He tasted like dark coffee and Ted. She fisted the front of his dress shirt in her hands, trying to get even closer. His hand slid to the back of her head and he tugged until their lips parted. He pressed his mouth to her cheek, her jaw, her throat. Leaving open-mouthed kisses with just a hint of teeth.

"We need to stop," Ted said, as if she were the one kissing his inflamed skin. He pressed another kiss to the tender spot behind her ear.

"You're right," Eden said, but didn't pull back. "I just got out of my legal trouble. I don't need to be arrested for public indecency."

That got Ted's mouth off her neck, and his eyes flared with heat as he stared down at her. His lips were shiny and damp, and Eden shivered at the thought of kissing him again.

"You aren't wrong," he said and moved a few inches further away.

"About an arrest?"

"About why I came here. The legal information was just a convenient excuse." He dropped his hands from her face and head and turned his body away from hers. He drew up his legs, looping his wrists over his knees, and Eden tried not to be disappointed that he'd hidden his impressive erection from sight. They were in a public park and she was acting like she was in heat.

Her heart soared at his words and then the second half hit her. "Why did you need an excuse?"

Ted smiled at her. He'd been doing that a lot, smiling. She could barely remember the time when his smiles were hoarded like precious gems. Now he gifted them to her every time their eyes met.

"I've been trying to give you space," Ted said. "You'd been so adamant about not starting a relationship, so I was trying to give you the breathing room you needed."

"To not feel crowded?" She loved him for listening to her, but her heart broke just the same at the idea that he'd been that willing to let her go.

Ted laughed and looked out over the pond. He shook his head. "To figure out that we were already in a relationship, Sweetness. That we have been since—"

"Since the day I walked into your office and kissed you." Eden said. When he turned stunned eyes to face her, she bumped her shoulder into his. "I know Bear. It took me a while, but I did figure it out."

At her words, the tension rushed out of Ted and his whole body relaxed with a sigh.

"I was going to call you," she said.

"Your phone died? Ted finished for her, and Eden dipped her head to nestle in next to his neck.

"Yes, and I forgot to charge my extra battery. But I was coming out to see you before you delivered to the park."

"Looks more like you've been drawing." Ted's hand squeezed hers, his thumb brushing over the skin on the back of her hand.

Eden looked down at their linked fingers, feeling almost dizzy with relief that he was here. Still tucked into his side, she picked up her pencil and lazily sketched the older man's face. Just the line of his cheek, the shadows where his eyes would go, the curve of his mouth. She'd figured out what the picture was missing, what she'd struggled to capture on the page. Ted's arm moved to circle her waist, holding her up as she continued to sketch in the couple. His heart thudded against her back.

"I love you Ted," Eden said as she shaded in some more details. "It's too soon, but I can't pretend it isn't true." A drop splashed down onto the page, narrowly missing the figures she'd drawn there. Eden glanced up, looking for rain, and Ted's fingers were there, brushing the next tear from her cheeks. "I want to try, Bear. You get me. You listen and you get me, and you've never once expected me to be anyone but myself. You've stood up for who I am. I'm terrified of doing this again, but I'm more terrified of losing you. So I'm ready to try. I want to try."

Ted stared down at her. Under his beard, his cheeks creased into a smile. His eyes shone.

"I have good news and better news, Sweetness." He pushed a strand of hair back from her eyes.

"I don't think that's how the phrase goes."

"You just told me you love me. There is no bad news." Ted laughed, a hoarse burst of sound. "Because I love you too. Even though it's too soon, and it's terrifying. You get me too, Eden. Even when I buried me down so deep that no one would ever find him, you still saw me. Still got me. And thanks to you I'm done hiding Ted just to make other people happy."

Eden blinked the burn out of her eyes.

"That sounds like good news. What could be better than that?" Another tear slipped down her cheek, and he caught it with a thumb before cupping her jaw.

"We've already been trying, Eden. You said it yourself. We're already in a relationship. We've been trying every day. So—" he pressed a kiss to her mouth, a chaste peck, but enough to have her chasing after him as he pulled back, "we just keep doing what we're doing. Every day, we choose to keep trying. Sound good?"

"Yeah," Eden said. "Let's do it."

"Let's get out of here," Ted said as she closed her notebook and pushed it down into her bag. He pushed up to his feet and extended a hand to help Eden as well.

"It's a beautiful day," she looked at a group of kids splashing in the frog pond. "We could stay here."

Ted took her bag and wrapped his arm around her shoulder. He started steering her towards the parking garage.

"No, we really can't." His fingers twisted in the ends of her hair. "We're escalating the terms of our original agreement, Eden. No take backs. No pretending that we aren't, and I believe that means there is a specific part of the clause that I need to live up to."

"Your bike. It's here?" She dug her heels in to stop their forward momentum, making Ted stop and turn to face her. "I've only been dying for a ride for weeks, Ted. Weeks! At least since I found out about the bike." He stared down at her and she rolled her eyes. "And it was never just about going for a ride."

"I have a sparkly helmet for you," Ted said as he leaned down to rest his forehead on hers. "Don't ask me when I got it."

"Three weeks ago?" Eden pressed a kiss to the tip of his nose.

"I wanted to be ready, Eden."

"You believed in us that much?" It was humbling. It was exhilarating. It was everything.

"I *hoped* that much. I took a page out of your book. I manifested a relationship. Just in case. Even when I told myself I wasn't doing it."

"I love you," Eden said. "You're the best boyfriend in the world."

"Boyfriend," Ted repeated, his smile so large Eden thought the astronauts could see it on the international space station.

"Every day, right Bear? Just keep choosing to try every single day."

"I love you," Ted said and slid a kiss across her mouth. Their teeth clacked together; they were smiling so big. "Did I mention the helmet I bought my girlfriend isn't just sparkly, it's rainbow and sparkly. It reminded me of her."

"You're right," Eden said against his lips. "We do need to get out of here. We don't need an audience for what happens next."

And then she kissed him again.

Join Stella's NEWSLETTER for bonus scenes, sneak peeks of upcoming stories, and more…

If you enjoyed this story, please consider leaving a rating/review, or telling your book-loving friends.

ALSO BY STELLA STEVENSON

The Trope • November 2022

Mother Knows Best • February 2023

The Escalation Clause • June 2023

COMING SOON

On Ice • Fall 2023

Blind Luck • Early 2024

ACKNOWLEDGEMENTS

As always, writing and releasing a book takes a village. I was sure that each book and each release would leave me a little less panicked as I stared down the finish line. I was wrong. What each release has brought is a larger community of writers and readers that I am lucky to call friends. Without them, I would still be staring down an empty page and a blinking cursor, wondering why I decided that I needed a summer release.

As always, my first thank you is to my mother. She listened to me plot this book, parse out the characters, read the very first draft, and patiently served as another set of eyes when it came to the grammar and spelling I'm not so good at correcting (know when tell my college advisor that I still don't know where to properly use commas).

Thank you to my husband who is graciously giving me time to become the next NYT Bestseller while also 100% believing that this journey is worth it. His love and support is unwavering and he's the biggest inspiration for all my characters' Happily Ever Afters.

Thank you to my writing soul mate Bailey. I can't imagine navigating this author world without you.

Thank you to my writing sister Cerissa. Your octopus love is exactly what I need in my moments of crippling self-doubt. Everyone needs a hype-person just like you, but I'm too selfish to share. Thank you for drafting with me, giving me advice, and loving my characters as if they were your own.

Thank you to Callan for your quick and insightful feedback into Ted and Eden's motivations and love. This book would be very different without you to help guide the arcs.

Thank you to the Baby Romance Author Group for their marketing help, supportive words, and insider tips. There's always more to learn and this group makes it fun.

This book came at a very difficult time in my life. I finished the first draft the same day I lost my dad. This is the very first of my novels that he will not read cover-to-cover and share with all his friends. This transition has been difficult for my entire family and without the love and support of the friends and family in my life I may have set this story aside with no plan to pick it back up.

Thank you too, to everyone who reads, rates, reviews, and shares my stories. You're making my dreams come true.

Thank you,
Stella★